MW00654327

# SEIZE THE DAY

## The UnBRCAble Women Series, #2

### By

# KATHRYN R. BIEL

KATHRYN R. BIEL

SEIZE THE DAY, The UnBRCAble Women Series, #2

Copyright © 2019 by Kathryn R. Biel

Ebook ISBN-13: 978-1-949424-06-5

Paperback ISBN-13: 978-1-949424-07-2

This book is a work of fiction. Names, characters, places, and incidents are either products of the author's imagination or are used fictitiously and any resemblance to actual persons, living or dead, business establishments, events or locales is purely coincidental.

All rights reserved.

No part of this book may be reproduced, scanned, or distributed in any printed or electronic form or by any electronic or mechanical means including information storage and retrieval systems, without permission in writing from the author. The only exception is by a reviewer, who may quote short excepts in a review. Please do not participate in or encourage piracy of copyrighted materials in violation of the author's rights. Purchase only authorized editions.

Cover design by Becky Monson.

# DEDICATION

To Mackenzie:

Thank you so much for your time and insight about a day in the life of a zookeeper. I don't know why you took the time to help a stranger, but I am in your debt.


To Kris:

You raised an incredible daughter. But I'm sure you already knew that.

KATHRYN R. BIEL

# CHAPTER 1

"It's not like you're getting any younger, you know."

Mackenzie laughs, flattening her voice to sound like our mother's. If Mom's said this once, she's said it to me a thousand times. Mackenzie nails the impression. I know she's trying to be funny, but I don't need my sister to point this out to me.

I know.

Every single day, I know.

Most women my age probably hear a faint tick every once in a while. My biological clock clangs like Big Ben every fifteen minutes.

The moment you receive the news that you are BRCA-1 positive, that clock speeds up. Yah for the likelihood of developing cancer that attacks my reproductive organs!

Clang.

"I'm aware," I mutter.

"Well, what are you going to do about it?" Even though she now sounds like she's in a wind tunnel, I can hear the change to her tone. Gone is the jesting. Concern fills her voice.

As an aside, I hate when she uses speakerphone. It takes a minute for the background noise to settle down. I'd rather text than talk, but my sister is usually multitasking more than a circus juggler. I'm appreciative that she's able to carve out any time at all for me, even if it means we have to talk. To each other.

Like in the olden days.

In the meantime, I stretch out on the couch.

"Nothing today." I stifle a yawn. "I was at work until three a.m." The late night has ruined all hopes of a productive day off.

"Everything okay there?"

"Another day in paradise at the Pittsfalls Zoo. Talbert, one of my spider monkeys, had to have emergency dental surgery. I wanted to stay until he was awake and moving around again."

As such, my only plans today call for tacos and a nap. Maybe cruising the internet a little.

And when I say cruising the internet, I mean spending a few hours creating the perfect life on Pinterest.

I pinned the most adorable baby zoo animal collage today. It'll go perfect with the giraffe mural I pinned last week.

Basically, the perfect day.

"Carpe diem, sis. You can't keep putting this off," Mackenzie says.

Even if my biological clock wasn't going off like gangbusters, I've got Good Ole Kenzie to remind me that time is *not* on my side and encouraging me to seize the day.

She's always good for a pep talk, whether I want to listen or not. Most of the time I feel lucky to have such support.

Most of the time.

"Oh, but I can and I will." I cross my arms defiantly, even though my sister can't see my pout.

It's not as if a solution has magically presented itself to me. Nothing has changed since last month, last week, and yesterday, when we had the same conversation.

In other words, I haven't found a husband.

I hear Mackenzie rustling on the other end of the phone. She's always doing *something* while we talk. I swear, she doesn't know how to sit still. She never did and being mom to a toddler hasn't changed that.

"Erin, you have to do something. You just turned thirty-two."

The Mylar balloon proclaiming "Birthday Princess" still dances above my kitchen table. It hasn't even started to lose air yet. I tell myself I've still got time.

"Kenz, I'm tired. I was at work all night. I probably have to go in to check on Talbert, and I have to work tomorrow. Can you harass me about this another time?"

"How can you just lay there? These things take planning and time. Time that you don't have. You have three years, at best. The doctor recommended you take care of everything by thirty-five."

I sigh. I hate it when she's the voice of reason, especially when I'm trying to be lazy. "How do you know I'm laying here?"

7

"Because I know you. You're draped on your couch, cruising Pinterest. You look like hell, and you can't even remember the last time you had a date. You're probably eating a taco. You will *never* find a husband like that."

I say my goodbyes, but not before sticking my tongue out at the phone. Normally, Mackenzie doesn't care about my social life, or lack thereof. She doesn't care that I'm not married. She does, however, have a valid point about the timeline.

But right now, I don't care about husbands or babies. All I want to do is sleep.

*Current mood: fatigued.*

Except, thanks to my well-meaning but intrusive sister, I can't seem to drift off. I toss and turn, moving from the couch to my bed and back again. Thirty-two isn't old. I think current statistics have the average age for first time motherhood at around thirty. That means for every twenty-year-old first-time mother, there's a forty-year-old giving birth.

To be clear, those are Facebook statistics but should be considered reliable for my argument.

Even cruising Pinterest, as my sister so astutely guessed, doesn't bring comfort. Not my board about animals of Central America with cute pictures of sloths. Not my board about tacos which is making me hungry. Not my board about organization which seems like it requires too much energy.

Not even my super secret board.

I shove my phone under my butt, but visions of my pins dance in front of my eyes when I close them.

Rocking chairs. Changing tables. Bassinets draped in flowing fabric. That giraffe mural peeking out from behind a crib.

Things I'll never have if I don't do something soon.

Dammit.

I pull out my phone and stare at the List2Love app. My finger hovers over the heart symbol, but I can't bring myself to click. Last time I logged in, it didn't go well. Let's just state for the record that "DTF" does *not* stand for "Date, Tacos, Friday."

Now that was an awkward date.

Not to mention that in the past, all I seemed to get was pictures of men holding dead animals. I wonder if List2Love is sponsored by the NRA or National Fishing Association or something.

Surely there's got to be another way.

I mean, it has been a while since I've received an unsolicited dick pic. Let me ask, has anyone *ever* actually asked for a picture of that or is including the word 'unsolicited' redundant?

This is what my sister doesn't understand. First of all, she doesn't have the time constraints I have. Her body is not a ticking time bomb, waiting to kill her at any minute.

She also has Luke. And Trey, the most perfect two-year-old in the world.

Luke is the dream guy. He's hot. He's smart. He's loyal. He's fertile. And he is so totally devoted to my sister that it's not even funny.

I hate Luke.

I hate Mackenzie.

9

I hate my nephew.

I hate their stupid, perfect life.

None of that is true. I love them. And if it weren't for the fact that I have the BRCA-1 mutation and will most likely develop breast or ovarian cancer any minute now, I'd say my life is perfect.

I've got the best job anyone could ask for.

I've got a great family.

I have no one harassing me to stop eating tacos or watching movies or creating my dream life on a Pinterest board. For the record, that doesn't include my sister because, in the sisterly contract, she's bound to be on my case about one thing or another.

It's her job.

I don't need no stinking man to make my life better.

But, as it turns out, I do actually need one to have a baby.

It's not like I need to get pregnant today, though that wouldn't be a terrible thing.

Impossible, probably, considering I've been single for so long that I doubt I even remember what sex feels like. I imagine my nether regions looking somewhat like an old, dilapidated house in a ghost story, complete with creaky floors, hanging shutters, and a plethora of cobwebs.

Not exactly sexy.

And if there's a man out there who gets turned on by mentioning my crotch and cobwebs in the same sentence, I don't want to know him.

Still, other than the pressing need to get married and have kids ASAP, I'd say my life is pretty damn perfect.

As a zookeeper at the nationally recognized Pittsfalls Zoo, my days, and even a few nights are spent with primates and other really cool animals. I've applied for a transfer to the brand-new exhibit we're opening up, which would be even cooler.

Sloths.

And frankly, I prefer ape behavior to some of the men I've dated in the past. Apes don't leave their dirty socks on the floor or try to explain things to me, like biology.

Which I have a college degree in.

It's not that I don't want to date or fall in love or get married. Quite the contrary. It's more that I'm having trouble gathering up the motivation I need to put myself out there again.

Let's face it: no one likes being shot down. Or rejected. Or told they were too geeky (nerdy, tall, fill in the blank). It seems I'm always *too* something for the guys I pick.

And now, it's all I can think about. Why won't decent men date me? Am I ever going to have the family I want? Something like my sister has.

These thoughts continue to assault my brain. No matter what I try, I can't fall asleep. My nap eludes me.

It's not time to go to my UnBRCAble meeting yet. I get up and stretch. Rather than face the obvious, I take a few minutes—okay an hour—to scroll through Facebook. I don't often get the time to peruse through the social media sites like this, reserving my free time for creating vision boards of my perfect life, as well as finding pictures of Chris Evans looking hot. But after reading the hundredth vague post and challenge that I wouldn't 'copy and paste' this post (they were right, by the way), I close the app.

I know what I have to do.

Might as well try the online dating thing again. What do I have to lose? Oh right. What's left of my frail self-esteem.

Dating has always been the one area of my life that remained elusive. Let's face it, I'm better with animals than I am with members of the opposite sex. Not to mention, Kenz has always been the "pretty" sister.

You only have to hear that so many times before you give up. I guess I never stopped to think through how avoiding dating would significantly limit my potential candidates for marriage and kids.

I figured it would somehow happen though. Maybe someone from work who shared my passion for animals and wouldn't balk at hand-raising a wombat in our kitchen.

But that hasn't come to fruition. Despite the large staff at the Pittsfalls Zoo, the only available guy within the correct age demographic is Xander Barnes and no. Just no. He's so not my type.

More accurately, I'm not his type. The super hot, super flirty player stud rarely dates the nerdy, awkward girl.

This is real life, not a rom-com movie.

Since work hasn't dumped appropriate candidates into my lap, there's only one thing left to do. I login and go right to my profile.

The picture isn't bad. Actually, it's sort of awesome.

Me, holding one of our flamingoes. I mean, who gets to hold a flamingo? That should make me stand out and look interesting. My arm muscles look ripped, most likely because Freido the flamingo was trying to get down, and it's pretty badass. My hair is pulled back, but at least you can't see the frizz that often plagues me. There's a good view of my favorite T-shirt that says 'Conservation through education.' It's probably the best picture of me I've taken in a while.

I visit my profile and still stand by my original post. *I take care of animals all day. Looking for someone who doesn't need their cage cleaned. I am single and ready to flamingle!*

I check my criteria: single, male, age twenty-five through forty, employed. Not that picky. Let's see who's looking to connect.

My first swipe reveals Eric, who apparently likes to fish. Nope.

Then there's Dave, who obscures his face. Big red flag. Nope.

Toby who is married and looking for someone to join in with him and the missus. Nope.

Eric number two, nope.

Chad, nope.

Todd, DTF, nope.

All the nopes.

13

Also, I think about writing to the app designers suggesting one of the exclusion criteria should be for stupid hipster beards.

After I swipe left on Phil, with the bare chest, and Bobby who's wearing a shirt that says—let's just leave it as tasteless—I finally, maybe, have a possibility.

Craig.

Age thirty-eight. Engineer. Divorced.

Wearing a white button down and jeans. No dead animals, no guns, no whips or chains. No stupid hipster beard.

I swipe right and wait.

I've little hope that Craig will be Mr. Right, but Mackenzie has a point. I'm not getting any younger, and I won't meet someone laying on my couch, unless he's delivering my tacos.

My phone pings with a notification.

Holy crap! He's making contact already! This is unheard of in the dating world. What about the carefully timed-out, nonchalant messages spaced enough so you're almost positive you've been ghosted?

*I know this is soon, but I'm better in person than online. Heading to Cali for a conference in the morning. Any chance you want to meet tonight?*

Wow. He put it all out there.

I've got my UnBRCAble meeting at six. It's almost three now. I should probably go into work to check on Talbert. Xander is on today, covering my territory in Central American primates. He was supposed to let me know how Talbert was doing today, but of course, he didn't. He was probably too busy schmoozing. Or flirting. More likely the latter.

I might be the only female under the age of sixty on staff at the Pittsfalls Zoo that Xander hasn't made a pass at.

Apparently, he also feels that we would not be a good fit to date each other.

I shoot Xander a quick text to ask for an update.

*No news is good news. I've got him covered. You know that.*

What a pompous ass. He's not wrong though—he is good with the animals. As much as I hate to admit it, Talbert is in good hands with Xander. Even if those hands are attached to a pretty boy who lives on female attention. I text him back.

*Should I come in to check on him after hours? Trying to make plans.*

*What kind of plans?*

Without thinking, I answer truthfully.

*A date*

As soon as I hit send, I'm filled with more remorse than my stomach after Thanksgiving dinner. Why did I tell Xander that? He doesn't need to know.

My regret is validated when Xander sends me a gif of someone laughing hysterically.

Asshole.

I start to type to Xander to take good care of Talbert for me, but stop. He doesn't need me to tell him that. He's my backup for days off, which means he's as familiar with my charges as I am. He may be the most

15

arrogant man I've ever met, but he does care about the animals. It's his only redeeming quality.

That and he has a fabulous butt. He could give Chris Evans a run for America's Ass.

Instead, I message Craig back.

*Free before six or after seven. Coffee?*

Coffee. Not drinks. Drinks means you want to get drunk and have sex. While I don't have tons of time, I don't need to jump into anything tonight. I'm being proactive, not desperate.

*Five works. Do you mind if I bring my brother and his girlfriend too? Transportation issues.*

Yes, I mind.

*Sounds fine.*

We firm up details, and I start making the mad dash to get ready. I glance through my extensive collection of funny T-shirts but decide to pass. I rarely need to wear anything besides khakis and polos, so this is the once chance I have to look nice. On the other hand, I don't want him thinking that I dress fancy all the time, because no way in heck is that happening. No point in getting his hopes up.

But it's just coffee, so I settle on a dressy flannel shirt, leggings, and booties. Casual, yet comfortable.

Even though I keep telling myself not to, I'm starting to get excited. I took action, grabbed the bull by the horns, and now I have a date. Sure, it's a long shot, but at least I'm going out.

Craig could be the one.

# CHAPTER 2

"His brother?" Millie asks.

I'm explaining my date from hell to the UnBRCAble group, which I made in plenty of time. No need to worry about not wanting to leave Craig.

"But not his brother-brother," I explain. "Craig is a Big Brother. The volunteer kind. So we were at the table with two horny teenagers, mauling each other. I wanted to give them condoms so Craig doesn't become a Big Uncle anytime soon."

I shudder at the memory.

That date was the longest forty minutes of my life. Thank goodness I had UnBRCAble right after that I couldn't miss.

"Eeew." Millie's nose crinkles up.

"Eeew is right. But that's not the worst thing."

Claudia shakes her head. "What could be worse than that?"

I sigh. "He asked where I had to run off to, and I knew the date wasn't going anywhere, so I didn't want to get into it about the BRCA stuff. I told him I was going into work to check on my animals."

"Understandable." Claudia nods.

"He said, 'do you see yourself as chicken or an egg?' I thought he was getting all deep and philosophical, like, which came first. He kept looking at me for a response so I said chicken."

Millie's eyes dart side to side. "What did he say?" She's cringing a bit.

She should. It's totally cringeworthy.

"He said, 'I see myself as more of an egg, because I'm looking to get laid.'"

There's a stunned silence throughout the group.

"I ... what ... how did you even respond?" Millie stutters.

"How else? Awkward silence, a confused look. I had no idea what to say." I shrug. I'm still baffled. Not that it's ever acceptable, but I've never had anyone have the nerve to say something like that to my face.

Claudia opens her mouth and closes it, unable to say anything. I know the feeling. "So, needless to say, Craig is not the one."

Understatement of the year.

*Current mood: disappointed.*

The UnBRCAble meeting shifts away from my pitiful love life and onto important matters, like nipples and cleavage and whether over the muscle implants are better than under the muscle. Things that are life changing, like hysterectomies and men who can't handle the life-altering measures we have to take to beat cancer before it starts.

Even though membership in this club is wholly undesirable, I'm super lucky to have found this support group. I'm the odd-woman out here, as I've put off my surgeries, though statistics indicate over thirty-percent of BRCA-positive women delay having prophylactic surgery. It doesn't seem that way in this posse.

I'm in the "wait and see" group.

I understand why this choice isn't for everyone. There are days where it's not for me either. It's hard, marking months between scans and ultrasounds. Fighting the insurance companies to use ductal lavage for cancer screening rather than mammography to reduce my radiation exposure and therefore my risk of developing cancer. Waiting for the results to make sure that cancer hasn't yet reared its ugly head. The anxiety and dread, fearing the doctor is going to tell you he "found something."

It's not that I don't feel the devil breathing down my neck. I do. But I've got things to do first. I have a life to lead.

"Erin?"

I look up to see Claudia looking at me inquisitively.

"Oh, sorry. Was lost in my thoughts. Can you repeat the question?"

Claudia smiles. "Sure. Kelli here wanted to know who was waiting and why?"

I spot Kelli across the room, her hands knotted tightly in her lap. She joined us last fall and is still on the fence about surgery. I'm guessing she's coming up on her first set of six-month scans.

Otherwise known as the worry week. Or misery month, depending on how long it all takes.

Then, six months later, lather, rinse, repeat.

It's not for everyone.

So many women with the BRCA mutations and other genetic predispositions opt for surgery immediately, that it's hard to find someone to actually talk to about it, despite online statistics that about thirty-percent of women wait.

But I read it online, so it must be true.

I've connected with a few other women online, but everyone else here in the UnBRCAble group is either in the process of scheduling surgery or has already had it.

I'd been glad that Kelli was in the group with me. I didn't feel as alone anymore. But once Millie got her pathology back—what a crazy story there—most of the newbies who were considering waiting went ahead and scheduled.

Except for me.

I'm still in surveillance mode.

Makes me feel like a badass ninja or something.

"Kelli, since you asked, I'm picking surveillance because of a few things. I'm working on banking sick time. I don't get much, so it's taking me awhile to accumulate it. I'm saving money as well, because all those copays and expenses add up."

I look around to see the ladies in the group nodding. I've been to a lot of spaghetti dinners and silent auctions for members helping to cover medical bills.

I hesitate before saying the last part. I know what's coming. Even if no one says a blasted thing, they'll be thinking it.

"And I want to get married and have kids." I look at my watch, as if it reads my actual biological clock.

Tick. Tick. Tick. You have three years left ...

"Probably just one kid at this point. I'm not getting any younger." Even though Kenzie isn't here right now, I bet she's still smirking at me. "I know it's frivolous, but I want to carry a baby and not be able to see my toes and get hemorrhoids and give birth and nurse. I don't want to miss any of those things."

There's a tug deep in my abdomen, as if the absence of a baby growing in there has created an actual vacuum. There are a lot of downcast eyes. It's a touchy subject in this group. Enough members had preventative salpingo-oophorectomies and hysterectomies that it'll always be a fresh wound for someone.

It's one thing to choose not to have children. Lots of women make that choice, and I respect it. It's another thing to have the choice ripped from your body and thrown away. I want my choice while I still have it.

"But if you're meeting people online, then you're not even close to that, are you?" Kelli is being brutally honest, which we all need at times.

I shrug. "Not really. My sister reminds me every day, which only makes me feel like it's going to be that much harder."

"Your sister? Is she positive too? What did she do? Is she waiting also?"

The question is reasonable and innocent, yet I feel like Kelli slapped me. It's my turn to knot my hands and look down. "She's negative."

And married.

And mom to the cutest toddler on the planet.

And pregnant.

Again.

I love my sister. I do. I don't begrudge her these things. I don't wish her ill. I simply want them for myself more than words can say.

"Family's really important to me, and I'm not ready to give up on that dream yet." Another tug from deep within. Although, and I haven't admitted it out loud, I'm thinking I might have to.

That knowledge is harder to process than knowing that my mutated genes are too damn broken to suppress tumors, and cancer's almost a certainty for me.

I can handle a lot of things. I know I'm going to lose my breasts. I want the chance to use them for their intended purpose first. It's not too much to ask, now is it?

Kelli nods thoughtfully. "I guess. I mean, it seems like a lot to pin your hopes on, especially considering you aren't even seeing someone."

I shrug. I've been defending my choice for the past three years now. When I made the decision to wait, I was twenty-nine. I felt like I had all the time in the world.

The sand's definitely emptying into the bottom part of my glass now. I did not see myself as single at thirty-two. Yet, here I am.

Of course, I don't know when I thought it would all magically happen. Maybe I need a new fairy godmother or a wand replacement or something. My life is definitely a little lacking in the marriage department.

I leave the meeting and drive over to work. Might as well. It's not like I'm busy or anything. I'm sure Talbert's fine but checking on him will ease my mind.

Except he's not fine. He's spiked a temp.

Xander is holding Talbert while Dr. Val reports the temperature.

Damn. I knew it. I shouldn't have believed Xander.

"Why didn't you call me?"

He doesn't look up, as he continues to stroke Talbert's black fur with the gentlest of touches. While the rational part of my brain knows that Xander is as capable of nursing Talbert back to health as I am, the judgmental part of my brain hopes he washed his hands because Lord only knows where he's been. I can't seem to separate the player from the caretaker.

"He seemed fine. Temp just went up. Plus, you had that date. How'd it go?"

"Um, fine," I answer, startled. Xander and I don't make small talk. Mostly because he's a conceited ass and I hate him.

He's still not looking at me. "I doubt it, if you wore that."

This is why I hate him.

Also, he's a woman magnet. He flirts with every female here.

Everyone except me, that is.

"Craig and I didn't hit it off, but it had nothing to do with what I'm wearing." So much for my cute flannel. Maybe I should have worn my "Freddy Purrcury" shirt. Every time I see "Don't Stop Meow" I smile. If my dates are going to be lame, at least my clothes should make me happy.

"Mmm hmm," he murmurs.

"But that doesn't excuse you not calling me."

Xander looks at me. "You're always here. I didn't want to ruin your chance at a social life."

Hmm. He even seems sincere, cradling Talbert in the crook of his arm like a newborn. His arms are so strong, but his touch with his charge is delicate. Nurturing. Maybe he's not as bad as I make him out to be.

"But it looks like you did that all on your own."

And there's the Xander I know and hate.

"I thought you'd be all dressed up." He shrugs.

I look down at my outfit. *Maybe* it's a tad frumpy. "Why does it matter to you?"

He smiles. "You got my hopes all up."

What's *that* supposed to mean? What did he want me to wear?

And why is Xander Barnes thinking about my clothes at all?

# CHAPTER 3

The notifications on my phone are annoying the piss out of me. In the three weeks since I re-activated the app, it's been driving me crazy. If I wasn't practically up to my elbows in poo, I'd uninstall List2Love. As soon as I'm done here, that's what I'm going to do.

This is why I don't do online dating. I don't have time for this nonsense.

I don't even need to look at the hits to know what I'm going to find. They've all been the same, including more pictures of dead fish and antlers than I would have believed possible. Perhaps they're missing the fact that the bird on my arm in the profile is *not* dead, or that I spend my life taking care of animals, not killing them.

If they can't even understand that, my expectations are pretty low for anything else.

"You seem pretty popular today. Something going on?" Terry, my work partner, grins as she walks by me, carrying the large bottle of disinfectant and the hose.

Disinfectant day is easier in the summer, when we can put the animals in the outside enclosure while we clean the inside one. It's more of a hassle in the cold. I'm counting the days until the temperature stays above freezing. It's March, so that could be tomorrow or it could be in three months. Early spring in western Pennsylvania is a fickle thing.

"It's this stupid dating app. It's so bad out there. I need to delete my account."

"No Prince Charming yet?" Terry laughs. Her smile is wide and easy and she bears more than a passing resemblance to Terry Irwin. They're both the same age and build. Sometimes my Terry likes to tell people she was once married to Steve Irwin.

RIP Crocodile Hunter.

"Not hardly. But more hunters and fishermen than I ever knew existed. So many pictures of camo and dead animals."

"You'd think a hunter or fisherman would understand how to use the correct bait."

"And that, my friends, is what we call irony." I shovel the last bit of waste into the wheelbarrow and proceed to hose down the enclosure. We're going to repeat this process all day today.

Some zookeepers work on their own, but Terry and I like to tag-team for disinfecting day. I'm on sweeping and scrubbing; she's on spraying and washing. Can you tell who has seniority?

Most people think working in a zoo is glamorous. It's anything but most of the time. It's fun, to be sure, if you don't include the poo. I spend my days providing input and cleaning output. Not to mention checking locks and counting animals. I've become so OCD about checking locks that I catch myself checking my own apartment lock several times throughout the day.

Not gonna lie, about ninety percent of the job is dealing with bodily functions. Add in that we work long days with little time off for very little money, and it's nowhere near as glamorous as most people think. You can only do this job if you really love it.

"I didn't know you were doing online dating. When did this start?"

"I reactivated my account a few weeks ago." And I've been sorry ever since. "It's about time I meet someone and settle down."

I hope it sounds more sincere than it feels. It's not that I don't want to settle down—I do. Just not maybe yet.

Terry frowns a bit. "I'm surprised. From our previous talks, I thought you were going in a different direction. You don't seem like the type to be all focused on catching a husband."

She's not necessarily wrong, yet her comment rubs like too-small shoes. My jaw clenches. "What's wrong with wanting to settle down and start a family?"

"Nothing. Jeez. You've never seemed to be in a hurry about it. You never even really talk about dating. In fact, I'm surprised you're thinking about it now. You never seemed to spend a lot of energy on dating. I thought you were more focused on your career. I heard you applied for Sloth Central."

Terry is too astute for her own good, raising my defenses even more. FYI, I'm terrible when backed into a corner. "Yeah, well, I don't have the luxury of forever."

27

Crap. I can't believe I let that slip. I'd been deliberate in not sharing my BRCA status at work. This is a competitive field, and I don't want anyone thinking that I'm a liability or a risk, especially not when applying for a new position.

Not that I think Terry would think that. She knows me too well.

Terry straightens up. "What do you mean by that? Erin, is something going on?"

Better rip off the Band-Aid.

I take a deep breath. "I'm probably going to have to have surgery in a little while." I busy myself sweeping, even though you could probably eat off this floor.

Not really. It hasn't been disinfected yet. Gak.

"Probably? Are you okay? What's wrong?"

"Nothing's wrong. I'm fine. Totally fine."

Yep, that's me.

*Current mood: fine.*

"If you're fine, then why are you having surgery? Is it elective?"

Oh, that's a loaded question, indeed. To the general population, totally. To the women in UnBRCAble, absolutely not.

"So, it turns out that I carry the BRCA-1 mutation. You know, the breast cancer gene. I'm going to eventually have to have a mastectomy so I don't develop cancer."

Terry's face falls. Might as well drop the hammer.

"And a hysterectomy. So, if I want to have kids, I've got to get on that sooner than later. Hence, the 'I don't have forever' thing."

Terry moves in to hug me, which surprises me. And smothers me a bit. "I didn't think you were a hugger," I mumble.

"This is a hugging occasion. When are you having surgery? What can I do to help?" She steps back, and I'm grateful for the space.

*Lend me your uterus?* That might be a tad much to ask of a work acquaintance, especially considering Terry hit menopause about five years ago.

Those were fun days, working with someone getting hot flashes in a simulated rainforest climate. She almost stripped down nude in front of guests to hose herself off.

More than once.

We move on to the next enclosure while the disinfectant sits, eradicating the pen of germs and other creepy crawly things that could make the animals sick.

"I'm waiting for the time being. Like I said, I want to get married and have a baby first."

"Is it really that big a deal to have a baby?"

Terry's question freezes me in place like a punch to the gut. A big deal? My entire life? Of course, it's a big deal.

"Um, yeah. Family is important to me. You know that."

"No, I get that. But you don't have to *have* a baby to be a mother. There are lots of kids out there who need you. There's lots of different ways to be a family."

Terry's watch beeps, alerting her it's time to hose out the previous pen, rinsing all the disinfectant away to make it animal-safe. It couldn't have come at a better time. I continue on with my area, getting it ready for her spray. Hopefully by the time she gets back, she'll forget what we were talking about.

"Have you ever looked into adoption? Think of it—you not only get to be a mom, but you're literally saving a child's life."

No such luck. You know how they say an elephant never forgets? Terry's practically part pachyderm.

"I know. Both my parents are adopted." Which is how I started on this journey in the first place. Stupid DNA testing.

I mean, great for DNA testing, but there are moments I wish I didn't know.

"I didn't know that. That's cool. You should look into it, especially since you know how well it works out."

"Sometimes it does, sometimes it doesn't. My dad's family is great. Big huge Irish family. He's one of eight kids."

"All adopted?" Terry stands up straight. This usually stops people in their tracks. People tend to think the McAvoys are akin to circus freaks when I talk about the size of the family. I guess eight is more than enough for some people.

"No. My grandparents didn't think they could have kids, so they started adopting. After the first three, suddenly they couldn't stop having kids."

"Wow. And what about your mom?"

While the disinfectant is sitting in the second enclosure, I head back to the first to let the seven tamarins into their newly cleaned area. After several head counts and lock checks, I'm satisfied they're good and head back to cleaning.

Lucky for me, Terry gets pulled away for some reason or another. I'm too busy cleaning and disinfecting to think about dating or adoption or my mom's family.

Disinfection days always pass quickly because there's so much to do. Before I know it, we're in base camp for the end of the day meeting.

Terry slides into the chair next to me and whispers, "I have a cousin who adopted a baby from Guatemala. It was pretty easy, I think. Do you want me to get information for you?"

I shake my head, not looking at her. Instead, I pretend to be absorbed inputting my information on ZIMS, the database where we track medical and husbandry, amongst other things, for all our animals.

"Oh, do you want a US adoption? I think those are harder to get, but I know a couple who adopted. I can put you in contact. It's easier if you're willing to accept minority or special needs babies."

Inhaling deeply, I grit my teeth.

"Or you could do foster-to-adopt. I think those are mostly older—"

"Terry, stop!"

"What's got your panties in a twist?" Xander strolls by and casually plops into the seat next to me. Great.

"Isn't there somewhere else you can sit?" My nerves are frazzled enough. His presence is going to continue to grate on me like nails on a chalkboard.

He leans forward and as he does, his arm brushes against mine. Did someone turn the heat up in here? Suddenly I feel flushed.

"You know they like us to sit together by exhibit."

Sigh. He's not wrong. Xander's primary job is the big and small cats of South America, while I'm with primates of South America. We are the back up for each other, meaning he helps Terry on my days off, and I help Cass in his exhibit on his days off. Cass and Terry flip flop as well. We're all one big happy continent.

As if Xander Barnes needed any help stroking his ego, working with jaguars, ocelots, mountain lions, and the super rare small bay cat of Borneo, is the cherry on the "I'm a big deal" sundae. He's got quite the reputation—no pun intended—for working with cats. He hand raised two of our white lions and is the tiger whisperer. His head is so big, he needs to use the elephant door to get in.

He's probably overcompensating.

He looks over at me. "What are you all upset about?"

"I'm not upset." I try to focus on getting the last of my entries done.

"Dating not going well?"

I think they frown upon punching co-workers, but I may be willing to risk it.

"It's fine."

Xander laughs, which earns him a glare from Don. He leans in and whispers, "No, it's not. Don't lie to me. You wouldn't be so grumpy if things—" he waggles his eyebrows at me "—were going well."

Ick.

Though, he has a point. It's been a while.

But no matter how long it's been, I'm not desperate enough to date the losers who apparently find me attractive.

Also, I refuse to analyze that thought.

On the other hand, I don't want Xander to think that no one is interested in me so I slide my phone over to him which shows my latest person looking to connect. It's a dude (can't see his face) with a tattoo of a ruler on the inside of his calf, and he's holding a fish up to it.

Yep, another dead animal.

Xander leans in and whispers, "Wanna bet he has that same tattoo further up his leg as well?" Xander's breath is hot on my neck. It takes me a minute to get the mental picture he's painting.

"Oh my God, gross." My voice is waaaaay too loud.

"Excuse me, Erin, is there a problem?" Suddenly, I'm back in third grade and just got caught passing a note.

"I'm sorry Don. Xander doesn't respect my personal space and is making inappropriate comments to me again. I think perhaps he may need to sit through the HR training. Again."

It's a running joke about the annual HR trainings, including lifting techniques, using personal protective equipment, and sexual harassment. The sessions are boring, and anyone who doesn't know to put gloves on while handling poop doesn't deserve to work here.

However, Don has little sense of humor about the ongoing dysfunctional relationship between Xander and me. What can I say? Xander is the perfect example of why I'm single. Years ago, when I was young and stupid, he would have been my type.

I've developed higher standards as I've aged and stopped letting beer make my dating decisions. He's not hard on the eyes, but the minute he opens his mouth, I want to shush him because undoubtedly, his words will somehow make him seem very unattractive.

At least to me. There's not enough beer for that. Plus, it's not a super great idea to be drunk while at work. I hear that's frowned upon as well.

Along with getting naked in front of guests and punching co-workers. They really are a drag here.

I'm not sure anyone else at the Pittsfalls Zoo finds Xander quite as repulsive as I do. In fact, from the amount of notches I suspect are on his Leatherman's case, I'd say I'm in the minority. Xander loves when the new seasonal employees are hired. He's always chatting them up. I swear, there's not much separating him on the prowl from some of our most primitive animals here. The ladies flock to him like he's some kind of god. Or peacock.

Still, the girls seem to fall for it every time. Hook, line, and sinker.

I mean, they must.

For all the flirting and joking, Xander is relatively discreet at work. At least I'll give him that.

It seems like he's better at catching and reeling in than most of the guys popping up on my dating app. Maybe he should put out a video tutorial on suave pick up lines. The women he dates don't seem repulsed by him, so he must be doing something right.

I can almost see him like one of the lions, lounging on a large rock while his pride of lionesses swirl around, all vying to give him offspring and bring him the biggest antelope. Of course, in this vision, he's got long, flowing golden locks instead of his short dark hair.

Okay, so maybe not a lion.

Not to mention lions tend to be stocky and broad. Xander is broad, but more lean. Sort of like a cheetah.

I glance over at him. One ankle crossed casually over the other knee. Calf muscles tight. Forearm muscles tight, holding onto his lower leg.

If there was such a thing as a forearm fetish, I would develop one just looking at Xander.

Except for his personality, that is. He always seems to be talking to someone new. And walking them to their cars. And making them giggle and flirt. It doesn't take a rocket scientist to figure out what else he's doing with them.

I'm not sure why he gets under my skin the ways he does.

At least he doesn't try to act all chivalrous and stuff with me. That is a line I do *not* want him to cross.

But I mean, would it kill him to smile at me every now and again? Or to offer to carry a bale of hay. He has big, strong muscles to do that.

And now I've wasted entirely too much brain space on Xander Barnes, and I don't like wasting brain space. He's made me look bad in front of Don, which I can't afford. The brand-new sloth encounter program is scheduled to open in May, and I'd do anything to be one of the staff educators working that exhibit.

It'd be a step-up, going from keeper to educator. And the extra-added bonus is that I'd get to stop job sharing with Xander. Of course, if I keep acting like this, there's no way Don will recommend me for the position.

Getting this job is just like finding a suitable husband—all I need to do is focus and apply myself. Hard work will surely pay off in the end.

And if I get that job, Xander will *have* to stop picking on me, right? Now that I think about it, he's over the top nice to everyone *but* me. What's wrong with me that he won't even look my way?

Not that I want him to.

Obviously.

# CHAPTER 4

"I thought it would be super hard, and well, it is," Millie says as she flops onto the chair. "Sorry I'm late."

We're used to the way Millie comes into the UnBRCAble meetings now, a bundle of energy and usually already midway through a story. Such a difference from last summer when she used to cry all the time. It's not abnormal. We all go through those crying phases. This is a safe space to do so where we can let it all hang out without being judged.

"What happened?" Claudia asks. Her voice is so soothing that it's like a tonic on all of us, but especially Millie.

"Lisa had the baby. I ... I had to help deliver it. Him. It was the grossest thing I've ever seen." Millie crinkles her nose.

Yikes and wowza. Having been present and assisted with numerous animal births, I can only say that most people are not prepared for the ick factor. Mackenzie asked me to be there when she had Trey, but she ended up with an emergency C-section. It was just as well, because I was working when she went to

37

the hospital, and it would have been hard to leave in the middle of a shift like that.

"But Dexter is simply perfect, and after seeing what happened to Lisa's nether region, I'm getting more and more okay with adoption." Another nose crinkle. Millie leans forward, "Did you know that when you push, you end up pooping? Like, for everyone to see?"

There's nervous laughter. Some of the women have had kids, and I look to see some color rising in their cheeks. After all they've been through, mastectomies and reconstructions, bodily functions are still embarrassing.

That's why this group is so important. At least to me. Other people don't seem to understand. And let's face it, it's hard enough to talk about the women parts. But then when people tell you you're overreacting or laugh that you want a free boob job ...

Kelli pipes up, "Let's get back to 'you helped deliver him.' How did that happen?"

Millie laughs. "Well, you know Lisa. She's was trying to get all her work done before she went out. After the appendicitis scare, she'd been afraid she'd go early and leave too many things hanging. Basically, since then, she's been doing too much."

Ah, the old 'trying to shove ten pounds of crap into a five pound bag' routine. I can empathize with that. It's exhausting trying to be everything for everyone, all at the same time.

"I went to her office to pick her up and help her move some files home," Millie continues. "Crazy nut is planning on working with a newborn instead of taking a full maternity leave. Anyway, turns out, she'd been in labor for a while. She dismissed it as back pain from moving boxes in her high heels."

"She was lifting?" Frances asks.

Heck with the lifting, what was she doing wearing high heels? I look at my own Sperrys and smugly smile. I think I'd die if I had to wear fancy shoes every day.

I'd die if I had to wear them more than twice a year.

"Yeah, and apparently, by the time I got there and realized why she was stopping every three minutes, it was too late. I called 9-1-1, but then,"—Millie shudders—"I had to ... look in places and there was a head and ..." She breaks off. "I don't think the carpet in her office will ever be the same."

"Were the paramedics hot at least?" Leave it to Frances, the romance novelist, to think of this.

Millie shrugs. "I dunno. I was too busy looking for bleach to pour in my eyes to notice."

She doesn't need to notice. She's got Sterling, a tasty British dish. He's super supportive and has a kid. Millie's in good shape there, though I know it wasn't an easy road to this point for her.

"How are you feeling about the baby?" Claudia asks.

Millie's gaze drops to the floor. "I'm sad that I won't get to defile my carpet at work like that."

Millie's a teacher, so going into labor at work might really scar her kiddos for life, but I get what she means. It's why I'm waiting. The urge to carry and birth my baby, to nurse my baby, is as strong as the desire to raise a child.

She continues, "But I know I didn't have a choice. I don't need to give birth to a child to be a mother. I'm already a mother figure to Piper, and I know someday, I'll have my own little bundle of joy. I'm not sure if I'll use a surrogate or adopt or what, but I'll get there. I just turned thirty. I'm not even sure I'd be ready to have a kid yet anyway."

Her attitude is mature and realistic, which is one of the reasons I like her so much. No drama llama with her.

To be fair, llamas aren't really dramatic either. They are mostly smart, curious, and don't put up with bullshit. Also, their poop doesn't smell, which makes it much more pleasant to clean out their enclosures.

Here's a fun fact: llamas know their own strength, and if you overload it, it will lay down and refuse to move.

Some of us could learn a lesson from that, thinking of Millie's friend who worked herself into labor *at work*.

I keep thinking about what Milie's said about not being ready. I don't know that I am either, but I need to be. I've probably got to get a little more realistic about dating. It's not my fault I'd rather spend time with the animals than most men these days.

The animals are way cooler.

Pulling my phone out of my back pocket, I check the notifications from List2Love. I scroll right past the guy calling himself "Captain Underpants" that includes a picture of his genital region. Seriously people, what the heck?

The next is a message that starts with, "Hola Chesty McGee!" I don't remember swiping right, but I must have if he's able to message me. Swell. Must have been an accidental swipe while I was falling asleep.

Word to the wise, don't scroll while tired.

"Guys, this is why I'm single." I turn my phone around to show the group the message. My phone is passed around, murmurs of disgust and exasperation rippling through.

"What's with the 'Chesty' crap?" Claudia asks.

"I'm not sure there's any understanding this. I mean, who puts this in writing?"

Claudia leans over. "Doug does."

Obviously, Doug is not an actual viable dating candidate, but I can't resist. "I'm going to have some fun." Quickly, I type back:

*Chesty?*

Low and behold, Doug must be sitting there, waiting for his clever lines to nab him some high-quality tail. An answer pops up.

*Yes, you look like you have a good rack.*

What a prince.

I type back,

*Yes, well I'm also BRCA-positive so I am getting a mastectomy soon.*

*Are you going to get bigger boobs after?*

I read the answers to the group. "Tell him you're staying flat," Kelli yells.

41

*No reconstruction. Staying flat. Boobs get in the way.*

A message pops up that Doug has blocked me.

Millie says, "Guess that's one way to weed them out."

I didn't need any help weeding Doug out.

And as if dating wasn't hard enough, I've got the extra-added bonus fun of having a super good chance of developing cancer. I'm, like, the total package here.

"What if there's no one good?" Millie asks. It's easy for her to ask this. She found someone.

I shrug, not knowing what else to do. Sooner or later—most likely sooner—I'm going to have to start having my surgeries, whether I'm married with kids or not. I've almost come to terms with losing my breasts and ovaries. The only thing I can't accept is losing my chance to have a baby.

It's been so much easier to avoid dating and discussing this than to consider the very real possibility of not having a baby. No one blames me for not dating. I'm not sure where the eligible candidates are, but they don't seem to live in Pittsfalls, or within a twenty-five mile radius.

"You know, I wasn't super happy when I found out I was pregnant when I was twenty-one," Tracey says, "But even though it was tough, I got to do that before all this." She waves to her chest.

"When did you find out about BRCA?" I ask. I don't know why it matters.

"When I was twenty-five. I was having breast pain. They ran some tests. It wasn't cancer—not yet—

42

but it would have been. And now I have Tallon, and even though she drives me crazy, it's all worth it."

"Does she carry the BRCA mutation too?" Millie asks.

Tracey looks down at her hands. "She hasn't been tested yet. She's only fifteen. Probably soon, though. I—I haven't told her yet. She doesn't remember my surgeries. My mom took her for the time I was recuperating. Joe was no help."

"Is that Tallon's father?" I ask.

"Yeah, stupid me insisted we get married. Joe was a good-for-laughs, but not good for the long run kind of guy. We're much better off without him, frankly."

I try to think of how it would have gone over for me to get pregnant at twenty-one. It wouldn't have. At all. And there would have been no option of marriage. It would've been mandatory, shotgun and all.

Millie leans forward. "But isn't it hard? Doing it by yourself? I'm worried for Lisa who's going to have to do it all on her own. I don't know how she's going to have a career and be a mom and all."

Tracey nods. "I'd be lying if I told you it was easy. But then again, most things in life that are worthwhile are hard. And if I hadn't accidentally gotten knocked up, I would have missed my chance."

Tracey's words rattle through my brain for the rest of the evening. I used to head over to Kenzie's for dinner after UnBRCAble, but now that Trey is a little older, he goes to bed around seven. It leaves me with free hours that I don't know how to occupy.

Normally, I'd work on my Pinterest boards, but I can't bear to even open up the site. Seeing the landing page, full of nursery ideas and baby blankets is too much for me.

I'm restless and I don't want to be alone tonight.

I'd love to swing by, even to have a drink with Kenz after Trey goes to bed, but my sister is wiped out these days. Growing a person, apparently, is a lot of work.

What if I never get the chance to find out?

No, I can't accept that answer. One way or another, I need to find a way to make this happen.

# CHAPTER 5

"Sit down, Erin."

Oh crap, this is serious. Don doesn't call you into his office to chit-chat or ask what you did over the weekend.

Not that he needs to ask. I was here, working, just like every other weekend. I've only been on staff here for eight years, which means I'm about twenty more away from moving up to having a regular Saturday or Sunday off.

Gosh, it's taken me this long to move back to having Tuesdays and Wednesdays off. When I first started, I had Mondays and Thursdays off. It was a step up in the zookeeping world to get two days in a row off.

I was able to finagle Wednesdays so I could attend my UnBRCAble meetings. During the season, the zoo is open ten to six, which means my days are about nine to seven. And no, the pay doesn't make up for the hours.

Don was not impressed that I needed to attend my support group meetings. I didn't disclose why, and he didn't ask. I bet he thinks I'm codependent or a shopping addict. He doesn't seem to care either way.

If in the past, I hadn't seen Don making all gaga faces at the animals, I'd wonder if he has a heart. I think he honestly does better with non-humans than humans.

Yet here he is, my manager. Swell.

My stomach's been off all day, and this is not helping. I try to ignore the tightness that's spreading across my abdomen. It's like menstrual cramps and a gas bubble had a baby, and it's growing exponentially in there.

Maybe it's gas bubble triplets.

Certainly feels like it.

"As you know, we need to make final staffing decisions for the new sloth encounter. I understand you're interested in being considered for this."

Of course, I'm interested. I applied the day it was announced. Plus, I've been through two rounds of interviews so far. But Don knows this, so why is he putting me on the spot?

The large lump in my throat prevents me from doing anything other than my impression of a bobble head. A sharp pain stabs through my lower abdomen, and it takes all the strength I have not to double over. I try to take a subtle breath in through my nose and out through my mouth.

I need to find words before the opportunity passes me by.

"Yes, as much as I love working only with the animals, I've always hoped to move into the education aspect. In fact, from the time I was little, my mom would say she could see me as the person holding up a snake for everyone to pet, explaining how they're not poisonous, but venomous."

Don nods. "I do think you are one of those people who likes the people as much as the animals." He looks at me and shakes his head slightly, like he can't understand that concept. "We don't get tons like you here. In fact, I'm not sure we have enough qualified candidates for staffing the way we are envisioning."

What does this mean?

It would be the best thing ever if I didn't have to do the final interview. I can talk to people all day everyday, but when it's to someone in authority, suddenly stringing together more than one syllable seems daunting. My first two rounds were ... less than stellar.

"We've opened up your position for hire. I wanted to tell you in case someone told you about the posting."

The pain in my abdomen is making it hard to focus. I might actually be sick. What is he saying? Am I fired? Is he terminating me because I want a different position? They need to staff the sloth enclosure, so they're hiring anyway. A wave of cramps rushes through me, and I'm not sure if I'm going to vomit ... or do something much worse.

"Okay ..." I finally manage to squeak out.

*Current mood: terrified.*

"You're going to start training with Ed from Education on Tuesdays." He quickly adds, "As in tomorrow."

About seventy questions flood my brain all at once. I try to streamline. "So can I assume that since Ed's in charge of the education department, it means that I'll be working in the sloth encounter? Also, I'm off on Tuesdays. Is that in exchange for another day?"

Don sighs, tired of me already. I don't know what I've done to piss him off, other than the occasional squabble with Xander, but it's clear he does not care for me. "You'll be primarily in sloths but still help Terry in South American primates. Until we can fill your position, your schedule stays the same."

Except it's not.

"I'm off on Tuesdays."

"Oh well, now you're not."

Think. Think. Think. I can't freak out now, but the pain is definitely putting my brain into freak out mode.

Jesus, Erin. Pull yourself together.

I can use this to my advantage. I hunch forward, trying to ignore the pressure building in my abdomen. It's like there is a party in my gut, all with knives trying to stab their way out.

"Since it's over time, I'll get time and a half, right?"

The extra money will certainly help. Zookeepers aren't known to be rolling in the dough.

Okay, I make practically nothing.

Don nods.

"Okay then. I'm in. Would you please send me an email with the details, including the additional time and pay for my records?"

Dad always taught me to get everything in writing.

It takes every ounce of energy I have to keep what little composure I have together while I walk down the hall and back to the locker room. In my head, I'm dancing like Hugh Grant in *Love, Actually*.

In reality, I'm not that coordinated, but my feet don't seem to care as they take over, sashaying down the corridor.

"Do you want me to call EMS or something?" Xander's dry voice stops me cold, my feet freezing in place. Slowly I turn to face him, praying that he didn't see my moves.

"Um, no, I'm fine. Clearly."

An evil grin spreads across his face, reminding me of the Grinch. "Oh, I thought for a minute you were having a seizure or something."

I hate this man.

Partially because he's an arrogant asshole, but mostly because when he taunts me, I lose all ability to come up with a witty come back. So, I stick my tongue out at him. Super mature.

Xander laughs. "You're lucky you're not in with the gorillas. You'd be getting poop flung at you for that."

He has a point. Gorillas see staring as a major threat and when combined with a sticking out tongue—well, them's fightin' words.

And one of our adolescent silverbacks, Ujasiri, does have a penchant for flinging fecal matter. In fact, they're talking about separating Ujasiri from his current troop to form a new one. He has all the indications of being an alpha, and there's concern that he'll try to assert dominance in his current setting. I wonder if that's how Xander ended up here—was he too alpha for the staff at the last zoo he worked in and they sent him away?

He's been here eight years. That hope—that he's too alpha for Pittsfalls—as well as the hope of sending Xander to another zoo, doesn't hold water. Though if he left, in a strange way, I'd miss him.

I try to regroup. "If you must know, I've been selected to be one of the educators on the sloth encounter."

I don't know what I expect his reaction to be, but it's surely not the stony-face expression that's staring back at me. He's always ready to fire back with the witty retort. His silence unnerves me.

"What?" I shift my weight from side to side, trying to figure out how I can get around him.

He never seemed that big before, but suddenly I'm aware that he takes up a fair amount of space. He's definitely over six-feet tall and his shoulders feel as if they take up all available space. Okay, maybe he could be the male lion of the pride.

As I move to the right, he moves left. Then we repeat the dance to the other direction. Finally, I stop and look at him.

"What? Why won't you let me by?"

"You got the position? Who told you? When did you find out?"

Testifying on the stand would make me feel less on the spot. I do half-expect him to fling some dung in my direction, based on his current sneer and posture.

"Don told me, just now."

"I applied for that position. He hasn't called me in."

I think about how Don said they didn't even have enough qualified applicants to fill the position. Either that means Xander is definitely in or definitely out. If it were anyone else, I'd probably reassure him and be super positive.

I know I should tell him that. I really know I should.

But it's Xander.

Xander who picks on me and goes out of his way to make me look bad.

Xander who won't keep me updated when my animals are sick.

Xander who won't let me pass, and I really need to go to the bathroom because there's a fair chance something is exploding in my abdomen.

Screw Xander.

I shrug. I want to give him some flippant answer about how I must have been the best person, but that seems a little mean. Xander's nice to the animals, and that's got to count for something, right?

And while I'd like to stay and torment him at least a little, the pressure in my abdomen kicks up again. I have all I can do not to double over.

I shove past Xander and dash off to the ladies' room. This is the greatest day. I got my dream job *and* I got to stick it to Xander Barnes, at least a little.

Sloth Central, here I come.

~~~***~~~

But it can get worse, which is what I discover when I hit the restroom. My abdomen is bloated. No not even bloated—swollen. I look like I'm six months pregnant, which I assure you I'm not. Not to mention that I woke up with a flat stomach this morning.

Not flat-flat obviously, but certainly not this.

Now I understand the pain and cramping all day. My utility pants have an elastic waistband so they've been forgiving ... up to a point. But even they are stretched to capacity, and I hesitate to button them.

Panic floods my system.

Oh God, is this how it all starts? Did I wait too long?

I know that this is cancer, and I'm going to die.

My fingers fumble as I pull my phone out of the side leg pocket of my pants. Thank goodness I don't have to dial any number as I'm sure I'd never be able to coordinate my hands that long.

Two taps and my Mom's on the line. "Hi honey. How was work?"

My voice shakes. "I think I need to go to the hospital. Can you meet me there?"

Mom's tone shifts dramatically in response. "Are you on your way? Do you need me to drive? What's wrong?"

Mom might be intense and controlling at times, but she's definitely the person you want in your corner during something like this.

I start to head out of the bathroom, grabbing my coat and bag quickly while I keep the phone pressed to my ear. It's hard to stand up straight, and all I want to do is curl into a ball.

As I pass through the door, I fill her in on my current symptoms. "I know it could probably wait for me to get in with Dr. Lee, but ... I have to know today."

Mom assuages me. "Erin, you don't know what it is. It could be anything. Chances are it's not cancer."

Her words should soothe, but they bounce off the surface of my brain like water off a duck's back. "Chances are it is. I shouldn't have waited. It was stupid. And now I'm going to die—" I break off before I can say, "because of you."

It's not her fault, not really. She's not even the one who passed me the stupid defective gene. That came from my dad's side. But my mom's family—the stories she can tell.

And does tell.

Adoption didn't work out as well for her as it did for my dad. Her parents and brother never really accepted her. They kept driving through her head that family is about blood. And since she didn't have it, she was never really part of the family.

Which is why it is so important to me to have my own child. My own blood. My mom's blood. Someone that she knows really belongs to her, as I do. As Mackenzie does.

I pick the smaller of the hospitals around us. I'm hoping that everyone thinks to go to the big trauma center, and I can get whizzed through to find out I have cancer. I mean, being time-sensitive is the least they can do.

It's a slow Monday evening in the emergency room, which means I only have to wait about an hour before I'm through triage and being handed a gown and a cup to pee in.

As I prepare to give the list of my current complaint for the third time, something in me snaps. "Can you please call Dr. Lee? She covers here, I know she does. Can you call her in for me? She knows me. She'll know what this means."

The young resident pats my hand. *Pats* my hand like I'm some old lady she's trying to shush. "Why don't you tell me what's going on?"

I look at my mom, sitting in the chair next to me. The worry is etched across her face. This is going to kill her.

"I'm all bloated up. Look at this! I'm not pregnant but throughout today, my stomach has grown to look like I am. I'm BRCA-1 positive, so this is probably a tumor."

"Ma'am, tumors don't grow that fast." She sets about pressing here and there, and when she gets to my right side, I nearly jump off the table.

Holy crap that hurts.

"Hmmm ... we'll have to get some blood work. It could be your appendix."

Okay, so I'm not a doctor, nor do I play one on TV, though sometimes I play one at the zoo, but even *I* know this is not my appendix.

"It's not my appendix."

The doctor smiles benignly at me. "We'll have to do a CT to rule that out."

She disappears, I assume to order the cat scan. Fine with me. I know it won't show an inflamed appendix, but will probably show a massive tumor.

I can't believe I let this happen. Just when my career picks up, my life is going to end.

# CHAPTER 6

*Wop-wop-wop.*

Holy crap. That cannot be what I think it is.

*Wop-wop-wop.*

I mean I don't even understand how it would be physically possible. I haven't been with anyone in six months.

At least six months.

Probably even more than that. There's no way I can be one of those "I didn't know I was pregnant" people. But there I am, listening to the heartbeat, while the ultrasound technician scans and clicks.

"Um, what is that?" My voice shakes, and I can feel my heart thudding in my ears. This isn't how it's supposed to be. I'm exposed to x-rays at work and I drink beer and I ...

"Oh, that's your blood vessel. I'm making sure your ovary has good blood flow. Sometimes, the ovary can twist around, and it cuts off the blood supply. You're good here."

Huh? I ... what? Am I not? "So that's me?"

The tech laughs. "Oh, yeah. Just you here."

As fast as it seemed to race, my heart thuds to a stop. "I'm not pregnant?"

"Did you think you were?"

I look over to the side, trying to decide which is worse: the sharp pain in my abdomen or realizing that this was probably my only chance, even if it would have been the Immaculate Conception.

Ouch.

The pain wins.

"I'm sorry. I know this is painful. We're almost done."

A few minutes later, I'm being wheeled back to my area in the Emergency Room. I feel like a VIP patient, not even having to walk anywhere. Not that I really could. I'm not sure I could stand up straight at this point. I roll to my side, clutching the sheet around me so I don't accidentally moon anyone.

Mom's reading a book, waiting in my space. I want to tell her about the "heartbeat" I heard. I want to make it a funny story. Instead, I blubber through, tears stealing any last iota of humor.

"Sweetie, it'll be okay. You'll have your time. I'm sure you'll meet someone and get married and you'll have your family, just like we've always planned."

If I was feeling better, I'd bristle at her use of we. She, most assuredly, will not be included in my family planning ... uh ... plans.

Ick.

But my whole life, we have talked about the future, and for me that did always include a white wedding, an adorable husband, and a few kids running around our farm.

Sometimes Mom has boundary issues. Especially with letting go of control over Mackenzie and me. I think Mackenzie has set the line more firmly, now that she's married and a mom.

I should probably work on that.

I'll put it on my list of things to do when I'm not dying.

A bit later, the doctor comes back in. "We want to take you for a CT, to rule out appendicitis. You do have an ovarian cyst, but that's no big deal."

"It is a big deal. Can you look at that on the cat scan? Can you tell if it's cancer?"

"It's not cancer." The doctor doesn't even bother to look at me while she brushes off my concerns like a pesky mosquito.

"How can you tell? I have the BRCA-1 mutation. Do you know what that means? I have about a seventy-percent chance of developing ovarian cancer. Odds are better for cancer than anything else."

"Odds are, it's your appendix."

I don't like this lady and if my rear end weren't exposed, I'd probably storm out right now. "Odds not," I mumble as she walks out of my curtained room. I hear her on the other side of the curtain, with her next patient.

"I think it's a kidney stone. We can check with an ultrasound, or we can do an MRI. Which would you like?"

I frown, looking at my mother. What is this? Since when do patients choose their own tests? Isn't that why she went to med school and the rest of us didn't? I have no confidence in this quack. "Should we leave?"

My mom shakes her head. "Get the cat scan first. It could provide useful information, either way. I mean, she *could* be right about your appendix."

I roll my eyes. If this doctor is right about my appendix, then I'm Abe Lincoln. I need to talk to Dr. Lee about all this. I need to talk to all the UnBRCAble women to see what they have to say. I'm tempted to call the answering service for Dr. Lee, but I'm sure whoever is on call is busy doing things like delivering babies. They don't need my problems.

Cancer probably won't kill me by tomorrow.

Probably.

Following the cat scan, the resident comes back in. I don't think she's actually made eye contact with me yet. "So, it looks like it's just an ovarian cyst. Your appendix is fine."

She's still looking at her computer.

"And?" My pain isn't any better. I still look pregnant. I'm still dying of cancer.

"Your blood work is normal. We're going to give you something for the pain. Follow up with your doctor."

"WAIT! Stop. Can you please slow down and look at me?"

The doctor does, but doesn't bother to hide her irritation. Apparently, she has more important patients. Like the ones she lets pick their own diagnostic tests.

"How do you know what it is? How do you know it's not cancer? How do—"

She cuts me off. "You have a small follicular cyst. It's common."

"How small is small?"

She looks at the computer. "Um ... three-point-one centimeters. It will go away in a month or two. There's a chance it could rupture, in which case you'd see some bleeding, but even then, it's fine. Follow up with your gynecologist in a few months. It should be gone by then."

"There's no treatment?"

She shakes her head. "No, it's really nothing. Very common. You're fine. Try not to worry so much."

*Try not to worry?* What is this lady smoking and can I have some?

She doesn't offer me wacky-tabaccy but does hook me up with a shot of toradol which makes me feel instantly drunk before discharging me. Mom has to drive me home, and she assures me that Dad and Luke will get my car to me by morning.

Mom pats my hand. "At least this happened on a Monday, and you can rest for the next two days. I never thought having Tuesdays off would be a good thing."

I'm trying to think, but fog rolls through my brain like morning on the Maine coast.

"Yeah, I know. Wait, no. I have to work tomorrow." I'm going to need to write that down as soon as I get home, otherwise I know I'll forget.

"No, honey. You're confused. Tomorrow's Tuesday. You're off." Mom pulls into my parking spot and comes around to help me out. My abdomen is still bloated, though I'm feeling no pain. In fact, I'm feeling pretty damn good.

Almost like I'm not worried about dying.

I should ask for this injection pain medication thingy more often.

Me likey.

~~~***~~~

I'm not prepared when the alarm jolts me out of my sleep, mostly because I was dreaming about giving Robert Downey, Jr. a behind-the-scenes tour at the zoo. I was doing a stellar job of laying the groundwork for convincing him to take me and a sloth on a movie tour with him and—

GAH! What time is it? I start with Ed in the sloth enclosure today! I can't be late on my first—

Ouch.

The memories of last night come flooding back. The emergency room. My freak-out during the ultrasound. The doctor dismissing me. That lovely pain shot.

Mmmm ... that was nice.

I look down at my stomach, which has now regained its former shape. Not to say flat, but at least I don't have to wear maternity clothes today. This is so weird. The pain is still there, especially when I press on my right side. I set an alarm on my phone to call Dr.

Lee's office on my first break and take an ibuprofen, as per my discharge instructions.

A record twenty-three minutes later, and I'm out the door. I'm lucky I don't have one of these jobs where I have to do things like pick out an outfit or try to find pantyhose without runs (does anyone even wear pantyhose anymore?) or style my hair. I have three ways I wear my hair to work: a bun, a braid, or a pony. Today's a bun day. It's the easiest of the three. Also, coincidentally, it's still up in a bun from yesterday. Even easier.

I don't even bother with makeup, since I won't be seeing guests today. The sloths won't care if I have circles under my eyes. They'll get the being tired thing.

Actually, sloths aren't lazy, though they do really sleep over eighteen hours a day. Most cats sleep that much, though you'd never name a deadly sin after them. Sloths have an incredibly slow metabolism, and their slow speed allows them to evade predators. It's a survival tactic. However, my slow speed only makes me late for work.

While I'm driving, I do put on some lip balm. It's not a vanity thing—I can't stand dry lips. I have several tubes stashed everywhere, including always carrying one in my pants pocket.

By the way, anyone who eschews cargo pants is a fool. Do you know how much you can fit in these puppies? I don't understand why more women's clothes don't have super utilitarian pockets like this. If I ever do get married, pockets in my wedding dress are a must.

Everything about my appearance for my job is utilitarian. I used to wish for a job in which I could look pretty and nice. Pretty and nice is not compatible with poop. Plus, shiny things like earrings and rings are distracting to the animals and make me look like food.

I've heard that sloths can actually move quickly when threatened or reaching out for food. Those claws that keep them hanging are pointed, as are their teeth. Who knew in that cute little face was a bunch of razor-sharp teeth? I don't want to tempt them with something silly like an earring because I was trying to look good.

But that's not important right now. All that matters is that Ed thinks I can do this job, and that I learn the best way to work with not only the sloths but the people entering the exhibit as well.

So once at work, I try to focus on what Ed's saying. I really do. But this sharp, nagging pain in my lower abdomen has other ideas. Each time I get absorbed in what I'm supposed to be learning, the red hot poker is back. Nagging me. Taunting me. Reminding me that I am not in control.

I will show my body. I will take control. I will show it who's boss.

I will not let cancer invade.

As soon as I pop another handful of ibuprofen.

Seriously, though, this is bull. If a dude had a three centimeter growth on his nad, the treatment wouldn't be "take some painkillers, and it'll be fine eventually." Even without the increased risk of cancer, this is scary, not to mention costly.

My deductible is small, and the emergency room visit last night will undoubtedly take care of that. I guess working six days a week and the resultant overtime will be a good thing. I'll need to bank every single cent to save for when I go out on maternity leave.

If I ever get to.

Who am I kidding? I've got to get into the doctor and see about having all my potentially cancer-causing and also reproductive organs removed. I am done with surveillance. Time to get active.

"So, read through the binder provided. You will be responsible for the information in it, in case a guest asks. And if prior experience is indicative, they will ask," Ed concludes.

Crap. What did I miss? I look at the binder with the zoo's logo on it. There are three of us in here, besides Ed.

That's not a lot of staff. Not when you consider that there will probably be two of us on a day, not including the private tours.

I wonder why Xander didn't get the position. As much as I hate to admit it, he'd be perfect here too. He'd be perfect anywhere in the zoo really.

He's annoyingly good at this job.

Not that it wasn't a *little* entertaining to see him sweat about this job. Now I feel badly. He would be an asset here.

I look around again. I'd think we'd need at least two more people, minimum, especially if we're still covering other exhibits. I wonder who they'll hire for that? Tours will run every hour and a half, with each group receiving an information session first followed by thirty full minutes with the animals.

Thirty minutes can be a long time, if the people can't follow the rules. I'd say it would be the kids, but I have a feeling the adults are going to be worse. I need to check in with Millie to see if she has any handling techniques. As a veteran second grade teacher, she's probably got more than one trick up her sleeve.

From the warnings Ed is giving, I get the impression that the wild animals will not be the most difficult thing in the exhibit.

It will be good. I handle difficult people all the time. The questions I get from zoo patrons would make you shake your head. Mostly about watching the animals procreate.

And yes, they actually do it like they do on the Discovery Channel.

People are creepy.

Plus, I hate to break it to them, but most of the time, animals only get the chance to mate under carefully controlled circumstances. There's a whole department of husbandry. All of us have assisted in impregnating one animal or another.

Perhaps I should hire them to help me on my quest.

And that's when it hits me, sitting there in Sloth 101. I don't need a husband. All I need is a donor.

And maybe a detective to help me find my mind.

Apparently, I've lost it.

Can I really do this? Can I have a baby without the husband?

# CHAPTER 7

"I need advice."

I can't even believe I'm thinking about this. Not thinking, but actually considering. *Really considering.*

The ladies of UnBRCAble, from all walks of life, are sure to tell it to me straight. Is this idea totally lunatic? Is it feasible? Is it smart?

The thoughts have been running on an endless loop in my brain ever since yesterday. What if my benign cyst isn't a cyst? What if I need to start with treatment?

It's last call. I'm out of time.

I have no other options.

After relaying the events of the past few days and my revelation, the ladies sit in stunned silence. Claudia finally breaks the tension, "So you want to abandon all your plans and find yourself a ... sperm donor?"

Okay, when she puts it like that ...

"Well, I guess. I mean, we're all here because we've had to abandon our plans. I don't think any of us *want* to be here."

Heads nod throughout the group.

"I mean, I'd still rather meet someone and fall in love and get married and have a baby, but ..." I look down at my hands. I don't need to say anymore.

They all understand. I see tears well up in Millie's eyes. She knows.

I take a breath and then continue. "I've never been that successful with dating and waiting at this point seems—literally—like putting all my eggs in the same basket. I can't control who I meet, but at least I can control this one thing. And I don't want to wait too much longer to have my surgeries. I can't." A wave of cold rushes through my veins, even thinking about those scary hours in the emergency room.

"Have you thought about how you're going to do this? Do you have a fertility doctor?" Claudia inquires.

"I've been researching it all day. I stopped in at the clinic in this building earlier today." Good use of my one day off. "I have an appointment next week to meet with a counselor and doctor."

"Have you told your family yet?" Tracey asks.

My smile drops, much like the pit in my stomach. I shake my head, wishing we weren't talking about me anymore. Maybe I should bring up the current hot topic of under the muscle versus over the muscle implants. That's sure to distract everyone away from my family and me.

One thing I've been trying hard *not* to think about is how my family is going to react. Because I know exactly. There will be yelling and tears. This is probably going to go over like a fart in church.

And maybe not even that well.

Let's put it this way: motherhood out of wedlock is going to be a no-go with my conservative family. There's a good chance I'll be shunned or disowned. At very least, my parents will be *deeply disappointed* in me, the guilt of which may be worse.

Old-school Catholic guilt. The best deterrent on the market.

I figure I need to start out with Mackenzie. If I can get her on my side, Mom and Dad will have to jump on board. They won't want to risk alienating both kids. Especially Mom.

Nothing's more important to her than family. True family. Real family. Family spawned from other family. People related to her by blood and genetics. Right now, Kenz and I are the only people she knows that fit that criteria.

"My mom has some very narrow views on what constitutes family. All of it involves love and marriage and shared genetics." I shrug. "She's conservative."

And in her eyes, the only way to do it is first comes love, then comes marriage, *then* comes baby in the baby carriage.

If you'd asked me two years ago, or even two months ago, I would have said I was equally as conservative in terms of what I wanted for myself. I never, ever would have considered having a baby without being married first. I know it works for lots of people, but I never thought about it for me.

Desperate times call for desperate measures, and I'm more desperate than a cat in a bathtub.

69

"Has anyone done this? Thought about it?" I look to the ladies of the group. A surprising amount are shaking their heads.

Claudia adds, "I think Sarah may have explored some of these options, but she's not here tonight. Perhaps you can connect with her another time to find out what her experience was. I believe that she looked into freezing eggs."

I mean, that's another option, but then I'd have to find a surrogate, which is another layer of complication. Obviously, Mackenzie would be my first choice in an ideal situation. I think she'd do it. After she has the baby of course. And recovers. And has enough time to forget how awful labor and delivery are.

I'm going to have to start buying her better birthday presents.

The vortex of thoughts whirring through my brain make it nearly impossible for me to focus on anything for the rest of the meeting. I sprint for the door as soon as it's done and head directly to my sister's house.

"Erin, what's wrong?" The color drains from Kenzie's face when she sees me at the door.

"I really need to talk to you."

"I've got to give Trey his bath and get him to bed." Kenzie sighs, looking down over her burgeoning belly at the two-year-old who is literally clinging to her leg. "After that wrestling match, we can talk, if you can hang around and wait."

The fatigue on her face says what her words don't. She doesn't have the time or the energy for this. For me.

"No, that's okay. It's ... it's not that important. You looked wiped."

She sighs. "I am. This pregnancy is killing me. I'd like to make it one day without throwing up. Just one. And to make matters worse, I now have sciatica, and Trey wants me to carry him all the time. I don't think I'm going to make it."

Her face contorts, growing even paler—which I didn't think was possible—as she pushes past me, still dragging my now screaming nephew with her. I step aside just in time to watch her spew all over the rose bushes.

Eeew.

She wipes her mouth with the back of her hand. "Oh God, I cannot take this anymore. I am never going to make it until my due date. And Luke—I could kill him for this. This is his fault. He's not the one who goes through hell every day. I never, *ever*, want to be pregnant again."

All righty then.

"Oh, did I tell you?" Mackenzie keeps right on talking like she didn't just go all *Exorcist* on me. "The doctor says I probably can't go VBAC for this. Something about the placenta's not in the right spot. I don't know. I'm so pissed off."

She throws up again.

I'm so looking forward to pregnancy.

"What's VBAC?"

My sister rolls her eyes, like I'm the dunce in the class. "Vaginal birth after cesarean."

71

She doesn't add the 'duh' on the end, but it's implied.

"Right. So you have to have another C-section? That sucks."

*Totally sucks that your uterus has to get cut. Mine has to get cut out, but whatevs.*

Very rarely am I upset that I got the luck of the BRCA and Mackenzie didn't. However, it doesn't stop her insensitive comments from stinging.

"I'm crushed. I didn't get to enact my birth plan last time, and I wanted to do it with this one. It's my last chance to have the birth I envision."

I may not know a lot about being pregnant and all, but I do know that when it's time, it's time, and it doesn't always go to plan. I wonder who came up with the crock of shit called birth plans. Now Kenz is all upset and for what? Some crappy expectation that society told her she had to have.

My birth plan included meeting a fantastic guy who is head over heels in love with me, getting married, and then getting pregnant, none of which will be relevant at my birth. Really, all that matters is the baby and mom are healthy.

I want to tell her that, but after another round of heaving, I decide not to poke the beast.

She also gets a pass on being insensitive. It's hard to be tactful when your insides are exiting your body violently.

"Okay well, I'll be going then. Good to see you. Take care. Get some rest."

I back away, trying to avoid the sullied stoop. I get to my car and put the keys in the ignition before I stop. Getting out, I find the hose on the side of the house and proceed to clean up the mess in the front. If there's one thing I'm good at, it's hosing down animal waste.

My sister definitely does not have that pregnancy glow.

Plus, I know she loves me and all, but I'm not sure that it would be enough to convince her to go through a pregnancy again. With the repeated C-section, I wonder if she would even be able to.

I'm going to have to find a different option.

Once home, I pace my small apartment. My tiny apartment. My one-bedroom apartment that I've never felt the need to spend a lot of money on because I'm hardly ever here. It's comfortable and has all the amenities, but looking around, it becomes glaringly obvious that there is no room for a baby, let alone a mobile toddler here.

Certainly no room for a Pinterest worthy nursery. Yes, I've got a board for that. Okay, several boards. Obviously, I'd go with a zoo theme.

That does it. I'm going to need to move. Another thing to add to the list.

I should probably actually start writing these things down.

What do I need to do? Have my eggs harvested. Have my surgeries. Find a bigger house. Pick a sperm donor. Pick a surrogate. Win the lottery to pay for all of this.

Maybe I could just marry a billionaire. Seems to be easy in all those romance novels Mackenzie reads.

I sigh and crumple up the list.

It's not fair.

None of this is fair.

Stupid, stupid, stupid DNA test. Why did I have to buy it for my dad in the first place? I'd be so much happier if I didn't know. I wouldn't have all this pressure and this fear and this inability to control anything in my life.

It would be so stupid to pursue this lunatic idea of having a baby on my own.

But if I don't, I'll never be a mother.

The feeling hits me like a ton of bricks. I want to scream and smash something and vomit all at the same time. My chest tightens, and I can't seem to get any air in.

*Current mood: devastated.*

Since my sister obviously is in no condition to talk, I call my mom. She's barely said hello why my silent tears turn into large, wracking sobs.

"Erin, honey, breathe. Tell me what happened? Are you still in pain? Do you want me to take you back to the hospital?"

Finally, in gasping breaths, I manage to get out, "It's ... not ... fair."

"What's not fair?"

"This." I gesture to the lower half of my body as if she could see it through the phone. "Me. My stupid body and my stupid genes."

"I know, honey. It's terrible. But your genes make up who you are, the good and the bad."

"I know. I don't blame Dad. It's not like he knew what he was carrying."

Ah, the joys of having two parents who were adopted. Neither had any idea of their ancestry or heritage. The only thing we could guess at is that Dad, with his curly black hair and light brown skin, was most likely not as Irish as his McAvoy last name indicated.

We weren't wrong on that.

His DNA showed that he was about thirty percent Nigerian, in addition to being Western European, German, Italian, and a whopping three percent Irish.

He's practically St. Patrick.

Who was ironically not Irish either.

None of this mattered to my grandparents who considered their adoptive children as much family as their biological children. And in some weird way, my dad does look like Grandpa a little. *A very little.* Grandma and Grandpa McAvoy were always pretty awesome.

When Dad did the DNA testing, we expected to find out what his heritage was. It never occurred to any of us that we'd find his blood relatives. Until the emails started coming, that was.

There weren't that many contacts, but they all painted the same picture. Women dying young because of breast cancer. My father's biological half-sister and mother. Three cousins. It was enough to suggest that Mackenzie and I get tested.

We all know how that worked out.

Mackenzie and Luke were pregnant when the information started coming in. She was so upset when she found out that we all thought she'd lose Trey.

Thinking back, that wasn't the easiest pregnancy either.

My mom's voice brings me back. "Then what's changed? What's wrong now?"

I should blurt it all out and tell her, but, well, I'm too chicken. "It was the cyst. You know, it scared me. I don't know that I can stay in surveillance mode much longer."

"No, probably not. I bet you'd sleep better if you didn't have to worry. Worry is a terrible burden." Meaning *she'd* sleep better if she didn't have to worry. Meaning it's time for me to stop burdening *her* with this.

She's not wrong, just passive aggressive.

I can't imagine what it must be like, living with the fear of burying your child.

"I know, I will, but you know, there are other things I want to do."

"Yes, but we don't always get the things we want most." Mom's voice hangs heavy. She's had a lifetime of losing out, starting with her biological family and continuing on with her foster and adoptive ones. I can't imagine what it must have been like to lose one family after another and to never know what receiving unconditional love feels like.

All she ever wanted was for a family to love her.

She has it now, but carries the weight of a lifetime of being unsure. Most of the time, Mom's awesome. But during those trying, stressful times, her controlling nature takes hold. She manages, and micromanages, everything, attempting to bulldoze her way through.

Not the best trait perhaps, but understandable. She loves us and comes from a good place. She just doesn't handle it well all the time.

One of the things she tries to control is the future growth of our family. My mom's family tree is a new one—the roots are young and weak. She wants nothing more than strong, deep roots that extend for generations, and I intend to give that to her.

My dad may have passed onto me faulty genes, but my mom passed on crippling self-doubt and insecurity.

Woo hoo.

Also, I have hair that tends toward the frizz, but that seems like small potatoes right now.

I want to tell my mom what I'm thinking about, but there's no way she's going to be okay with it. At least until I'm pregnant. Maybe a lot pregnant. Like when I'm crowning.

But the feeling of needing to figure out a way to make this work won't go away. Instead it's only getting bigger.

It may be crazy, but I think I've got to try. Somehow, someway, I'll think of the right way to tell my mom I went out and got myself pregnant.

Maybe she won't take it as badly as I fear.

KATHRYN R. BIEL

# CHAPTER 8

I have never seen so many zeroes in my life.

This is ridiculous.

Completely and totally ridiculous. And I'd say I got bad information, but the hours I've spent researching this stuff tells me I'm not wrong.

Egg harvesting and fertilization. Sperm donation. Preimplantation genetic screening. Embryo storage. Fertility medications.

We're talking close to a hundred thousand before we even get started. Insurance doesn't pay for any of it. Maybe some do, but not mine.

And that doesn't include the cost of having the baby. It's hard to raise a kid when you've gone into bankruptcy just to have one in the first place. Not to mention the cost for my mastectomy and reconstruction and hysterectomy after.

Forget winning the lottery. Robbing a bank or embezzling bitcoin might be the only way to get this done.

Then I accidentally Google the cost of using a surrogate. I almost need someone to Heimlich me after I choke on the pretzel I am eating. I don't know why

78

more women with functioning uteruses don't do that more often. It seems like a cash cow.

I chew on this information as I drive into work. My exciting Sunday night was spent needing to defibrillate myself after finding out how much my dreams cost. I logged onto my bank account, just to see if there'd been some miraculous banking error that deposited an extra hundred-grand into my account.

There was not.

And to make matters worse, it's Monday. Which means tomorrow is Tuesday. My former day off. Otherwise known as day six in a row of work for me.

It's a good thing Barry is so cute.

Barry's my sloth.

Okay, my current suckfest of a life is probably worth it because I can say the sentence, "Barry's my sloth."

His little derpy face makes my day. Two more weeks, and I'll move into Sloth Central full time. Good-bye overtime.

On the other hand, good-bye overtime.

I'd say I need it now more than ever, but there aren't enough hours in the week for me to be able to finance my pipe dream of having a baby. I try to shove all those feelings down. I can't lose it at work like I did last night on the phone with my mom.

I slam my locker a little harder than I need to.

"Easy there, killer. What'd that locker ever do to you?"

I am not in the mood for Xander Barnes and his stupid perfect face right now.

"Shut up. I hate you."

Okay, that was harsh, even for me. "I'm sorry. I don't know why I said that." I add quickly.

I do know why I said that. Xander is cocky and annoying and everyone loves him, and he thinks he can do whatever he wants simply because he has chiseled arms and a face that belongs on the movie screen and a smile that is so bright it could be measured in wattage.

"Whatever, yo. But you're going to need to check that attitude when the guests are here. Especially when we're doing a show together."

Huh?

"What are you talking about? I'm moving to the sloth encounter. If we're doing a show together, someone's in trouble because your cats are likely to eat my sloth. In case you didn't know, jaguars are a primary predator of sloths."

*Duh.*

"You haven't heard the good news then? I'm moving to Sloth Central too. We're doing the big shows."

"We? Who's we? Do you have a mouse in your pocket?"

In the zoo, it's not unheard of to carry around one creature or another. Usually they're dead, to be used as enrichment with some of the animals, but still … dead mice don't go through the wash well.

Please let that be why he said we.

Xander laughs, leaning his elbow on my locker, right in front of my face. A lazy grin spreads across his face. If I didn't know better, I'd think it was his seductive grin. "We. Us. You and me. Didn't Ed tell you? You and I are the face of the new sloth encounter. They're even going to take our picture together and plaster it all over town. There's a big huge marketing campaign."

Shut the front door.

I cannot even.

"I take it from your fabulous poker face that this is news?" He puts his hand under my chin and pushes my mouth closed. I didn't even know it was open. "Careful, or you're going to swallow a fly."

I swallow and begin stuttering. "But ... I ... how ... what ..." There is not enough air.

He pushes off the locker and I'm relieved for the increased distance between us. "They had trouble finding someone to take my place in cats. Now that they've hired my replacement, I'm all yours. Although, maybe you should let me do the talking while you just stand there and look pretty." Xander turns and heads toward the door. He casts a quick glance over his shoulder. "Or whatever it is you do."

This cannot be happening.

Yet it seems that it is.

This job is the only beacon of light for me right now. And that says a lot considering the amount of poop I clean on a daily basis.

That is a bright spot of this move—sloths only have a bowel movement once every week to two. Sure, it's a doozy, but there's not a lot to clean on a daily basis. Sloths are the epitome of slow metabolism.

It can take them up to a month to fully digest one meal.

Also, I won't have to try to outrun any sneaky animals trying to get away. When I was in the Farmland exhibit, we had this one rabbit—Lola—who wanted more than anything to be free. She was sneakier than a raptor, looking for weak spots in her enclosure. I had to catch her on more than one occasion. Not a lot of people can say they move faster than a rabbit. On the other hand, she didn't like being caught, and I have the scars on my arms to prove it.

I look down at my forearms, which makes me think of Xander. He's got this interesting tattoo on the inside of his left wrist. I didn't notice for a long time because his watch band often covers most of it, but one day I saw it and now I can't stop looking at it, trying to figure out what it says. All I've been able to make out is "Never."

Never what? I can't picture Xander having anything he feels that strongly about, unless it actually says, "Never stop being an ass."

I could see that.

This day has gone from bad to worse. First realizing that I'm not going to be able to finance having a baby. Then finding out I'm working with Xander. And is that a cramp I feel?

Dammit.

Like I needed to get my period right now. Fantastic.

I run to the bathroom before I head out to start my shift. Great. It's like my body is sticking it to me, saying *look, we're fertile but there's not a damn thing you can do about it.*

I hate being a woman.

I'm still grumbling about it when I reach the first enclosure. Terry's already done first check on the locks and is lining up food and medicine. She glances at me, but doesn't say anything.

"Sorry I'm late. Had to make an emergency bathroom run."

"Yeah, and you were too busy flirting with Xander."

Her tone makes my eyebrows shoot up. "We were not flirting."

She laughs, "Right. Sure. I give you guys two weeks."

"Two weeks?" I have no idea what she's talking about.

"Yeah. You won't be working together two weeks before you'll be hot and heavy."

Um, no. Gross.

"I don't think so. The only way I'd hit that is if I could dip him in bleach first and replace his personality with someone—anyone—else." I shudder at the thought of getting up close and personal where so many others have gone before.

Ick.

"Uh huh." Terry doesn't sound convinced.

Plus, let's face it, Xander would never even look my way. I'm not his type. Which is code for I'm not slender and girly and pretty enough. He does have a thing for the model type. "He's a man-whore. I'm not going to be his next conquest."

Even as I say it, I feel guilty. As much as I like to think Xander's an irresponsible frat boy, he's actually a very decent, reliable co-worker. He's diligent about the job, thorough and compassionate. I've seen him trade days off with people when they ask. He never slacks on the job.

But still.

Terry glances at me out of the corner of her eye. "Sure thing. Two weeks."

"Seriously, Ter. I can't even think about that. I ... I've got a lot bigger things to worry about."

"Are you okay?" The smile fades from her face. "Is it the cancer thing?"

I look at the howler monkeys and count. All four are present and accounted for and have started breakfast. The oldest female is moving a bit slow, and we're keeping an eye on her. Arthritis doesn't save itself for humans, poor girl.

"Yeah, sort of. I'm fine. For now. But I need to make some important decisions, and I don't have the time I thought I might."

Terry gives me the cancer-face look. Even though I don't actually have the Big C yet, I might as well. I still get *the look*. Pity mixed with fear mixed with relief that it's not her. "What are you going to do?"

I hesitate before I speak the words, as if saying them out loud will make this *thing* real and permanent. "So, I'm thinking about having a baby."

"Okay. Aren't you missing something? Or did someone finally step up on *List2Love*?"

"Yeah, no on that." I break off a piece of cantaloupe and give it to one of the tamarins. This is one of the juveniles and we're still working on training them to take food from us so that we can medicate them if needed without having to trap and sedate. "I want do this on my own."

For the record, I don't *want* to do this on my own but don't see another option.

I wait for the shocked gasp and the clutching of pearls, but it doesn't come. "Makes sense. Are you looking for some frozen pop?"

Her brash tone alone makes me want to abandon my plan right now. I can see myself telling my kid someday, "Yes, and I looked through a catalogue and then picked the slushy that seemed best."

So romantic.

"I guess."

"Cool. I think it's badass that you're going to do this on your own. You don't need a man."

I mull over Terry's words all day. I don't need a man. I don't need a man. I don't need a man.

Technically, she's right. But there's one little thing.

I want a man.

I want a partner. I want someone to share this journey with me. I want someone who thinks the sun rises and sets on me. I want someone to run to the convenience store to get me ginger ale when I feel sick, and I want someone to rub my feet when my cankles burst forth. I want someone to call when the baby does something cute, and I want someone to hold my hand when our little one steps onto the school bus for the first time.

I also want to have the choice of having a baby when I'm ready, not because I have to.

I don't want to find my baby's father through a list.

I don't want to go into debt to have this baby.

Am I being selfish even trying this?

# CHAPTER 9

"Are you crazy?"

All righty. Not quite the reaction I was hoping Mackenzie would have.

Suspecting, yes. Hoping, no.

"No, I'm being practical. I've got a lot of tough decisions to make, and this is the first step. I'm going to have a baby."

"Have you told Mom yet?"

"Are you the crazy one? I'm not telling her until it's a done deal."

"She's going to flip."

I nod my head, even though Mackenzie can't see it. "She's going to flip," I agree. "But once she sees the cute little bug, she'll be fine."

"Un huh. Are you sure we're talking about the same woman? She might disown you. Hang on. Luke's beeping in."

I doodle on a notepad while I wait for Kenz to come back on the line. Another week has gone by, and I'm no closer to getting pregnant than I was last week.

Also, I took the List2Love app off my phone. No use in being tormented by that anymore.

I hope Kenz isn't serious about Mom disowning me, though that woman does know how to hold a grudge. She's fiercely loyal, in both love and hate. This will be a disappointment to her, surely, but not enough for her to hate me.

I hope.

The only other thing that's different this week is I'm wrapping up my time as a primary keeper in primates of South America. My replacement, a scared kid named Tyler, will probably be fine, if Terry doesn't eat him alive first.

Probably.

Kenzie's voice pops back on the line. "Erin, this is terrible. I don't know what I'm going to do. I have my ultrasound today, and Luke can't come. He's stuck with people from corporate, and there's no way he can get out of it."

"Okay ..." I don't understand why this is a crisis, but the panic in her voice indicates that it surely is.

"Today's the anatomy scan." Her voice is impatient, as if she's explaining that water's wet.

"And? Sorry, Kenz, you'll have to explain that to me. I don't know what it means." All I can picture is the security guard from the airport, wanding the fetus up and down.

She huffs, and I can practically see her eye roll through the phone. "It's when they check all the parts and stuff, and we find out if it's a girl or a boy."

Ah, that makes more sense now.

"Can you reschedule?"

"No, because we have our big gender reveal party on Saturday, remember?"

I actually forgot because I never get to go to the Saturday parties. One benefit of moving to Sloth Central is that due to the revolving show schedule and encounters, I might end up getting about one Saturday every two months off. It doesn't sound like a lot, but I haven't had a non-vacation Saturday off since I started this job. If you include my intern time, that's almost nine years.

The lack of weekends off sort of sucks. Having occasional Saturdays off almost makes working with Xander worth it.

Almost.

"Okay, so go to the ultrasound and call Luke later. Let's face it, it's a boy or it's a girl. As long as he or she is healthy, does it matter?"

Kenzie huffs again. This pregnancy has made her moody and snippy. Maybe the prolific puking has something to do with it. Maybe not. Either way, she's not a barrel of laughs right now.

"Can you come with me? I can't do this alone."

"What time? I've got a hair appointment at eleven and UnBRCAble at six."

Normally, I'd cancel the hair appointment. Heck, normally I'd never even have a hair appointment. But desperate times call for desperate measures.

If I could cancel it, I would.

"A hair appointment? Are you unwell? Have you been possessed by aliens or something?"

"I get my hair done." I run my fingers through my bushy mane of hair which is way too long and has way too many split ends to admit.

"When was the last time you went to a hair salon?" Mackenzie asks accusingly. She goes every six weeks without fail to maintain her perfect coif. She gets keratin treatments, and her hair wouldn't dare disobey her by frizzing.

"Well, I need to do something with it. I am getting pictures taken tomorrow, so I thought I'd at least try to make it look decent."

"Pictures? For what?"

"Just some zoo publicity. Nothing big. There's something going up on the website about the sloth encounter. I always get caught when I look like I went ten rounds with a gorilla. I thought I might go in at least attempting to look pretty. I might even wear makeup."

Shoveling animal waste doesn't usually require much maintenance in the face department. It's been a long while since I've done anything wild and crazy like used blush or foundation, but I need to look the best I can if I have to be in a picture with Xander. I mean, I'll still be wearing cargo shorts and a polo, so there's not much you can do when you look like your wardrobe was designed by Dora the Explorer.

"Do you even own makeup?"

"Yeah, I have the stuff I used in college."

There's silence on the line.

Finally, my sister speaks. "Erin, you're thirty-two. You've been out of college for almost a decade."

I fail to see her point.

"No wonder your dating life is a disaster," Mackenzie mutters.

"Now you sound like Mom." If she can hit below the belt, so can I.

"I'll tell you what. My appointment is at two. I'll pick you up and after you go with me to the ultrasound, I'll take you to Ulta to get you some new makeup." She sounds like a mother bribing a young child to eat her vegetables.

Luckily, I'm not above bribery.

"Sounds like a plan. See you soon."

I disconnect before I realize what I've done. I just agreed to go to my sister's pregnancy ultrasound, as I'm trying to deal with the fact that I may never get to be pregnant myself.

I so did not think this one through.

*Current mood: screwed.*

~~~***~~~

"This product is a miracle. It says so right here. I need it." I clutch the eye cream that promises to reduce puffy eyes.

The sales girl looks a little afraid of me, as she should be. It looks as if I have some highly contagious skin infection. I wish the physical cause of this was contagious.

Unfortunately, pregnancy is not contagious. If it was, I'd be rubbing myself all over my sister.

I don't know what I was thinking. I know Mackenzie wasn't. I mean, she was thinking that she didn't want to be alone for this and thought it'd be cool to share it with me.

Yeah, really cool bringing your sister who wants nothing more than to have a baby but probably will never get to to your ultrasound.

Needless to say, my eyes are puffy and my skin is splotchy and this poor girl cannot find a product to fix me, though this cream did make my eyes look a skosh better.

Not enough for the pictures, but enough to show potential.

Unfortunately, I don't have time for potential. I need a facelift in a box.

Unless she has a magic wand that can change my mutant genes, she's outta luck on making me better.

It didn't help that my sister's ultrasound was at the Genevieve T. Wunderlich Women's Health Center, where UnBRCAble also meets. I come in and go to the meetings without ever really looking to see what else is in the center. Lots of my group mates have gone to physical therapy in the building, and there's also a mammogram office. It never occurred to me that the facility encompassed all aspects of women's health—not just us with broken systems.

To make matters worse, now Mackenzie is crying and neither one of us can stop.

"I'm so sorry. I didn't think about it. I know you can't have any babies. Do you want this one? I want to share it all with you so you get to experience it."

"That makes no sense, and no I don't want your baby," I sob. "I want my baby, growing in my uterus, pressing on my bladder, and tearing apart my hoo ha on the way out."

This is way too much for the sales person, who slinks off. Out of the corner of my eye, I see her point to us and then run into the back. Yup, she's going to be telling the story of us for a long time. I'm still clutching the tube of eye cream and at this point, they probably don't care if we steal it, just to get us out of the store.

I drop the tube on a shelf, and we leave the store and head to the food court, where I shamelessly dunk my napkin in my cup of ice water and dab at my eyes, attempting to decrease the swelling.

"I'm so sorry, Erin. I thought you'd like it."

"I did like it. But it doesn't mean it's not hard for me. I really thought it was going to happen. I really thought I'd get to have it all and have a baby and then do my surgeries. Like I'd pull a fast one on Mother Nature."

I shrug. No fast ones here.

"I think you should."

"Should what?"

"You need to get a sperm donor and get yourself pregnant. Totally. You need to do this. You are meant to be a mom. And then I can come with you to your ultrasounds."

"Why?"

"Erin, you're super kind and compassionate. You're great with kids. Trey loves his Auntie, and I know this little ..." she drops her voice to barely a whisper, "*girl*

93

will too." Mackenzie looks around to see if anyone heard. I don't have the heart to tell her that probably no one cares. "I want my kids to have cousins."

"A cousin, at best."

"One cousin is better than none."

"What if I don't want to have a baby?" I don't know why I even say that. All my focus has been on to *have* a baby. Maybe it'd be better to start thinking about life without one. I could start a Pinterest board for a house that has lots of white and glass and sharp corners.

"Then don't have one. But you make that choice. Don't let a bad roll of the genetic dice pick for you. If you want one, we will figure out how to make this work. I'll save all my baby stuff for you. Either way, you'll be set with hand me downs forever."

I nod, thinking about it. We have tons of cousins on the McAvoy side. We're not as close with the ones on Mom's side, only because she's not close with her brother. It would be sad for Mackenzie's kids not to have any cousins. It's the least I can do, right?

I wipe my face one more time. "So you think I should? Do this on my own? Sperm donor?"

Mackenzie nods.

"I will on one condition."

"Shoot."

I laugh. "You have to tell Mom for me."

# CHAPTER 10

Holy crapballs.

I didn't know this was possible.

*Current mood: impressed.*

I look hot.

Not just decent, but actually hot.

Like sexy Dora the Explorer.

Mackenzie got up super early and came over and did my hair and makeup this morning. She's still feeling guilty about the ultrasound, and I'm not above reaping the benefits of that guilt. I know I was with her when we bought the products last night, but she must have cast some sort of special spell on them because they worked magic.

And my hair—maybe I should get it cut more often. It's falling in soft layers and waves around my face and shoulders. I'll still be able to pull it back, but man, I feel sexy right now. I want to flip my hair and have Beyonce wind for the photo shoot.

Mackenzie tries to tie up my shirt to show midriff and roll my shorts, but I draw the line there. This is a family experience. I'm not trying to channel my inner Lara Croft.

Though with my hair and makeup, for the first time, I feel like maybe I could. Watch out Angelina Jolie.

I just hope we take the pictures first thing, before I get all sweaty and nasty. It's a beautiful April day, but many of the enclosures are humid. There's significant doubt that the Brazilian keratin can actually stand up to Costa Rican level humidity.

Ironic.

"Take my picture before I go." I hand Mackenzie my phone. I never have mastered the art of the selfie. I can't find an angle that doesn't make my head look tiny on my shoulders or that doesn't look like I have six chins.

She snaps a few, and I even like one well enough to immediately change my social media profiles.

"Don't take this the wrong way, Erin, but what if," Mackenzie shrugs a little, trying to act super casual, which is a dead giveaway for this is not a casual suggestion, "you know, you tried a little more with your appearance. I mean, you get more flies with honey than with vinegar."

My sister just told me I look like vinegar.

"I'm going for a natural look."

"And you're naturally beautiful. But you know, peacocks show their tail feathers for a reason."

"Peafowl—and peacocks especially—are some of the dumbest creatures on Planet Earth. We lost almost our entire flock because they thought it'd be a good idea to roost in the lion's den for the evening. While I'm sure the lions thought that was great, the cleanup was hellacious. We had to get all the feathers and blood out before the guests came in in the morning."

That was a sucky day. Although our pride of lions were in an especially content mood.

"Eeew, gross." Mackenzie wrinkles her nose as she finishes cleaning my brand new makeup brushes and beauty blender. Before this, I thought a blender was what you made drinks in.

"Yeah, and we lost another peacock to the soda machine."

That gets her attention. "Huh? The soda machine."

I laugh. This is one of my favorite zoo stories. "Yep. Pablo the Peacock decided to try and get amorous with the soda machine. He electrocuted himself. We found fried Pablo wedged behind the machine. Apparently, you can't stick it anywhere without repercussions."

Which immediately makes me think of Xander.

Ugh.

My high is ruined.

Why do I have to do this photo shoot with him?

On the other hand, I was simply stoked to be picked for the sloth encounter at all. I never expected to be the face of it. Word on the street is that this campaign could even result in some local news appearances. Usually it's the big wigs, like Don and Ed who handle that stuff, plus the vets like Dr. Val or Dr. Sophie who get their faces on the news.

I wonder if my face will be on the side of a bus or a billboard. Should have skipped those tacos yesterday.

When I tell this to Kenz, she smiles. "Um, duh. I've seen Ed and Don. They're not going to appeal to all the demographics."

"What do you mean by that?" I finish packing my lunch (leftover tacos, naturally) and head toward the door. Mackenzie follows me, but not before straightening the blanket and pillows on my couch and hanging up a sweatshirt that I'd thrown on the back of the chair.

I try to remember that she's nesting and that it's not a personal comment on my housekeeping.

I lock the door and wait for my sister's answer. "Look at you and Xander. A lot more people are going to be interested in coming to look at an animal that sleeps twenty-two hours a day if they get to look at you two, too."

It takes me a minute to process that. There were too many twos in that sentence. "So you think I got the job because of my looks?"

That would be a first for me.

"No, I think you got the job because you'll be great at it. And Xander probably the same. But I think they're being smart using you two as the face of the new program. It's not cheap. Four-hundred bucks is a lot to ask a family to spend for an hour."

I freeze mid-step when she says that. *Four-hundred dollars?* Holy cow. That's outrageous. And if we have four encounters a day times seven days a week, we're talking a veritable gold mine for the zoo. Not to mention merchandising.

Merch is the true cash cow. That, and bottled water.

I should see if the zoo will fund regular trips to the hair salon for me. Maybe I can even expense a pedicure every now and again. I should have done a manicure last night.

I think about this as I'm driving in. This needs to work. The zoo needs Xander and I to be appealing and approachable, all while educating. My spirit is soaring knowing that for the first time in my life, someone is seeing me and appreciating all I have to offer, including the aesthetically pleasing part. I've never been singled out because of my looks. I bet this sort of thing has happened to Xander his whole life. I'd wonder if he has the brains to backup the position, but I've seen him with the animals, and I know he does. He's good. He's got the gift.

I cannot disappoint the zoo. So the first thing I need to do is to be professional toward Xander. I won't let him get under my skin. I won't let him needle me. I won't let it bother me that he's slept with practically every female ever employed by the Pittsfalls Zoo.

I will be professional.

I will be kind.

I will be courteous.

"Holy crap, what happened to you? Did you get abducted overnight by a rogue band of drag queens?"

I hate Xander Barnes.

Then when I thought it couldn't get any worse, he starts laughing. "Did you do this for the pictures? You know it's literally going to be your hands holding Barry or Bonnie. Did you get a manicure too? How about adding some contouring. Don't want your hands to look fat."

I ball up my non-manicured (thank goodness) hand and think long and hard about punching him. "If our faces aren't in the pictures, then it won't matter if you have a black eye."

That makes him stop.

He puts his hands up, as if surrendering. "Woah, easy there, killer. I'm just kidding with you. I just didn't know you were so ... girly." He looks me up and down, which makes me squirm a bit. "I didn't think it ... mattered."

I get neither the chance to punch him nor to decipher what he means by "girly" because suddenly we're not alone. All the higher ups and publicity people are here. There are lights being set up. Casually, I turn away and run my finger under my eyes, trying to wipe off some of the eye makeup. Not that it matters, because no one will even see my face. They didn't want me because I was attractive.

It doesn't matter what I look like.

At least I have the pictures Mackenzie took to remind me that I can be a little pretty.

~~~***~~~

I have to laugh. Because if I didn't, I'd be crying. I am *such* an idiot.

The stars of the sloth encounter are obviously the sloths. There's no use for me. There's no use for Xander's ugly mug.

Okay, he's not ugly, but still.

They needed us to handle Barry the sloth. Not to pose with him. We had to keep him awake and moving so they could get pictures of his adorable face. Bonnie wasn't cooperating so we let her sleep. Let's face it, there's no *letting* a sloth sleep. When they power down, it's game over.

Oh, to be a sloth.

Needless to say, my face will not be on a billboard. Even if I'm in the background, I'm sure to be photoshopped out.

I'm glad I had those tacos last night. And this afternoon.

I think part of my chest might make it in one promo picture. That's it.

That's all.

We had Barry on his perch, but the photographer wanted me to hold him so he could get a different angle. We don't handle the animals a lot in this way, but Barry and I had an instant bond.

Barry held tight with his front claws digging into my shoulder blades and his hind claws firmly implanted into my hips. If it weren't for Xander's quick thinking stuffing a sweatshirt down the back of my shirt, I'm sure I'd have deep scratches down my back. But Barry, who doesn't love being held, arched his head back and looked totally adorable. My green polo shirt probably faded right into the background trees. I should have asked them to focus on my chest, knowing that I won't have it forever. Something to remember my girls by.

I wonder if I can return opened makeup?

If not, I'm probably set on cosmetics for the next decade.

At least they did a little interview with Xander and me. I'm not sure how it will be used. Maybe one of those videos embedded into the website or something. I don't know if they were filming us or the sloths, with our voices simply providing narration. Ed told us to act as if we've been taking care of the sloths everyday instead of one day a week. It was tough though, because I'm still not totally used to how slow Barry moves.

Monkeys are a whole lot faster.

Seems like time is speeding up everywhere else in my life but inside the animal enclosure. I'm sure there's some sort of metaphor here or something, but I can't find it.

All I want to do is wash my face. The hair ended up in a ponytail hours ago. Someone remind me of this the next time I consider getting up over an hour earlier to put on my face. Sleep is so much better.

Barry the sloth is already rubbing off on me.

I plop down on the bench in the locker room. At least I didn't have to do any weird or awkward poses with Xander. Though I have to say, after our initial confrontation, he was actually decent today. Once he's with the animals, a totally different side of him emerges. The swagger melts away into kindness and compassion. He really seems to love what he does.

I mean, we sort of have to. No one puts up with what we do if they don't have a passion. You can only clean up bodily fluids for so long, even when you love it.

Nonetheless, he's my arch-nemesis.

And he made fun of me this morning. Every morning really. At least once a day and usually twice on Sundays.

"Guess you didn't need to get all gussied up. They didn't take any pictures of our faces."

Have I mentioned that I hate Xander Barnes?

"Go away." I don't look at him as he plops on the bench next to me. "I can't believe they only got a picture of my chest."

I see his eyes wander down slightly and then quickly correct to my face. It's hard to tell if he's trying not to be a creeper or if he doesn't want to think of me as a female. Either way, it doesn't matter.

It's not like I'll have this chest for long.

"I'll always have that for posterity I guess," I sigh. "I hope the photographer got their best angle."

He tilts his head slightly. "Okay, I guess." He trails off.

Sometimes I forget that you're not supposed to talk about your boobs or other people's boobs in public.

"Now I can remember them when they're gone. They won't be here much longer."

I glance out of the corner of my eye to gauge his reaction. It's not what I expected. His face has gone ashen, and he clutches the edge of the bench, as if to keep from falling over. "What?" He shakes his head, like his ears are clogged.

"I'm getting a mastectomy soon. The girls are going bye-bye."

And because Xander is Xander, he never does what I expect. He gets up and walks out of the room. Hell, had I known it was that easy to get rid of him, I would have mentioned the mastectomy sooner.

I could say his reaction doesn't hurt, but that would be lying. I don't know why he bothers me so or gets under my skin. I can *almost* handle the teasing and taunting because that's who he is, and it's not like I'm kind in return. We have a mutual hate-hate relationship. It works for us in a completely unprofessional, dysfunctional sort of way.

But this was unexpected. I didn't think it would phase him at all. It's not like he's attached to me or my tatas. On the other hand, lots of guys can't handle the seriousness of living with the BRCA mutation.

Heck, lots of girls too.

Marriages crumble, friendships dissolve. It's why the UnBRCAble support group is so important.

It's a lot to live through.

The guy Millie was dating dumped her when she got out of surgery. Like, she was still in recovery and not totally conscious when he told her she was no fun anymore. He wasn't her true love or anything serious, but he noped outta there so quickly it made her head spin.

I guess I'd rather know that someone can't handle my stuff right up front than have that happen. It's one more reason why my crazy plan is not seeming so crazy. I'm going to have enough to deal with that I can't handle some unreliable guy who may or may not flake out at the first sign of hardship. At least I know I'm dependable.

And Xander, not that I expected him to be, is not.

My Thursday night will be spent just how every single girl dreams—reading online profiles to pick a sperm donor.

Jealous?

# CHAPTER 11

"You're not really doing this?" Mackenzie whines. "Come on, Erin. There's got to be a better way."

Suddenly, my sister has done a complete one-eighty and is totally against me having a baby. With the way she's been acting lately, it's hard to tell if she's lost her senses or come to them.

"Says you who has all the time in the world, a great husband, and no fertility issues."

"You don't have any fertility issues," she counters.

"Right, other than having no regular source of sperm—heck, no source of sperm actually—I don't have a ticking time bomb in my ovaries, which have already decided to go rogue and cystic on me. Nope, no issues here. Hang on, I'm putting my headset on." I've pulled into my parking spot and need to get out of the car. I switch over to my Bluetooth. "You still there?"

"But a sperm donor?" Mackenzie doesn't waste any time. I don't know what changed her mind. I thought she was on my side yesterday. It's like she forgot Cry-Fest 2019 in the middle of Ulta.

"What else am I supposed to do? Pick up some rando in a bar and get knocked up? That doesn't seem safe or responsible. At least these guys have met some standards and have been tested and all."

"I guess."

"And I can pick some specifics. Like height, coloring, that's sort of stuff." I make my way through my apartment, cleaning up from the mess we left this morning. There's makeup debris all over my table. How did it get everywhere?

"There's no guarantees. Look at us."

It's true. I'm about five-foot-eight, while Mackenzie is about five-three. My eyes are a light blue, which look odd with my skin tone. I've got skin that trends toward olive and bronzes up nicely in the summer. It's not super-evident, but I can see traces of my Nigerian heritage. Not so much with Kenz. She freckles and her skin color perfectly complements her dark blue eyes and light brown hair. Mom's pretty fair, but we don't know what her background is. She was too scared to take the test initially, wanting Dad to go first. Once she realized that relatives could contact you, she never sent her test in. I think she threw it out, unopened.

I'm literally the American melting pot, at least on my Dad's side. Can't imagine what we would have found out about my mom's heritage.

I once heard someone say I looked like I was put together by committee. Sure, I was ten and going through a very awkward stage, but those words have stuck with me. It's like all the ingredients that went into my soup didn't blend enough. There's something inherently not right about me, and potential partners have always been able to spot it.

Frozen pop isn't going to reject me because I like corny T-shirts or make animal puns. I'd be *lion* if I said I didn't.

I don't care what a donor provides in terms of ethnicity. I'm not picky.

"Yeah, but what's your type?"

"Frozen?"

"Erin, be serious." Mackenzie's using her mommy voice now.

"I am. What am I supposed to say? I think it's hypocritical to strive for ethnic or genetic superiority when I myself am faulty. This isn't an exact science. We're not living in Gattica."

"What's Gattica?"

I sigh. I forget that Mackenzie hasn't watched a movie or TV since Trey was born. I tend to binge on movies at night, so there's not much I haven't seen. The perks of being single. "You know that 90s movie with Ethan Hawke, Uma Thurman, and Jude Law. Everyone is judged at the moment of birth by their genes and if you're not perfect, you don't get any opportunities in life."

"Never saw it."

"You should because hot Ethan Hawke and hot Jude Law, but that's not the point. The point is I'm entering into this knowing there's a fifty percent chance the kid will have the BRCA mutation like I do."

"I know, Erin. I know it's tough. I wish there was some way to only use your eggs that don't have the mutated gene."

I sink down on my couch. I should get something to eat, but I need to get through this discussion first. I have a feeling I'm making my dinner in a blender, and I don't mean a smoothie.

"There is a way. Kind of."

"OMG, really? You should do it!" Mackenzie screeches into the phone. I hear Trey let out a wail. Kenz curses under her breath and then I hear a door shut. Ten bucks says she's hiding in the bathroom now.

All the perks I have to look forward to.

But seriously, I could get whiplash from how fast she's changing her mind.

"Okay, I have about three minutes before Luke finds me and hands me Trey. What's this about using only the good eggs?"

All I can think about is the dollar signs as I tell my sister. "Not my eggs but the embryos." I pause to let that sink in before continuing. "I'd have to do in vitro fertilization where they harvest my eggs, fertilize them, freeze them, test them, and then implant good ones. The bad ones are destroyed."

There's silence on the line, so I keep talking. "So, even if I could afford that, which I can't, there's too many other problems."

"Yeah, wow. How would you consent to that? Willingly destroying your embryos? What do you do with the leftover embryos? You won't be able to have kids so the extra embryos won't do you any good."

"I know. In theory, I like the idea of using preimplantation genetic screening, but I don't know that I could."

Mackenzie doesn't need to say anything to me. Her mind works much like mine does. We were raised in a very conservative family. I don't talk about it much because not everyone understands—or agrees with—the beliefs we hold onto. To us, life begins at conception. Those embryos are each an individual life. To destroy and discard some—I don't know that I could make that choice. And not to mention I'd have to pay for storage of the ones I don't use. Cha-ching.

"So, that's off the table. What's the other option?"

"I get a sperm donation and spend a romantic night at home with a glass of wine and a turkey baster and hope for the best."

"Maybe by the time the kid grows up, there will be a cure for the mutation or cancer, and it won't be an issue," she says quietly.

I take a slow, deep breath. "It's the best I can hope for. Actually, the best I can hope for is that my kid doesn't carry this genetic mutation, and it dies with me."

"Okay, so turkey baster is your best option. Sounds romantic. When are you thinking about doing it?" I can't tell if she's on my side or not, but at least she hasn't told me not to do it yet.

"I need to get some stuff in order first. Mostly work stuff. Sloth Central opens next week, so as long as Dr. Lee thinks I'm okay to hold off, I'm going to try to wait about three months. If it happens right away, I'm looking at April of next year. Hopefully, I can be back for the end of the year field trips and summer, when it gets super busy."

"How long do you get for maternity leave? Is it only six weeks?"

I have no idea. "I haven't checked yet. Is there a legal minimum? I mean, when our gorillas have babies, they don't go back out into the exhibits for at least two months."

Mackenzie adds, "Wouldn't the zoo extend the same courtesy to their humans?"

"I hope so."

I hear a banging, followed by my sister sighing. "Okay, they've found me. I'm sorry this is so hard for you."

I disconnect, willing myself not to wallow. Instead, I login and start reading through profiles.

This is so weird. It's like online dating but without the pictures of dead animals. Also, there are no tasteless acronyms, like DTF. Some of the sites even have technology so I can combine my face with his to see what my kid might end up looking like. It's sort of like doing the face swap and gender swap on Snapchat. I bookmark potential candidates and send Mackenzie my login info so she can look.

It's the new age version of taking him home to meet my family. I'd love Mom and Dad's opinion, but I know this is too far out for them. I'm not sure they're big supporters of fertility stuff. In fact, I have a feeling they're not. Definitely not in a single mom. They talk a lot about "God's plan."

I'm going with God's plan is that I have the ability to impregnate myself with a turkey baster and have a baby before cancer moves in.

That's my story and I'm sticking to it.

They'll get over it eventually. Hopefully by the time the kid starts Kindergarten.

I've got ten potential candidates by the time I'm so tired I'm nodding off while still scrolling. That's a good start.

I awake in the morning to find a series of texts from my sister. My optimism that she's weighed in on preferences fades as I realize they're all links to stories.

I don't even need to open one to know they're probably horror stories.

Apparently, she's changed her mind again. Currently, she's in the 'con' camp.

The first link is one in which a man found that he has nineteen half-sisters because his father was a sperm donor to pay the bills. Another is about family horror stories in which a man and a woman started dating and had a kid, only to find out that they were half-siblings.

Eeew.

The last is a story about a man who sued for custody of the baby conceived through artificial insemination, and he ended up kidnapping the kid and hiding out in Brazil for years.

Guess which way Kenzie is leaning on this whole issue? So much for support from my sister. If I can't get her on board, there's no way my mom will ever come over to being okay with this.

And here's one more story about a fertility doctor who was found to be the father of the babies of twenty-six of his patients. My sister doesn't do subtle well.

This day doesn't get any better when I find Xander waiting for me at the door.

"Nope, not today, Satan." I brush past him, my shoulder clipping his.

"Erin, wait. I need to talk to you."

Anger fills me. It may not be *all* his fault, but the straw that's breaking the camel's back is that the moment I said something serious to him, he walked out. I can handle the teasing and ribbing.

I can't handle the insensitivity about something so … sensitive.

I've always called him an ass, but seriously, who does that?

"I have nothing to say to you. You are an ass. I will speak to you when we have to and in front of guests, but that's it. Leave me alone."

He reaches out and grabs my arm. I look down, feeling his firm grip on my bicep. I look from his hand to his face and back again. He doesn't get the message to get his paws off of me.

"Erin, I really need to talk to you. Can we … talk … after work? Maybe grab dinner?"

"Are you touched in the head or something? Why would I go to dinner with you?" I glare at his hand, and he finally gets the message. My arm feels hot, like it's on fire, where his hand was. I hope he washed his hands before he touched me.

113

"Because I need to talk to you. I really need to clear the air before we start working in close proximity on Monday. And also, I know how grumpy you get when you don't eat. I need you to be available to listen without being hangry."

Unfortunately, he is not wrong.

"I'm not giving you one iota of my time."

"Please, Erin," he pleads. If I didn't know better, I'd think he's actually being sincere.

This had better be good.

Also, I don't feel like cooking dinner tonight. That thought buoys my spirits immediately.

"Fine, but it's not a date."

He laughs and says, "Obviously," before he turns and walks away. My mouth is probably hanging open again. Partially because of his rudeness. Partially because I agreed to go out to dinner with him.

And partially because I just noticed how fine his backside is as he walks away.

Damn.

# CHAPTER 12

Well, this is awkward.

I adjust my silverware, straighten my glass, and reposition the napkin in my lap.

Xander is late.

He texted me to go in and claim the reservation, as well as to put in an order for nachos.

I've done all that, and he's still not here. If he stands me up, I swear to God ... oh, the nachos are half-price if I get my order in before seven. I flag down the waitress.

For the record, normally I would have bristled at his directive, but this *El Charro's* really does have the best nachos. Normally I'd say this was blasphemy, but the nachos here are better than their tacos and the tacos are da bomb. I've come here on several dates because it's a good way to automatically screen out someone who doesn't want the nachos. I don't have time for that kind of negativity in my life.

I'm actually surprised Xander suggested *El Charro's*. It's not flashy in the least. It's comfy and real, and not at all what I'd expect from Xander Barnes. It's off the beaten path, and probably nowhere you'd take someone you were trying to impress. Doesn't seem like his kind of place.

I'm allowing myself to order one beer. It's going to take that kind of social lubrication to listen to his bull. Also, in addition to the nachos, it's pretty much mandatory here. The menu includes over one-hundred draft beers from all over the world. I'm working my way around the globe. Today's selection is a German Hefeweizen.

It's good.

Too good.

Going down way too quickly good.

I'm going to have to pace myself if Xander doesn't show up soon. Drinking on an empty stomach probably isn't the best idea.

I can't believe he's not here yet. What could he possibly want from me? I have nothing to say to him.

If the incident in the locker room hadn't happened yesterday, I'd say it would be reasonable for us to try to figure out a way to work together better. But him leaving after I told him about the mastectomy ... I don't know if I can forgive that.

I'm glad I at least took the time to go home and change. I'd be even more pissed if I'd come right from work. If I'm not in my uniform of cargo shorts and polos, I'm content to be in jeans and a T-shirt. Today's shirt says, "Sometimes I'm Hungry. Other Times I'm Asleep."

I wore it especially for Xander. I mean, he's not wrong about me getting cranky. I'm also sporting my Chuck Taylors to complete the look. Nothing says 'I have no interest in you' more than dressing in clothing that he could wear too. Not that Xander could fit into my stuff. He's broad and muscle-y, if that is even a word. Suddenly, the memory of his backside flashes into my brain, and I literally shake my head to dislodge that image.

That fine image.

"That's it, you've officially gone off the deep end."

Fine ass or no, his smart alec mouth has the same effect as a bucket of cold water to the head.

"You finally made it." My voice comes out sharp and acidic, and I'm sure to someone eavesdropping, I sound like a bitter nag.

"Oscar," Xander offers as he plops into the seat across from me. He doesn't need to say much more. The fatigue around his eyes is evident.

"Again?"

"Yep. Stupid animal."

"How'd you get him out and are you sure you should be breeding him if he's this stupid? You don't want to pass on those genes."

Oscar the ocelot is the bane of the South American Cats exhibit. As a rule, we try to crate train all the cats for movement and containment purposes. Seeing as how they are predators and carnivores, it works best to have them come willingly into their crates if we need to get into the exhibit space, for cleaning and whatnot. It's taken forever to crate train Oscar. But here's the thing. We can get him to go *into* the crate but can't get him out of it.

Normally it's the other way around.

The current plan is to introduce him to Harriet, our new female ocelot to see if there's any chemistry. Apparently Oscar wasn't on board with moving about.

Again.

"I will not miss Oscar. In general, the big cats of South America are not as cool as the other cats I've worked with. I have a feeling the sloths are going to be much more fun." Xander reaches across and picks up my beer. He takes a long swig of it. "That's good. What is it?"

My nose wrinkles before I can stop it. I push the glass toward him. "It's yours now."

Xander picks it up and drains the rest of it in one foul swoop. "Let's get a flight."

Immediately, I miss my beer, so his suggestion for a sample of different beers sounds like a brilliant idea.

Our waitress brings the nachos and Xander picks out six beers to try. I'm impressed with his choices, not that I'll tell him that. He looks at me sheepishly. I didn't know he could look sheepish. "I hope those were okay. I'm not a big IPA fan. I'm sorry, I should have asked you first."

I laugh nervously. His insight to me and my tastes is unnerving. It's almost like he knows me well. "Me neither. Too hoppy. And it seems like all the microbrews are IPAs."

We both dive into the nachos, settling into a comfortable silence while we stuff our faces. Wiping my mouth, I ask, "How'd you finally get Oscar out of his crate?"

Xander mumbles. "With the hose."

I shake my head. "Dumb cat."

"Yeah, and I feel like that creepy killer guy from *The Silence of the Lambs*. I even found myself telling Oscar that he needed to put the lotion in the basket or he'd get the hose again."

"Yeah, but that guy was spraying his victims with cold water to torture them. Oscar's hose is a little different."

Oscar hates rain. This is from a cat who lives in the *rainforest*. He freaks out at the slightest hint of moisture. So someone discovered that when Oscar won't budge, they use the hose and a filter to create a gentle misting rainfall over his crate and that's usually enough to get him moving to dry ground. In this case, into the den of his girlfriend.

"I still feel bad. Like it's cruel or something."

"If he weren't in the Pittsfalls Zoo, he'd be living in the rainforest where he'd get wet every day. Now it's at least only when he's not doing what he's supposed to do." I'm a little less sympathetic, but it's probably because I've never been able to form a good bond with Oscar.

I'm sure if I did, I'd be just as big of a pile of mush. When you bond with an animal, you tend to overlook their idiosyncrasies, much like a parent does with a child.

Speaking of which, Xander seems more torn up about the stupid ocelot than he does about all the times he's been mean to me.

Also, this is the longest and most civilized conversation we've ever had. Maybe it's this realization, or maybe it's the flight of beer which has gone down way too easily, but I call him on it.

"What's your deal?" Okay, that was perhaps a bit more abrupt than I intended.

"My deal?"

"Yeah. You're an ass to me. But now you wanted to have me out for dinner. You know there's no way in hell I'm going to be one of your conquests, so spill. Why are we here? What's your deal?"

That's enough to stop Xander mid-chew. Oops. I backpedal, which I find myself doing more often than I'd like to admit with Xander.

"I mean, you know, you're sort of mean to me. Actually, not sort of. You are mean. And yesterday, in addition to being mean, you literally got up and left when I was talking. I was telling you something big. Something that not a lot of people know about. Something that I'm having trouble dealing with myself."

He's looking down at his plate, but I see the top of his head nodding a bit. "That's what I want to talk to you about. I'm sorry."

"Sorry that you were rude or about that I even told you?" I don't know why it matters.

Yes, I do.

I don't want anyone feeling sorry for me.

"Both, I guess." He's staring down at his plate as if nacho debris is an advanced calculus problem that he needs to solve to save the world from an alien invasion.

"Xander, look at me." I wait until his gaze meets mine. "I don't want your pity—"

"Are you sick?"

Our questions collide against each other. I shake my head in case he continues talking.

Which he does.

"But you said you're getting a mastectomy. That's for breast cancer."

Now onto the educational yet awkward part of our evening. "I have the BRCA mutation. It means I'm more—"

He sags back into his chair. If I didn't know better, I'd say he looks relieved. "I know what it means. I was tested for it. My mom died of breast cancer, but not the genetic kind. Apparently hers was the run-of-the-mill bad luck kind."

Now it's my turn to apologize. "I'm sorry. I ... I didn't know."

He shrugs. "Not many people do. I don't exactly advertise it."

My mind is like a car screeching to a halt and thrown in reverse. Xander lost his mom. I can't imagine. I fumble, trying to come up with something that's not insensitive. "How long ago?"

"Eight years, next month."

That's so long to be without your mom. While Xander's a little older than I am, I can't imagine losing my mom before I hit thirty. I do some mental calculations. God, he lost his mom and moved all in the same year. Suddenly I'm seeing Xander in a whole new light. "Oh, right before you came to work at the zoo?"

"I'd been at Columbus before while she was sick. She got sick while I was a senior in high school. After ... I needed a change of pace. I'm still not too far from my family, but I don't have to see reminders all the time, you know?"

I see him absentmindedly stroke the inside of his left arm, where his tattoo is, which has me wondering if there's more to him than I'd initially thought. Perhaps he's a deeper puddle than I gave him credit for.

Xander looks up at me, his gaze suddenly intense. "When is your surgery? Do Don and Ed know? What's this going to do for the sloth encounter?" he asks.

I'm using more muscle control than should be necessary to control my face. I have a slight buzz on, but I don't want him to know it.

I shake my head. "I don't have it scheduled yet. I've ... uh ... got some things to take care of before I can have all my operations."

"What could be more important than your health? I've seen what breast cancer looks like. Trust me, you don't want to go down that road. You need to get it done. Soon." He's wearing the same passionate look that I've seen on his face when he talks about his animals.

Maybe it's because of the beer. Maybe it's because I've lost my ever-lovin' mind. Or maybe, just maybe, it's because I'm seeing a side to Xander Barnes that I never knew existed.

"I've decided to have a baby first. As soon as I do that, I'll have my prophylactic surgeries."

I probably should have waited until Xander swallowed his mouthful of beer before saying that. He promptly spits it out all over the table, drenching not only the remnants of our nachos, but me in the process.

Truth be told, I'm a little more upset about him ruining the nachos. I'm still hungry.

I start mopping up myself and look at Xander to see his reaction. He sits, stunned, for a moment more before jumping up into action. He grabs his napkin and begins wiping my face. As his napkin starts to descend southward, I grab his hand. "I can get that."

His gaze drops to my chest for a minute and then jerks back up to my eyes.

"I didn't mean to spit on you." He sets about wiping up the table while I finish mopping up myself.

"Yeah, well, I guess it's a good thing I'm used to spending my day covered in bodily fluids."

Xander stops and cocks his head at me. "You're not like other girls."

"Nope."

I shrug. I've heard this all my life. It's not usually a compliment, but for once, I don't think he's insulting me.

What else am I supposed to say?

I don't want to be like other girls. From an early age, I knew that the things that were important to other girls weren't important to me. They'd want to be princesses and lawyers, and all I wanted was my own zoo on a farm that my husband and I ran with all our kids serving as staff. I'd picture a pasture full of zebra and giraffe where cows and horses would normally be.

The waitress comes over and clears the soiled dishes. We order more food, agreeing to split an appetizer flight.

Flights are big in this place. They're good because you get a little bit of everything. I should suggest they put a taco flight on their menu.

"So where were we before you spit all over me? I always knew you were a drama llama." I wink at Xander.

An easy grin spreads across his face. Suddenly, I see why women fall all over themselves in front of Xander. There may be a flutter in the nether region. I must be drunk. That's the only logical explanation.

"I might be a drama llama, but that's not why I spit on you. I wasn't prepared to hear what you had to say."

It occurs to me that I've told him something deeply personal. Cripes, my parents don't even know yet. "Yeah, I guess I'm still digesting it myself. It's not what I'd wanted or planned, but I had a bit of a health scare a few weeks ago, and I'm not sure I can wait too much longer to have my mastectomy and hysterectomy. I don't want to wait. It's not safe."

I take a long drink of water. It's probably best if I focus on sobering up. "I figure since we're pretty much experts in animal husbandry, I might want to apply that knowledge to myself."

Xander looks at me blankly. Finally he says, "Now that I've reacted totally inappropriately, I don't know what to say or do. I have lots of questions but am unsure if I should ask them or not."

"Let's go with not. I don't really need to explain myself to you, or anyone else for that manner. I want to have a baby, and I have a narrow window, so I'm going for it. My options, as well as my time, are limited."

I don't want to get into the hours I've already spent reading through profiles or the fact that my finances—or lack thereof—are my biggest constraint.

We're saved from more awkward, confrontational conversation by the arrival of our appetizer flight. It's got fried cheese, quesadillas, potato skins, fried green beans, and calamari. I'm not a calamari person, but it turns out that Xander isn't a green bean person, so we work out a deal. After munching in silence for a bit, we go back to a safe topic—animals.

"Did you hear about Dallas? It's so sad," I say. The zoo world is small and when tragedy happens at one, it resonates with all of us. Especially when it makes the national news, as it did this week.

"Yeah, my ex-girlfriend works there."

Of course he has a trail of exes at every zoo in the country.

My facial expression must give away my thoughts. Damn stupid automatic eye roll.

"Yeah, I know, but don't believe everything you hear. I know what you think."

I raise my eyebrow. "Did you leave a trail of broken hearts and empty beds at zoos across the country?"

"Alas, no. She dumped me for a vet. She said everyone's torn up down there."

Whenever we lose an animal, it hits hard. This situation in Dallas is doubly worse. They were introducing a new female African wild dog to the pack and two of the young males, vying for alpha, attacked and killed her. The animals did what pack animals do, and the zoo staff was following a plan we all follow. It's a shame that it turned out like that.

"I can imagine. When Roscoe died, I wanted to cry for a week." I feel my eyes fill.

"That was tough. He was a great giraffe. So much personality."

We sit in silence for a minute, thinking about the different animals we've taken care of and lost. Xander's hand snakes across the table and covers mine. "I'm sorry."

I look from our hands to his face and back again. There's that flutter again, though I'd swear I'm sober now. I have no idea what's going on here. "I was the one who brought Dallas up."

"No, I'm sorry about the breast cancer thing and not taking the news well."

"Oh, we're back to that?"

His hand squeezes. "We're going to be working together. I think it's high time we started being friends."

Friends? With Xander Barnes?

What is this world coming to?

Yet somehow, having Xander in my corner, rather than the opposing one isn't the craziest decision I've made recently.

At least, let's hope it's not.

# CHAPTER 13

"Erin."

"Mom." I try to match her tone, which is stern. I have no idea what's wrong, but I know it's something. Something big.

"Care to tell me what you're up to, young lady?"

"Um, driving home from work." I know it's got to be bad. While I was at work, my mom called seven times. *Seven.* She didn't leave any messages, which means she's really fired up.

She takes passive aggressive to a new level.

"I talked to Mackenzie."

"Okay." I still have no idea where this is going, but my sweaty palms and clenched stomach tell me wherever it is, it's probably not good.

"Are you secretly in a relationship?"

"Um, no." The closest thing I've had to a date in weeks was dinner with Xander last night and that was so *not* a date. Though, in reality, it was much more enjoyable than my coffee date with Craig the Big Brother. In fact, aside from the beer spit, it was better than any date I've had in at least a year.

Cripes, even with the shower, it was still better.

I check over my shoulder and change lanes. My exit is coming up soon and more than once, I've whizzed by because I couldn't get over.

"Are you secretly married?"

"Mom, get to the point. I'm driving here."

"Do you have a husband?" Her tone is clipped.

Ugh. Two can play at that game. "You know I don't. What do you want?"

"Why does your sister seem to think that you are going to need her maternity clothes soon?"

If I wasn't driving in rush hour traffic, I'd probably stop and bang my head on the steering wheel. I cannot believe my sister ratted me out.

Actually, I can. She's decided she's in the anti-insemination camp for good now and most likely thought this was the best way to put the kibosh on it once and for all. The biggest way to do that was to let Mom know. Mackenzie knows I've never been able to stand up to Mom.

Obviously.

"I'm not pregnant." In my head, the sentence is, "I'm not pregnant *yet*" but Mom doesn't need to know that. I am not *technically* lying.

Not yet.

"You'd better not be. I thought I raised you better than that, going out and getting yourself knocked up."

Yeah, I could do without this old-school judgey Mom. I understand she's got baggage—lots of it—from how she grew up. I'm carrying lots of it for her. But I cannot get on board with her attitude anymore. I used to think there was only one way to go about having a

128

family, and that it always had to start with marriage. Or a relationship at least.

Being married doesn't guarantee you happiness or together forever. Plenty of my friends' parents are divorced, which is what I tell my mom. The divorce rate still hovers around fifty-percent, according to my statistics knowledge gained from Facebook.

Totally reliable source. They couldn't put it on there if it wasn't true.

"You are not plenty of friends. You were raised to respect the family."

Big sigh.

I was. And I do. And if I had my way, I would, which is why I've been waiting to meet the perfect man and have the perfect wedding and then the perfect family. Probably also why I'm still single.

"Wouldn't family include my kids? However they are brought into this world? You've always told me that blood is thicker than water and nothing is more important than family. When I have a baby, would all that other stuff matter?"

Stick that in your pipe and smoke it.

Yet somehow, my rock-solid argument doesn't even phase her. No pause, no stuttering, no nothing. "Are you telling me you are having a baby?"

Even bigger sigh. I get off the exit and pull into a parking lot because I know this is going to require more mental power than I have to give while safely operating a motor vehicle. "What if I am?"

"Are you bringing him to meet us soon?"

"What if there's no 'him?'" That should throw her nice and good.

I wait through her silence. One ... two ... three ... four ...

"Is there a *she*?"

I want to laugh. "Mom, think that one through. Would I be pregnant if there was a she?"

"I ... I don't understand. How are you pregnant if you aren't with anyone?"

"A. I'm not pregnant. B. There are ways."

"I thought we taught you better than that. Are you telling me you're a loose woman?"

I want to laugh again. I don't think she has any idea how ridiculous she sounds.

"Being sexually active doesn't make me loose. It makes me in charge of my own body and pleasure. But that's not the point here, Mom. The reality of the situation is that I don't have the time to wait for a husband to have a baby. I'm not pregnant yet, but I plan on becoming pregnant soon."

Oh my God, I can't believe I just said that to her.

"But how?"

There's part of me that wants to get super detailed and clinical to gross her out, but I'm not sure that's enough to back her down.

Also, it's not like I'd give her a blow-by-blow, no pun intended, of my conception if I was doing it the traditional way, so why start now?

"You don't need to worry about that. I've got it covered. Thanks for your concern, and I'll let you know as soon as I know so you can start knitting a blanket, like you did for Mackenzie."

I don't need to see her to know what's going on on the other end of the line, which I would bet includes lots of my mom opening and closing her mouth as she's trying to figure out what to say.

Her face is probably a nice shade of magenta right about now as well.

"Well, it was great talking to you Mom. I start my new job tomorrow in Sloth Central. I'm sure you meant to wish me good luck. It's a promotion and a better position. I even get the occasional Saturday off now. Okay well, I'll let you go."

With that, I disconnect while simultaneously wishing my sister a toe fungus for blabbing to Mom like that.

So not cool.

~~~***~~~

"And then she sent me an email, listing all the reasons why having a baby is a terrible idea," I tell the UnBRCAble women. In the three days that have gone by since the phone call with my mom, I've been in a perpetually grumpy mood.

"I don't understand. Why is she so against you having a baby?" Millie asks. Bringing this subject up is selfish of me, I know. There are many in the group, Millie included, who won't get the options I'm currently struggling with.

"Amongst other reasons, listed in bulleted form: I work too much, toxoplasmosis, I don't make enough money, passing on my lethal genes, I'm on my own, and I'm in no way prepared to be a mother. She called me selfish." That was the part that hurt the most.

"Don't you keep creatures alive everyday?" Claudia asks.

I nod. "Yeah, I mean, other than that, according to her, I am in no way prepared to be a mother."

"Do her other points have merit?" Millie asks. "Playing devil's advocate," she adds quickly. "I'm not saying I agree with her."

"Toxoplasmosis, not really. The others, unfortunately, yes."

For the record, pregnant women can get toxoplasmosis from cat feces. I don't have a cat, and obviously I wear gloves when cleaning up after animals at work. That's Zookeeping 101. Also, farmers have a higher risk—especially those who assist with birthing lambs—than cat owners do of contracting toxoplasmosis.

But then there are the things Mom forgot to list, like the fact that I need to move to a bigger place and how would I care for the baby when I had my surgeries. The hysterectomy will leave me down and out for a week or two, but the mastectomy and reconstruction is serious, and I won't be able to care for myself, let alone a baby, for at least six to eight weeks.

I don't even get into the in vitro versus intrauterine insemination debate. It's not up for discussion with the group. Even if I could come to terms with the ethical matter of what to do with the fertilized embryos, the cost on that is one-hundred percent prohibitive.

Going out on a limb to have a baby on my own is far enough outside my comfort zone. I'm not up for challenging my ethical beliefs, which still hold.

Millie gives me the pursed lip nod. In here, it's basically what we do when we have nothing to say because it sucks, and there's no way to change it. We were all dealt this crappy hand, and we're trying to play it the best we can.

Normally I feel better after group. Tonight is not that night. I should just go ahead and schedule my surgeries now because having a baby doesn't seem like a realistic or feasible goal.

Nor does it seem the responsible thing to do.

Not that I want to admit my mom might be right.

Instead of driving home, I head back to the zoo. It's my first week in Sloth Central. I can certainly spend more time with Barry and Bonnie. Bond with them more. Plus, they're a little more active at night. Two-toed sloths are mostly nocturnal, so we don't get to see them act spontaneously during the day. Sloths in the wild sleep fifteen to twenty hours a day, while sloths in captivity sleep more, mostly because they don't have to hunt for food or evade predators. Not that there's much evading. In fact, the sloth's defense is blending in and not moving. Obviously, they're not going to outrun a jaguar.

Not to mention, Bonnie's in heat which means she's climbing down to go to the bathroom every night, instead of the usual every eight to ten days. I can clean it up now rather than let it sit until morning. Yes, I'd rather spend my night cleaning poop than at home, alone, thinking about how my faulty genetics have screwed my chance for having a baby.

While wearing gloves of course.

Also, the bodily functions tell us a lot about how an animal is doing, and since this is so infrequent with sloths, I really need to learn.

Me and poo. Great way to spend the night.

But unless I want to have a pity party for two, I've got to put my plans on hold.

Xander is in the sloth enclosure.

"What are you doing here?" My tone is anything but friendly.

"Who pissed in your Cheerios?" He fires back without missing a beat.

"I wanted to be alone."

"I thought we agreed to be friends." He looks genuinely hurt but quickly turns away.

His words cut off my next retort. He's right. For once, my bad mood has nothing to do with him.

"Got in a fight with my mom. She doesn't approve of my plans to have a baby without a husband."

"I can see that. My mom would have freaked on my sister too."

"But not you?" I don't know why it matters. I stroke Bonnie's fur and she turns her head toward me, the ever-present smile on her face. For once, she doesn't show me her teeth. We're making progress.

The light's dim, so I can't read his face. "No, she would have been disappointed in me too. She was from a pretty conservative family. If my math is correct, my sister was born only six months after my parents got married. I don't think she was an eight pound preemie."

I'm somewhat relieved to know that there wasn't a double standard in his family, not that I know why it matters to me.

"Yeah, same here. To my mom, there's only one way to have a family, which is a courtship, a wedding, and then the acts that result in pregnancy. She actually asked me if I was a loose woman."

He laughs. At first I'm not sure if he's laughing at the idea of me having sex with people or my mom's comment. *Please let it be the latter.*

"Oh God, that's uncomfortable. What did you tell her?"

Good thing he clarified. At least he doesn't think me hooking up with someone is ridiculous or funny.

"I told her that being responsible for your own body, including your own sex life and pleasure, does not make you loose." As I say it, I look at Xander and think about my own bias and double standard I've applied toward him. "I'm sorry," I add quickly.

"Sorry for what?" He walks over to where I'm standing and begins to stroke Bonnie's fur. His hand is next to mine. I let my hand drop.

I look down at my shoes. "Sorry for all the times I called you loose."

"You called me loose?"

"Actually, I think I used the term 'man-whore.'"

135

Why did I say that out loud?

A small smile flits across his lips, but I see the pain flash in his eyes. "I'm not, you know."

"It shouldn't matter if you are. If I can take charge of my sex life, why can't you?"

"HEY—Who's in there?" A booming voice calls, forcing Xander and I to jump apart as if we were caught with our pants down.

"Carlos, it's me," Xander answers. "And Erin. We were just getting a little time in with Bonnie, since she's never awake during the day."

"Is she okay? Do I need to call Dr. Val in?"

I walk over to the cage door where Carlos is on the other side, shining his flashlight in. He had to have seen us on the security monitor. I wonder why he came all the way down here. "No, she's fine. She's in estrus, and we're checking that. We're good. I was heading out anyway."

Xander follows me out and steps aside as I check the locks three times before walking away. Not that Barry and Bonnie would or could get far even if I left the door wide open. Sloths can't really walk on the ground. They have so little muscle mass that they can barely drag themselves. It's one of the reasons they're becoming endangered in their native Costa Rica. As roads are carved out through the jungle, the sloths can't get across and often get hit by cars while trying.

On the other hand, sloths are excellent swimmers and have been known to drop from trees right into rivers and do the breaststroke to traverse.

That's something I'd like to see.

Xander and I wash up in the locker room and start to head toward the employee parking lot. I don't want to go home, to my empty place. Unbelievably, talking with Xander is infinitely more appealing than cruising Pinterest.

"Want to get a drink or something?" I'm pretty sure there's no way for me to be *more* awkward.

Xander stops and I nearly run into him. "It's not a date," he says, mocking me.

"Of course not. I ... I'm not in the mood to be alone right now."

"Your place or mine?"

"Mine."

Oh God, what did I just do?

# CHAPTER 14

On the drive back to my place, I mentally run through the condition of my apartment. It's not terrible but certainly not in neat enough order to excite Xander with my housekeeping skills. Who has time to clean their own house when they spend all day cleaning out cages?

Whatever. I'm not trying to impress him in any way, shape, or form. It's the same as if I was having Terry or Millie over. He's simply someone to talk to.

A surprising discovery, if I do say so myself.

I should probably apologize to him at some point for the man-whore comment.

I pull into my spot and watch as Xander parks in the guest parking area. I wait for him to cross to me before going in the lobby door. Suddenly, I'm super nervous, which for me equals verbal diarrhea.

Awesome.

"So, this is me. Well, not me. My place. I mean, I don't own it. I rent. Do you own or rent? Where do you live? Is it nice? Do you like it there?"

Xander stops. "Dude, calm down. This isn't twenty-questions." He smiles, but is that a hint of nervousness I detect? Maybe I'm projecting.

I regroup by focusing on unlocking my door, which suddenly seems like the front gates to Alcatraz. Good heavens, what is wrong with me?

"Seriously, I thought you were better with locks than this." Xander laughs as I drop my keys. For the second time. I mean, seriously? I lock and unlock cages literally *all day long*.

"You make me nervous." I might as well be honest. It's not like I'm trying to seduce him or anything. I still don't know what possessed me to invite him over.

Oh, right. My mother crushed all my dreams.

That'll do it.

Once we get in, Xander accepts my offer for a beer. All I've got is Guinness, so that's what he gets.

"Not many women I know like stouts," he says as he reads the label on the bottle.

"I don't think I'm the type of woman you usually hang out with."

He looks me up and down. "No, you're not. How's the quest for the kid coming?"

Cue waterworks.

Just like that, the floodgates open. Both from my eyes and my mouth. I recount the conversation with my mother, not to mention the cost struggles. My arms are waving wildly. "Look at this place! I can't fit a kid here. So on top of everything else, I'd have to move."

"Plus the travel. What do you do with the baby when you're out of town?" Xander nods, agreeing with all the evidence stacked strongly against me ever procreating.

That's enough to stop me cold. "Travel?"

"Yeah, didn't Ed tell you that we are doing some traveling for different shows and events? Sloths are big right now, so they're really looking to capitalize. We're taking our show on the road. I think he's working on booking our first gig."

I sink back into the couch, defeat washing over me. "Well, this just sucks. I can have a career, or I can have a family. I can't have both, and it's not fair."

"Lots of women have families and careers," he offers. "My sister is a CPA at a big firm and has two kid," he adds helpfully.

I know he's trying to be supportive, but I don't want support. I want to be mad and to rage and to get the best of both worlds. I want my Veruca Salt moment.

"Yes, but I bet she has a husband or partner or significant other to help, right?"

He nods.

"I don't have that, and logistically, there's no way to manage it all—financially or physically—on my own."

Xander's long since finished his beer, and he's helped himself to a glass of water from the kitchen. Normally I'd say it was presumptuous of him, but I'm too tired to get up. Glad he helped himself. He stands and brings his glass back to the kitchen. "It's getting late, and no matter how long we talk, I don't think we're going to solve your problems tonight. I'm sorry if you don't feel any better."

He heads to the door, and I don't bother getting up. I'm spent. The beer's gone to my head and I feel myself getting drowsy. "Thanks. Talking helped. Maybe. I don't know. I wish I could have it all," I mumble to no one in particular as I hear the door close.

All in all, this has been one bizarre evening.

~~~***~~~

My neck's stiff from sleeping on the couch, and I'm running late again. Long pieces of my bangs fall down from my bun, and I curse myself for ever getting my hair cut. I toss a headband on to keep the hair out of my eyes. I'm going to spend all day fussing with it, and it'll undoubtedly give me a headache. Par for the course right about now.

I'm certainly questioning most of my life decisions at this point. The only thing that makes sense is my job, but that's the one thing getting in the way of everything else.

Well, that and my genetics. And my personality.

You win some, you lose some. In my case, I lose more.

What I don't know is how I'm going to face Xander. I don't know what to make of this friendship thing. Tentative allies is more like it.

Except he's easy to talk to. And surprisingly supportive.

For some strange reason, I think I was more comfortable when he was my nemesis. At least I knew where I stood.

Especially as I see him get out of the car this morning with Sophie Stuart. *Doctor* Sophie. Xander's the only one who doesn't seem to pay attention to the hierarchy of zoo staff. The vets are on a higher level than the education staff or the animal keepers. Xander and I are a rare hybrid of the two which means we fit in nowhere. It's like sixth grade lunch all over again. Except Xander seems to make friends wherever he goes. He can sit at any lunch table.

Which leaves me the odd duck out.

Again.

Wait—he drove to work with Sophie. Does that mean he spent the night with her? Did he leave me and go to her? Was he trying to score with me and I was such a disaster that he decided to cut and run?

Not that he even attempted to put the moves on me.

And not that I want anything to happen with Xander, and him coming over *was* my idea, but still.

I feel like chopped liver.

*And now they're hugging?* That's it. I'm officially moving Xander back to nemesis status.

It's a much more comfortable fit.

"What's shaking, bacon?" he asks as I'm heading into the sloth enclosure. I open the lock and pull open the cage door. For some animals we have sliding doors that we open and close without ever getting into the same area as the animals. We don't need to take those precautions with Bonnie and Barry. I walk in and shut and lock the door behind me, with Xander on the other side.

"Hey!" he yells and then begins fiddling with the lock. This would have been so much more effective if he didn't have his own set of keys. "What's up with you? Are you still in a bad mood?"

"When your life falls apart, tell me how good of a mood you're in." I put on my gloves and start doling out their food. Breakfast consists of apples, grapes, sweet potatoes, romaine lettuce, and high fiber biscuits. There are leaves about for natural grazing, but we like to think of this as a five-star establishment, complete with room service.

"Your life hasn't fallen apart. You simply have a minor setback."

Minor setback? *Minor setback?*

"I know your life is so perfect that nothing is a big deal to you. But this is a big deal to me. And I know I have to deal with it, and I will, but I'm not going to be automatically cheerful, just because *you* think it's no big deal. I've only ever wanted two things in my life. To work in a zoo and to be a mother. It's a little bitter to know I can't have them both."

"Why do you think my life is perfect?" It's one of the first times I've ever heard Xander on the defensive. Usually he lets everything roll off him like water off a duck's back.

I feel another rant coming on, but hold back. I take a deep breath and count to ten. And then to twenty.

Okay, one-hundred.

It's one thing to be in a bad mood myself. It's another to attack a co-worker, even if it is Xander.

143

None of this is his fault. Nor it is his fault that his life is great. He does actually work hard here. He doesn't coast on his good looks or charm or charisma, which he has in spades.

He's sweeping up in the corner and as his arm moves the broom, I catch sight of the ink on his inner arm. It reminds me of when he talked about losing his mom, making me wonder if his life isn't as glossy and perfect as it seems.

Maybe we all have things we're dealing with.

And maybe, being short with Xander doesn't make me feel better. It's making me feel worse. Much worse.

We get the morning cleaning and feeding done just in time to greet our first group. The plan is to work in tandem for the sloth encounter tours. Xander and I won't always be paired up, but we are for today. We should be up to full steam by next week, but for today, we only have two groups scheduled to give us time to work out issues. Like the fact that I'm having trouble getting my mic to work. I don't know if I'm on the wrong channel or I have a dead battery or what.

"Check one. Check one." I fiddle some more. "Check, check, check."

It doesn't matter how many times I check. The stupid thing isn't working. I toggle the switch on the earpiece again, turning it off and back on. Suddenly, there's a hand on my lower back. The touch is warm and light and if I didn't know better, I'd say it sent tingles downward.

Hell I do know better, and there were definitely tingles.

"Here, try this." I feel a breeze where Xander's removed the pack from my waistband. I stiffen, knowing his hand is going to come dangerously close to my skin when he puts it back in. Reflexively, I suck in, willing my midsection to immediately tone up and lose all its softness.

He does something. "Now try."

"Check one." The mic is working. He slides the pack back onto my waistband. It feels familiar and intimate all at the same time. And that stupid zing is back.

And it doesn't necessarily feel wrong.

It actually feels all sorts of right.

"You good?" Xander smiles at me.

It's like his smile has wattage that amplifies the zing. Holy smokes.

"Yes, thanks." My voice booms, the amplification working.

"You nervous?" he asks.

I nod, not wanting to confess for the world to hear. Of course I'm nervous. I don't know how he's not. This is literally what I've been dreaming about since I was a kid. Probably since the first time I watched *Jack Hanna's Animal Adventures* on Saturday morning TV. I think I was about six.

I did have this fantasy that my mom's real family was actually the Hannas and they'd take me in and I'd get to live with them in Africa. As of yet, that has not come to fruition.

In this moment, preparing to greet my first group, I try to savor it. Spreading my love of animals to the world. Sharing it with kids. This is what I was born to do. It almost makes up for not being able to have any of my own. *Almost.*

"You ready for the first group?"

I'm going to give the lecture while Xander does the demo. When the time is right, he'll bring out Barry on a pillow for everyone to see. Then, he'll return Barry to his tree, and we'll lead the group in.

I nod and my career as a sloth educator is officially underway.

# CHAPTER 15

"You wanted to talk to me?"

Two weeks in, and the encounters are going great. We're totally booked through May and most of June is already full. Not bad considering it's still April. This word of mouth thing is awesome.

On the other hand, the word of mouth thing, otherwise known as social media, involves a lot of pictures, so I have to take the time to do my hair and makeup every morning. Gone are the days of sleeping in a bun or braid and wearing it the next day. I learned that after I saw the first group post their photos.

Also, invest in a good under eye concealer.

And I may want to lay off the tacos. Those khaki cargo shorts are not the most flattering on my hind end. Nothing a million or so squats can't change.

Ed sits back in his chair in the control room. He spends about half his days in here, watching monitors, keeping tabs on several exhibits at once. I wonder if he misses the direct time with the animals. I think I would.

"Come in, Erin. How's it going?"

I tip my head toward the monitors. "I think well, don't you?"

"I do. We've talked about doing some mobile education. Xander and you are the obvious choice to go."

"Go where?" I don't know why it matters. Obviously I'm going. It's my job. And it's not like I have anything else holding me back, like arranging child care.

"Albany. To the animal expo. You'd bring Barry. Your show would run once every ninety minutes between ten and six. It ends up being four shows. You give the spiel and walk around with Barry. Pretty straight forward. No one can touch him. Just education."

"Is it just us?" I can't imagine that many people would come out to see one little sloth.

"No. You'll be working with folks from ZooAmerica. They're bringing the birds of prey. And there's a group from Canada who will bring herps and other small animals. They're looking to pack the convention center. The animals will be housed there overnight. It's a two-day event, but we think you'll need to go out the night before, just to get Barry settled first."

This is the travel Xander told me about. Another nail in the coffin of my parenthood plans.

"Erin, is there a problem? Obviously you'll receive overtime pay and travel expenses."

I shake my head, unable to swallow the lump in my throat. The loss feels epic, like a tsunami washing over me. The extra money doesn't even matter at this point.

I get up and leave before I can fully fall apart. Ed doesn't need to know my issues. I can't even say my problems because how do you have a problem that doesn't exist? It's like an anti-problem. I'm glad it's the end of my shift.

Although, the end of my shift means I have to report to my parents' house for dinner. I was summoned with the enticement of pepper steak and chocolate cake.

Based on the photographic evidence of my backside, I should have said no. However, as said evidence indicates, it's obvious I never say no. Driving over, I hope that my mom hasn't said anything to my dad and that she doesn't bring up the whole pregnancy thing. I don't want to talk about it. It's still too raw and the wound too deep.

I'll run the offensive route by grabbing an alcoholic drink as soon as I walk in. That should keep her quiet.

Should was the operative word there.

"Erin! What are you doing? You can't have a beer!" My mother charges at me and grabs the bottle from my hand. Without missing a beat, she tosses it into the sink where the glass breaks and beer sprays all over the place.

"Jesus, Mary. What did you do that for?" My dad grabs a towel and begins mopping up the mess.

"Erin can't drink." My mom turns and looks at me. "I can't believe you're so irresponsible. Actually, I can, seeing as the mess you've gotten yourself into. Don't you have any shame? You really have some nerve."

I think my mom might be a little off her rocker right now. She can't be this mad at me for *wanting* to have a baby.

"Mom, simmer down. You're overreacting."

"I am not. I asked you here to talk some sense into you and to see if you can't better your situation any. Are you sure the fellow doesn't want to get married? Do you even know who he is?"

Have I been dropped into some alternate universe where my mom is suddenly a 1950s housewife? What the heck? I didn't think she was *this* conservative. Also, nice to know my mom has such a low opinion of me and my standards.

"Mary, what in God's name are you rumbling about and why did you throw Erin's beer? What's wrong with you?" My dad looks concerned.

"Erin's here tonight to tell us she's pregnant. And she does it by opening up a beer."

My dad turns and looks at my mom. "Mary, think about that. If Erin was pregnant, would she be drinking? She's more responsible than that."

I raise my eyebrow, waiting for her answer. When she doesn't supply one, I say, "I tried to tell you, Mom, but you wouldn't listen. I'm not pregnant."

"Were you pregnant? Is that what happened when you went to the hospital? Did you lose it?" She blesses herself quickly. I think I hear her mumble, "Praise Jesus," but I can't be sure.

"Mom." My tone is harsh. "You were there. It was a cyst. You know that." My hands are on my hips. As long as I'm on the defensive, I might as well go for it. "And would it be the worst thing in the world if I was? You know it's my only chance. I can't put off my surgeries for much longer."

I don't break eye contact with my mom as I say this. "I wish I could wait. I wish I could meet someone. I wish I didn't have an eighty-percent chance of cancer. I wish I could consider adoption." I see her suck in a deep breath. "I wish I could have a baby, but it turns out, I don't think I can. So, thanks for ruining my beer for no reason."

My dad promptly opens the fridge and hands me another. I don't actually want it now. My stomach's tight and clenched, and I feel like getting into bed and pulling the covers over my head for days.

My dad puts his arm around me and squeezes. "Erin, why don't you come in and sit down and tell me what's going on? I seemed to have missed some details. Mary, you might want to come and listen too."

He's always been the calming voice in our house. I don't know why I didn't think to go to him first.

Probably because all of this is related to my girl bits.

I sit down on the couch, while my parents take their usual side-by-side recliners. Mackenzie and I tease them endlessly about their old-folk chairs. My dad sinks back into his chair while my mom sits with her back ramrod straight.

We sit in silence, staring each other down. Fine. I'll start.

"I've tried dating. I've tried online and in person. I haven't met anyone remotely worth considering. I looked into freezing eggs, in vitro fertilization, embryo screening, and storage, as well as surrogacy. I can't afford any of it." The thoughts of all those zeros dance through my brain, making me a bit nauseous. "Plus, I don't want to have to decide what to do with the embryos I don't use. See Mom, I haven't totally lost my moral compass. Not to mention, storage is expensive too, if I don't make any decisions."

I see my mom nod her head. At least she's on board with that. Maybe it will restore some of her faith in me. I continue.

"So then I looked into just using a sperm donor and rolling the dice with passing on the BRCA mutation. Kenz started sending me all these internet horror stories, trying to talk me out of it. Then, you—" I look at my mom again, "brought up all the logistical issues, like child care. I also have to think about my surgical future and my apartment isn't big enough. And now, with this new job, I'll be traveling some, so there's that too."

I choke on that last sentence, the tears no longer able to be contained. "And even though I never wanted to think about it, adoption doesn't even seem like an option now because of all the other reasons you listed. I can't afford it, and I'm in no position to be able to raise a baby on my own."

With the mention of the "A" word, my mom bristles again. "I didn't think you'd even consider adopt—"

My dad cuts her off. "Mary, this is about Erin, not you. Of course, she should consider adoption. Honey, I don't think you should rule that out yet."

I sniffle. "I guess not, but it's not what I wanted. I wanted to be pregnant and give birth and—"

"To be married." My mom simply will not let this die. I don't know if she's overcompensating for the fact that her own biological mother was an unwed teen or what. It doesn't matter because I'm sick of it.

I stand up. Chocolate cake or no, I am not going to take this anymore.

"You know, Mom, for someone who is so set on the idea that family has to be blood related, you're certainly doing a great job at alienating your own daughter. Look at me. See what I'm going through. I know your childhood was tough, but you've had a great life since. Dad adores you and treats you like a queen. You've got two daughters who are doing pretty well for themselves. I am doing the best I can, and all I need from you is to shut your mouth for once and just be supportive."

I turn and storm out.

If she wants to be stubborn and obstinate, two can play at this game. You know what they say about apples and trees.

I am her daughter after all.

# CHAPTER 16

"It's going to be a long drive if you're hell-bent on playing the quiet game," Xander kids.

I grunt, looking out the window. Xander lost already. I win.

For a winner, I feel like the biggest loser.

"Things are bad with my mom, and it's got me in a funk," I offer. Why did I offer that? I'm not a sharer. Especially not with Xander.

Yet for some reason I seem to be. When I'm around him, the information flows from my mouth like a river spilling into the ocean.

I've yet to forgive him for the Dr. Sophie thing. Especially since she's started hanging around Sloth Central. She needs to stay in cats, where she belongs. Maybe the panthers have rubbed off on her. She's definitely on the prowl.

I don't know why it bothers me, other than ... nope, I've got nothing. But her hanging around is more irritating than an itch on the bottom of the foot.

And even though I told him I wasn't interested in dating him, I don't like the fact that he went to her after hanging out with me. It's not like he even put the moves on me and I rejected him!

Would I have?

That is *not* something I have the bandwidth for at the moment.

"You need to make up with you mom."

"I don't need to do anything. She's wrong and acting terribly, and I need an apology."

Xander stares straight ahead, his hands tight on the steering wheel. "But she's your mom. You only get one."

His words hang heavy in the air.

Crap. I'm a terrible person.

"I'm sorry. It's nothing. It's fine. It'll blow over." Like a hurricane blows over.

"No, it's obviously not nothing. You're distraught. But you should work through it."

"That's the thing. There's nothing to work through. She said hurtful things. She's holding ground that doesn't need to be held because it's a moot point. But her stance hurts me, and she won't see it."

As the miles fly by, I recount for him how Mom flipped out on me, both times, about the prospect of a pregnancy. He nods and asks occasional, thoughtful questions. Turns out, Xander Barnes is a good listener.

"I don't understand the adoption thing. Why is she so against it? You'd think that'd be the answer."

"Her own adoptive parents treated her like a second-class citizen because she wasn't 'really' related. Honestly, it doesn't have anything to do with adoption. They're simply crappy people overall. Her brother, who

155

was biologically theirs, was a god, and she was supposed to be his staff."

"Who would do that?" Xander glances at me, a puzzled look on his face.

"My grandparents, apparently. I've only met them once, I think. I don't even know if they're still alive. I don't care. My mom tries not to care, but she does. And so she's hammered into our heads over and over that family only counts if you are blood related."

Xander digests this for a bit. It's getting dark. We got a later start than intended, but should reach Albany by nine, I hope.

Finally he says in a low voice, "No disrespect to your mother, who I'm sure is lovely in her own way, but that's the stupidest thing I've ever heard."

It takes me a minute to remember what we were even talking about.

I shrug, not that Xander can see it. "I guess I've always understood where she was coming from. I don't think that shared genetics are the end all, be all. My dad's adopted too, so I know that it's not."

I recount tales of the Magnificent McAvoys, and before long, I'm laughing so hard I can barely breathe.

Xander's laughing too. I wipe a tear from the corner of my eye. It feels good to have these kinds of tears rather than the sobbing kind that threaten my eyes more than I'd care to admit.

"So, with that family, which you're obviously much more like, why wouldn't you consider adoption?"

I nod. I haven't said it aloud, but now seems like as good of a time as ever. "I probably will, though I'm not sure I'd be a good candidate, still. If I'm single, if my finances aren't right, if, if, if. There are a lot of ifs that I will have no control over. Maybe someday it will happen, but I feel like my chance for being a mother has slipped through my fingers." It's hard to express to a man—especially this one—the longing I have to carry and nurse my child. I don't feel complete, and I fear I never will.

He can't possibly understand that emptiness.

Damn these sad tears. They're no longer threatening. They've taken over.

"So, how 'bout them Steelers?" Xander laughs nervously. "I didn't mean to upset you."

I sniffle. "I know. It's a bad luck thing really. I mean, it could be worse. At least I know what's most likely coming. I'm not looking forward to the surgeries, but it beats the alternative."

"Sure does," Xander mumbles, and I immediately want to kick myself for being so insensitive.

"I'm sorry. I didn't mean—"

"It's fine. You didn't kill her."

And then he's quiet. Too quiet. Eerily quiet. So quiet that I can hear Barry over the hum of the van. He's rooting around, munching on the leaves and lettuce we put in the carrier with him. Though he's only about twenty-two inches long, he's in a large dog crate. This way, he can move and hang a little, if he wants to. We don't want him to be miserable while he travels.

I'm kind of in love with him. I loved working with the primates, but this is a whole new level of infatuation. Bonnie's great too, but Barry's my guy. He is starting to want to hang on my neck. He won't do it for Xander.

Tee hee. Barry likes me better.

"I want to sneak Barry into my hotel room. He doesn't smell. He's not due for a bathroom break this weekend. I can pop him in my bag and no one will be the wiser."

"You cannot smuggle a sloth into the hotel room. He'll be fine at the place."

We're supposed to unload Barry on site, to stay the night. There will be trained animal staff there, and we're only about five minutes away, should Barry need us.

"But I get lonely," I pout. It's not untrue. It's why I like to stay super busy and go into work during the evenings a lot more than I should.

"There are other ways to treat your loneliness, you know." Xander winks at me.

Oh no, he didn't.

"You are not hitting on me, are you?"

Xander laughs. No, not laughs. Guffaws. He *guffaws* at me. "Erin, be serious. We work together."

"Like that's ever stopped you before," I mutter under my breath.

Except apparently it was not under my breath, but plenty loud enough for Xander to hear it. "What's that supposed to mean?"

I lift my shoulder and drop it, as if I don't have a care in the world. "You've got quite the reputation."

"Do you believe everything you hear?"

Mmm hmm. "Seeing is believing."

"What's that supposed to mean?"

"You and Dr. Sophie. You were at my place and then show up the next morning with her."

"So I was at your place. Does that mean anything happened between us?"

"Ew. No. We're friends."

Xander turns and looks at me.

"Eyes back on the road, buddy."

"Did you just 'ew' me?"

Oh crap, did I really say that out loud? Oops. My bad.

"I meant, obviously nothing happened. We're friends."

"Then why would you think something happened between Sophia and me?"

"Sophia? Doesn't everyone call her Sophie?" I've never heard her referred to as Sophia before. Oh God, what if it's some cutesy nickname. Gack.

"Well, considering her brother Matt is my best friend and I've known her my whole life, I can say, no, not everyone calls her Sophie. Her family calls her Sophia. And since I consider her family, I call her Sophia. And, if you must know, her car blew the alternator, and she needed some transportation help. Also, she found out her girlfriend is cheating on her."

*Oh.*

"Oh."

"Why are you always so quick to judge me?"

I start to deny it, but I know he's right. "I don't like you." Even as I say it, I know it's not true. "No, let me

159

rephrase. I don't—didn't—want to like you. You're too suave, too ... I don't know. But despite my best intentions, I'm starting to think you're a really good guy."

I don't consider how hurtful my words might seem.

Xander purses his lips and doesn't say anything for the rest of the drive.

I guess he won the quiet game after all.

# CHAPTER 17

Show day one is hell. Barry is stressed. Xander is stressed. I'm stressed.

After we unloaded last night, some idiot decided that housing Barry's crate overnight in the same area as the birds of prey was a good idea. Whatever brain trust did this obviously did not know that harpy eagles are the sloth's number one predator, so Barry's fear of birds is ingrained.

And justified.

The set-up of the exhibition isn't the most well thought out either. We have a stage on a large floor area. The animals are all lined up behind a curtained off area. Each animal trainer pair brings their animals out through the same opening in the curtain. Which means it's hard to take one animal out until the others are corralled up.

All of the keepers and handlers, Xander and I included, feel badly about keeping our animals crated so much. This is not what they're used to. I'm not sure how were going to make this up to Barry, but we need to do something.

There's a large seating area with chairs, but since it's a flat space, it means the people in the back can't get a good look at Barry. Xander and I decided early on that he'd walk around with Barry so people can get a closer look. I have to keep announcing for the crowd to back up and not to touch him.

Barry, that is.

After one of my announcements, Xander laughed and said, "Ladies, you can feel free to touch me all you want." That earned him a good chuckle.

Quickly, he glances back at me and mouths something. I could swear he says, "Just kidding."

I look over and smile. Xander starts to return my smile, but then he remembers how terrible I am and a grim expression falls over his face.

He probably thinks I'm going to call him a man-whore again. His eyes dart down while his mouth tightens.

I deserve it.

I've got to make this up to him.

I don't want to see his mouth tighten when he looks at me. I want him to smile.

When the last stragglers clear out of the convention room, I sink down wearily on a chair next to Barry's crate. I think Barry's happy to be in isolation. I wouldn't mind some myself. There were a lot of people. And normally, I can handle people. I mean, I work in a zoo.

Xander pulls up a chair and leans forward, resting his elbows on his legs and his face in his hands. Fatigue sags at his shoulders. He reminds me of a deflated balloon.

I've never seen him so devoid of energy and personality. It's like everything he had went into the presentations today.

"You were great today. Really great," I offer. My voice cracks, harsh and hoarse from all the talking.

He shrugs, not lifting his head. After a moment, he rakes his hands down his face and extends back, now staring up at the ceiling. "I had no idea it would be like that."

"Me neither. I don't know how you walked around like that. I mean, it was great that you did, and the people loved it, but I think I would have freaked out with all those people."

"It's probably about as close as I'll ever get to feeling like a rock star. There had to have been at least five thousand people over the course of the day."

"Easily. And don't sell your rock star dreams short. You have the gift. I could see you working the talk show circuit." He'd be a hit on Fallon or The Late Late Show with James Corden.

Xander smiles. "You're ready to take our show on the road?"

"Not us. You. I don't have that charisma."

Xander's head lolls in my direction. "You think I'm charismatic?" His eyebrows shoot up while a slow grin spreads across his face.

Ah, there it is. I feel a small, personal victory.

"I said you had charisma, not that you are charismatic. Don't get too full of yourself here."

"You did a great job too. You kept the audience in check and engaged."

I smile at Xander. "Poor little Barry."

"Yeah, but I'll tell you what; he's not so little when you carry him around like that all day. When I can't lift my arm tomorrow, remind me this is why." He rubs his shoulder and arm a bit.

Xander's biceps were certainly working overtime. Not that I was checking him out. I simply noticed as I was monitoring Barry. I also noticed that Xander has a tattoo circling his right bicep. Similar to a tribal band, but knowing what I know about him now, I would bet it's not some random, drunken impulse tattoo.

He absently rubs his arm. "Okay, well, we should probably get the B-man settled in for the night."

"I still want to take him to the hotel with us."

"You know, after today, I'm tempted, but one of us has to be the strict parent. You want to be the fun one all the time, but someone has to say no to the kids every now and again." Xander stands up and arches his back to stretch.

I feel the smile fade from my face. It was a simple harmless comment, but nonetheless, I feel as if I've been punched in the gut.

Well, the uterus to be exact.

We settle Barry in a more quiet area for the night, far away from the animals who might want to eat him. The walk to the hotel should only take us five minutes, but I feel like it's twelve miles.

You know I'm tired when I forget to eat.

Xander and I part, agreeing to meet at the convention center in the morning. We're not attached at the hip, and it's not like we need to spend every moment of this trip together.

Once in my hotel room, I take the longest, hottest shower I can possibly stand. Upon finishing, all nice and pruny, I put on my shorts and oversized T-shirt for bed. I call in a room service order and comb through my hair. I don't have the energy to dry it, so I hope it dries in nice waves rather than the I-stuck-my-finger-in-a-light socket-look that it has the potential to spawn into.

The knock on my door comes a lot quicker than I was expecting. It's enough to boost my mood because I'm suddenly realizing how famished I am. I pull the door open with enthusiasm and say, "I didn't even know how much I needed this until now. I can't wait to get my mouth around this."

Only it's not room service.

It's Xander.

The shit-eating grin that spreads across his face means one of two things. One: that sounded as bad as I thought it did. Two: He now thinks I want him.

The only thing I want is a cheeseburger and fries.

"I don't mean you. I don't want you." Heat fills my face.

"I don't want you either." He's still smiling, and now there's a twinkle in his eyes.

"I thought you were my cheeseburger."

Xander laughs. "I'd feel the same way."

"Did you eat yet?"

We're still standing in the doorway. I don't know if I should invite him in or what. It's probably the polite thing to do. If I invite him in, will he think it's for that other thing?

Xander shakes his head. "I was coming to see what you were doing for food, but I guess you're all set."

I step aside and motion for him to come in. "Why don't I call down and add something for you?"

"That'd be great. Did you say cheeseburger?"

I nod, going to the phone. "Beer too?"

He nods and sits in the lounge chair in the corner. I've never spent enough time in a hotel room to be able to enjoy the chairs. I sleep in the hotel room and shower. Nothing else really. Never time to sit or lounge or contemplate the world.

"They say twenty minutes, even with the add on."

"Thanks. You didn't have to wait for me."

"It's the least I can do. I should have asked you before I ordered."

And now we're out of things to say.

A minute passes and then two. I've never known Xander to not have something to say. On the other hand, I don't know that much about Xander. He's a better listener than talker.

And suddenly I want to know more about him. I need to know what makes this man tick.

"So," he finally starts tentatively, "I've been thinking."

I want to interject with the comment, "so that's what I smell" but decide to hold back, not if I want him to open up. He's wringing his hands together and not looking at me. The confidence and swagger has slipped away. Whatever he has to say, it's serious.

He takes a breath and continues. "I've been thinking about your situation."

I'm not sure which situation he means. It could be the BRCA thing. Could be the mom thing.

Could be the super-unfortunate hair thing I've got going on.

I nod, trying to encourage him to go on without actually yelling at him to get to the point.

He may have been onto something about me getting hangry.

"Okay I need to say this before I lose my nerve—"

Holy crap, he's nervous. I didn't know he could be nervous. He always exudes such confidence and swagger. What could he possibly be nervous about?

Oh no. He's going to ask me out. Or ask me to have sex with him. What do I say? I don't want to ruin our working relationship, which is in a delicate state. On the other hand, Xander is quite attractive. It's not like I have much success on the dating front. He is attractive. More than attractive. He's not hard on the eyes.

Okay, Xander is hot.

And like it or not, now I'm thinking about mouths on various body parts.

But I didn't shave my legs. Why not? I was in there for long enough. Dammit, I should have shaved.

"I've been thinking about your baby problem, and I think I have a solution."

If that isn't enough to make my uterus wilt, I don't know what is. My hormones had even considered

KATHRYN R. BIEL

revving up. Okay, they were revved. All for nothing. He obviously wasn't going to proposition me.

Not that I want him to. Or do I?

Shit. Focus, Erin.

"I'm listening."

I'm not. I don't want to have this conversation. There is nothing he can say that—

"I know how you can have a baby."

Say what now?

He takes my stunned silence as permission to continue talking about my reproductive system. I don't know if he knows that's not okay.

"As you've explained it to me, I see that you have a two-fold problem. The first is the logistics of becoming pregnant. That seems like the big problem, but it's really not. Getting pregnant is relatively easy, with a sperm donor being the obvious choice. It's the second problem, which is your ability to care for the baby after you have it, that's the real issue. Not actual care of a baby, because we all know you can do that, but the logistics are where you're struggling."

Sadly, his analysis is spot on. "Thanks for the recap, Captain Obvious."

"No, bear with me. I'm getting to the point, I swear."

He'd better or else he's out of here. And I'll eat his burger. No remorse.

I wait for him to continue.

He swallows and finally looks at me. Then the words start tumbling out, so fast I can barely comprehend what he's saying. "You problems would be mostly solved if your baby had two people to raise it. I think that we should co-parent."

"Huh?" I understand his words, but still, they make no sense. What does he mean, 'co-parent?'

"My house is plenty big. It's four bedrooms and has a big yard. That solves the housing issue. We'd coordinate our schedules so that we don't have the same days off. That takes care of child care for more than half of the time. We won't travel together, so one can cover while the other is on the road. And we split kid expenses. You only have to be able to afford half a baby."

I have no words.

"Plus, then, when you have to take care of your ... uh ..." he nods toward my chest, "... BRCA stuff, I can take care of the baby, and you don't have to worry."

I know my mouth is hanging open at this point.

*Current mood: stunned.*

"I think we'd be able to come to agreement on lots of the parenting things. We'll hash it all out before. Plus, I've seen you with the animals. I know you're caring and nurturing. You'll be a great mother, and you deserve the chance to be one."

"I ... uh ... um ..." I cannot form a coherent sentence. I feel like I've been kicked in the chest. My lungs have lost their ability to move air in and out.

Who ... what ... when ... where ... why...

Most importantly, *why?*

"It's a great idea and everyone wins. You don't have to miss out on anything because of your diagnosis. You don't have to give up your job or your chance to be a mother. Come on, Erin, what do you say?"

Um ...

# CHAPTER 18

*Knock. Knock. Knock.*

Thank goodness. I'm saved from giving Xander an answer by the room service delivery. I step aside as the steward carries the trays in. I hand him his tip and then promptly retrieve the beer off my tray. I open the bottle and proceed to down the entire thing without stopping for a breath.

"Okay." Xander laughs. "That was impressive."

Oh no. The problem with chugging a beer like that is the inevitable gas buildup in my stomach. I let out the most unfeminine belch, but immediately feel much better.

"I rescind my being impressed. That was kind of gross." Xander picks up his beer and takes a small sip.

I wipe my mouth with the back of my hand. I need another beer. I need a six pack. I need a keg.

That's the only thing that might help make sense of this mixed-up conversation.

Xander Barnes wants to ... father my child? Raise my child? I still don't get the hows, and I certainly don't understand his whys. *Why would he do this?* My synapses start to fire but then short circuit. I can't even formulate a response.

"Huh?" That's about all I can come up with.

"It's super practical. We know each other. We respect each other, at least most of the time. We understand what our jobs require, which a lot of people don't."

*But why?*

Though, he's got a point about the logistics. Heck, he's got a lot of points, and they're all good. The few relationships that I've had have gone south because the guy didn't get my commitment to my job. What I do is literally life or death. Not for people, obviously, but some of the animals I work with are endangered. We are literally working to save species.

"But we don't really know each other."

"We know enough. We've seen each other almost every day for eight years. We both like to crack jokes and rib each other. We both have thick skin. We both value family. We're both caregivers."

Why is he making so much sense? Stupid logic.

But even his logic is illogical. There's no rhyme or reason to where this came from. I want to ask, but he's still talking.

He continues, "We already job share at work. We'd be job sharing at home too."

"Do you rent or own?" I'm not sure why this is the first question I ask. It's probably the least important detail. I know he said something about a house, so I glom onto that.

Plus, I'm not ready to process more information. Important information, like why he'd want to have a baby with me.

"I own. Four-bedroom, three bath over off of Powell Road. About a sixteen minute commute to work."

My current commute is twenty-two minutes. I could sleep for six minutes more every day. That's a plus.

Who am I kidding? With a baby I probably won't ever sleep again. Kenzie's tired face flashes before my eyes.

"I see."

"'I see?' That's it. Don't you have other questions for me?"

"Why?"

There. I said it.

Xander smiles as he takes a big bite of his burger. I suddenly have no appetite. "I thought you'd want to know my thoughts on how first."

I cannot even begin to process that. All the nerve endings in my brain seem to fire at once, resulting in a brain overload. It's like they burned themselves all out. Maybe one in the background is still fizzling and sputtering, but nothing else is working.

"I like you Erin. I always have. You're smart and strong and driven. You take my crap and give it right back. The same disease that is threatening to ruin your life ruined mine. We're touched by the same thing, and I want you to beat it. It can't win. Let's do this to stick it to cancer. We can finally have control."

"But why? Why me? Why now?"

He laughs. "I'm pretty sure you're on a relatively fixed timeline. I'm not getting any younger either, and it makes sense. I want kids too and I want to be young enough to enjoy them. I don't want to be the old dude moving my kids into college. Now seems like a great time to get started, and you seem like a great person to get started with."

Wow.

This is probably the most genuine, most compassionate thing I've ever heard. "Okay."

"Okay, you're in?"

Crap. Did I just agree to this? I can't agree to it. Not yet. I need to sleep on it. I need to talk about it with Kenzie and probably the ladies of UnBRCAble too. I need time.

I shake my head so hard I can feel my brain bounce around in my skull. "No, okay I hear your reasons. I ... I need time."

It's one thing to decide to have a baby. It's another thing to fill the slots with actual people for the job. It would mean I'd be tied to Xander for the rest of my life.

We've only been friendly for a few weeks now. It's new. Will we be able to stay friends forever? To co-parent?

"Understandable. Tell me about your family."

I start with Mackenzie. He already knows about my fanatical mother. "We used to be really close, but it's not the same as it used to be. She's got a two-year-old and is super sick with her pregnancy, so she's not as available as I'd like her to be. Stupid kids, cramping her style," I try to joke. Truth is, I miss my sister.

"Is it just the two of you?"

I nod. "Yup. We're two years apart, like her kids are going to be. She's having a little girl this time. Of course she is, because her life follows the script. She didn't get the BRCA gene either, so she doesn't have to worry about her kids."

There's no bitterness in my voice as I say it. I'm glad they won't have to worry.

"I have an older sister and two older brothers. My parents divorced when I was ten. My sister was already in college, so she was basically out of the house. I stayed with my mom while my brothers went with my dad. He lived in a better school district, and they were big football players. My middle brother played for Ohio State."

I feel like that's supposed to be impressive, but I'm not much into sports. "Was that hard being split up like that?"

"It was, but I couldn't leave my mom all alone. Then when my mom got sick, she moved in with my dad. He cared for her until ... the end. I had just graduated high school when she started chemo, so when I went to college, I lost my home base."

"But it was your dad's. Didn't you have a room there?"

"Of course, and it was my dad. But for eight years, it had been only Mom and me. My dad's place was always like a borrowed pair of fancy shoes. They're right for the occasion and they look good, but they never feel right on your feet."

"That's nice that he took care of her."

"They weren't in love with each other anymore, but there was a mutual respect that went a long way. My mom's family is out in California, so they couldn't really help. My sister was in grad school, and then she was trying to build her career. My brothers were out of the house. I was in college. It made a huge difference in the quality of her life that my dad was there for her. Especially at the end."

Suddenly, Xander's motivations seem crystal clear. Any doubts I may have had melt away. A warm feeling spreads through me like I've just downed a shot of whiskey. There will be lots to figure out, but at least I now know why he's doing this.

I can't believe I'm saying this, but Xander is a nurturer. He's a caregiver, and he wants to take me in. I know without a doubt that he'd do just that—watch out for me and help me.

It's like our whole relationship has leveled up in the past thirty minutes.

The idea of him being my nemesis or even frenemies now seems ridiculous.

Xander finishes his burger and wipes his mouth with his napkin. He drains the rest of his beer and moves his tray out to the hall. "You should get some sleep. Think about it. We can talk tomorrow. It's really a win-win."

Xander closes the door and is gone. What the heck just happened?

Needless to say, sleep does not descend quickly or easily. I toss and turn. Every time I start to doze off, my mind starts screaming at me. My jaw and teeth ache from the clenching I don't even know I'm doing. I put the TV on to try to occupy my brain. Somewhere after three I finally doze off.

Which means that when my alarm blares at half-past-six, I'm in no shape to get up and begin the day. I don't think my magic under-eye cream is going to get it done. I settle for getting a bucket of ice, sticking my spoon left over from my barely-touched dinner, in it. I take turns, icing my eyes.

Out of all of the things I could have imagined Xander hitting me with, this would not be one of them. Having a baby ... with Xander.

Without a doubt this is one of the most preposterous things I've ever heard.

There is absolutely no way I can have a baby with him.

Or can I?

I can't believe I'm actually considering it. Could we really? Could I have a baby with him?

Could I *make* a baby with him?

Oh God, what was he thinking about that? I was so busy thinking about the child-rearing that I didn't think about the child making. Does he want to have sex? It would be the easiest, I guess.

But then I'd have to sleep with him.

Is he going to get offended if I ask him to get tested and sanitized and wash him in bleach? Although he swears he doesn't deserve his reputation. Is it possible I misjudged him?

I'm starting to think so.

In fact, I think I know so, even though I hate to admit I was wrong. So very wrong. Maybe he wasn't flirting but listening. Maybe he wasn't making a play but offering support.

Regardless, I'm not even sure I could do the deed. While I'm not as conservative as my mom, I do want to have an emotional connection with the person I'm sleeping with.

Call me old fashioned.

But if we don't do that then we have to talk about samples and specimens and donations. Ick.

It doesn't seem so icky when I'm helping the vets inseminate one of our animals. Maybe Xander adds the ick factory.

But he shouldn't. And it's really no different.

And …

Holy crap! Is that the time? Did I fall asleep or doze off or what? I'm supposed to be at the expo center by nine and it's eight-forty-five. Good thing I showered last night. Quick bun, three-minute makeup, khakis and polo. I'm good to go.

I have time to grab a quick coffee and Danish in the lobby café before I'm practically running up the road. I think they increased the grade in the street last night, and I feel like I'm climbing Everest.

"You're late."

"I couldn't sleep."

He's quiet for a minute. "I take it you were thinking about things?"

"Obviously. How could you spring it on me like that?"

Xander reaches over and takes a swig of my coffee. "I'm pretty sure any way I brought it up was going to come as a surprise. It came as a surprise to me. It was a shower idea. And even though it came out of left field, it felt—feels—right."

The sad thing is that I totally understand what he means by a shower idea.

Oh crap, we're already on the same wave length.

He hands me my coffee back. "Anything we want to do differently today?"

I shake my head, not coming up with anything. We only have three shows today, since the expo ends at five, rather than six. "Think we can get loaded up right after we're done and hit the road?"

"I think so. If we can, we might be home by midnight or so."

It's sort of scary how in sync we are already, working together. I'm sure, if he were a woman, our cycles would fall in line with each other.

Why am I just seeing this about Xander?

Good Lord, my entire world is turning upside down.

Another long day, but we're rewarded with tomorrow off. I'm looking forward to that. What I'm not looking forward to is five hours in the van with Xander.

There's no way we're not going to talk about *the thing*. Maybe I'll just do a preemptive end-run and tell him I need to think, and I'm not ready to discuss.

I'm not. There's no way I can have a baby with Xander Barnes. I'd be tied to him for the rest of my life. I can't spend the rest of my life with a pompous ass. Except the more I know him, the less pompous he seems.

And the only ass I see is one fine-looking backside.

I look over to see him wink at a twenty-something who is obviously trying to catch his eye.

Okay, maybe not less pompous.

But then something happens. As Xander and I work in tandem to care for Barry, and then present him to throngs of kids and their parents, I can see it. I can see us doing this with a baby.

Human baby, not sloth baby.

I can't stop thinking about what he said about his parents. How he talked about family. How his family was conventional yet unconventional at the same time. The yearning and longing in his voice speaks louder than any volume.

We don't have to be in love. We don't have to be a couple. All that matters is that we are both in it for the kid. It's not ideal, and not what I'd dreamed about growing up, but truth is, with Xander Barnes, I'm a lot closer to my dreams than I've ever been.

Now how to tell him I want him to be the father of my child. Should be nice and awkward.

I wonder if Hallmark makes a card for that?

# CHAPTER 19

The moment we're in the van, I promptly chicken out.
This is such a crazy idea. There's no way it could possibly
work. Yet, it just might.

*Gah, I'm so confused.*

"Tell me more about you, Xander. I feel like I do
all the talking."

"That's because you talk a lot."

"Chalk it up to another on my long list of faults." I
shrug. "The list is numerous."

"Nah. Name one."

"Duh, for starters, I talk too much and usually
about animals, which people don't seem to like.
Weirdos. Second," I tick my faults off on my fingers, like
I'm making a shopping list, "Apparently, according to
*some people*, I dress poorly." I still don't understand
people who don't like funny T-shirts.

Today's shirt: 75% of brain capacity is filled with
song lyrics.

It's funny because it's true.

"Thirdly, I'm too tall."

"Okay, I call bunk on that one. You're not even
tall."

"In my family I am. My sister is five-foot-three and perfect. I'm in the five-eight range, which is tall for a girl. How tall are you?"

"Six-two."

"Great, so I'd pretty much be giving birth to a giraffe. Maybe I'll pass on your offer." I laugh.

Xander quickly glances at me. "Three faults is not a lot, especially when two out of the three are questionable."

"Which two?"

"The talking and the height. The clothes thing has some merit. Your T-shirt style is an acquired taste."

I laugh again. "Okay, there's more. I have fuzzy hair. It's not curly, it's not straight. It's … fuzzy. If I don't tame it down, I look like an alpaca. And I'm nothing to write home about in the looks department. Especially not compared to my sister. I was always the 'smart girl,' on the outside looking in. No matter how old I get, or how cool my job is, I'll always feel that way."

I might as well be standing in front of Xander naked. I can't recall ever being this candid about my faults. I wait for him to laugh or give me weak platitudes about how I'm not *that bad* looking.

"I hate the way I look," Xander offers quietly.

"Shut up."

His voice is a little louder. "No, it's true."

"Oh God, are you looking for compliments? Okay, Xander, you have nothing to hate. You are good looking. Very good looking. Like super hot good looking. And sexy. And freakishly photogenic. Seriously, have you ever taken a bad picture? I'm such a dork in pictures. I always look like I'm screaming or have seven chins. For the record, I only have three."

"You do not have three. It's more like two and a half. But I'm allowed not to like the way I look, just as you don't like the way you look. I can be equally as ridiculous."

"But have you looked in a mirror? What's not to like? You're angled and chiseled and symmetrical and you sparkle."

"Because that's all anyone sees. My face. My body. No one thinks there's anything more to me."

I open my mouth and close it, thinking of all the times I've judged Xander. He continues, "Growing up, math was not an easy subject for me. I was always in the remedial class, and even then I still struggled. No one else in my house had these issues. Quite the contrary. My dad, especially, didn't understand how I didn't get it. It's one of the reasons I didn't go to live with him."

"Oh, Xander, I'm—"

He quickly keeps talking, cutting off my apology. "So one of the things that I heard him say one time was, 'Good thing he's good looking, because there's not too much brain up there.'"

Oh my God.

"So the fact that people only talk about me in regards to my looks ..."

Like I do. I want to tell him he's smart and good with animals and even a kind person, but I know how I would have felt if he'd assured me that I was attractive

183

right after I listed all the reasons why I felt I was not. But there is one thing I can tell him. I need to tell him.

"I'm in. Let's do it. The baby thing."

I know it's the right thing. Xander and I may have known each other for eight years, but the last few weeks—and few days especially—have turned things upside down. I couldn't ever have imagined things going this way, but it seems right. Right?

Xander swerves a bit, hitting the rumble strip. I hope he doesn't wake Barry up. He looks over at me. "Really?"

"Eyes on the road. Yes, really."

Oh crap. What if he was kidding or made the offer to seem nice but didn't think I'd take him up on it? What if he didn't mean it?

Even though I've only just decided, it feels like my world clicked into place. The tension in my gut that has been an ever-present companion over the past several weeks releases. If he doesn't want this, there is no way I'll be able to keep it together. All the pieces will crumble. All the king's horses and all the king's men will not be able to put me together again.

"Okay ... why? Tell me your reasons for agreeing now." He glances over and then his eyes dart back to the road. It would be better if we made it home in one piece.

Is this a test?

I hate surprise tests. If I'd know it was coming, I would have studied.

"You're right."

"What?"

I say it a little louder, "You're right."

"What?" he yells.

"YOU'RE RIGHT!" I yell. There's no way, even with the rumble of the van cruising down the highway, that he can't hear me.

Xander smiles. "You don't have to yell. I can hear you just fine. I just wanted you to say it again."

I swat at him. "*You're right*. I don't have a lot of options. Not to have my cake and eat it too. You've found a way for me to do both. And it's not like I wanted to have a baby on my own. I've always wanted to get married first. Call me traditional."

"Right. This whole situation screams traditional." He chuckles.

"Honestly, that's been one of the hard parts. Giving up that dream. Plus we know I'm letting my family down. It's not going to go over well, I imagine."

"Did you talk to anyone about this?"

Fair question.

"No, not yet."

"Don't you think you should? This is a big decision."

"I'll call my sister when I get home." I look at my watch. "Make that tomorrow morning."

"Let's not consider this a done deal until then."

"What?"

*Is he backing out on me?* He can't do that. Not right after he offered and right after I accepted. That would be the most cruel, most hurtful thing to do. Two months ago, I would have thought Xander could do that. But now, it doesn't seem like him.

185

"This is a big decision. You sound pretty close with your sister, and you should run it by her first. Or someone else you're close with. There's a lot to think about and consider. Take your time. Make sure this is right, and you really want to do it. Don't get my hopes all up and then back out because during the light of day, you thought better."

I can't believe I'm going to say this, but Xander Barnes—cocky, arrogant, full of himself Xander Barnes—is a really good guy.

He's shown me his true colors.

I hope.

SEIZE THE DAY

# CHAPTER 20

"What are you doing here? It's Monday. You're not off on Mondays. Oh God, did you get fired?"

"Hi Kenz. Nice to see you too. I brought donuts."

She reaches out and grabs the bag. "Donuts first. Questions later."

I follow her in and am a little taken aback to see the condition of her house. Normally it could be in the pages of Better Homes and Gardens. Currently, it looks like an 'after' picture from a natural disaster. This pregnancy is kicking the snot out of her.

Oh God, if that happens to me, my place is likely to be condemned. I wish I had the money to hire a maid.

"So, I have news. I need to run it by you first."

"Don't put me in the middle," Mackenzie mumbles, donut crumbs falling out of her mouth as she talks. I swear, she must have shoved an entire one in there in a single bite.

I walk around, picking up Trey's toys. He's in for his nap, which is why I planned my visit for this time. I can

187

at least give her a hand while I'm here. Not to mention I'm too nervous to sit still while I tell her this.

"So it's about Xander."

"The hot one?"

"Yes, the hot one." *Wait*—did I just admit Xander is hot? Of course I did, because he is. "You know we're working together now, and we're traveling together for the zoo. Actually, that's why I'm off today. We were away together all weekend. But that's not the point."

"Well get to the point then. I want to take a nap before Trey wakes up."

I take a deep breath. How Mackenzie reacts to this is going to make or break it for me. I need to get her on my side so she can smooth things over with Mom and Dad. Probably just Mom. I think Dad'll come around.

Eventually.

"So Xander and I—"

"Oh, my God, did you hook up? Was it awesome? Did you see stars? I bet with someone like him, you'd see stars. Is that why you look so tired? Did he keep you up all night? Damn. I bet you could get pregnant just by looking at him."

If I had to guess, I'd think Mackenzie is going through the horny stage of her pregnancy.

"OMG, did he get you pregnant?" She shoves a donut into her mouth. Apparently, she is substituting her sexual needs with baked goods. No judgment here.

Without thinking I answer, "Not yet."

"But he's going to?" Her mouth falls open. Gross.

"Yes, we've decided to have a baby together. And close your mouth. I don't need to see your half-chewed donut."

My sister closes her mouth and tries to swallow, but ends up choking a bit. I hope she clears it because having to perform the Heimlich on a pregnant woman gets complicated.

After several minutes of coughing and sputtering, Mackenzie is finally able to talk. "Are you sure?"

I nod. "I'm about as sure as I can be. I don't have a lot of options."

"But you can't have been together that long. I didn't even know about him. I take it this isn't the first time you've hooked up? Isn't it rushing things?"

I should set her straight on the nature of our relationship.

*Should.*

But it occurs to me that if she thinks we're together—if *my parents* think we're together—then I'm going to get a lot less grief than if I disclose the true nature of the relationship.

It still won't be optimal, but it will be better than the truth. It's a harmless lie. Xander and I will both be protected by a legal agreement. I'm moving in with him anyway. It's not like they'll ask for details of our sex life.

"I'm not convinced it's a bad choice. In fact, it's a pretty good choice. A great choice, really."

"But Xander? Don't you hate him?"

Had she asked me two months ago, I would have said yes. Things are different now. I need to convince her of how different they are. I shrug. "Not really. Now that we've been working together more, he's grown on me."

"Like a fungus?"

"Did you know that a sloth's fur is full of fungus. It helps them to camouflage in the wild, but it is also full of natural anti-parasitic, anti-biotic, and even breast cancer fighting properties? How cool is that? Sloths might be able to cure at least one form of breast cancer."

"Great." Mackenzie's tone is less than impressed. My family generally doesn't care about the random animal facts I like to share.

Losers.

"But what do you know about him? What if he's a serial killer or something?"

"Should I ask if he has bodies buried in the yard before I move in?"

"*You're moving in with him?*" Her shriek is so loud, I'm sure she's woken Trey. As well as babies in China.

I shrug. Play this cool. "We've talked about it. Probably when my lease is up over the summer."

"That's so soon! You won't even have time to figure out if he's a secret slob or if he dissolves the bodies before burying the remains."

My sister apparently has a dark side. Or she watches too much *Investigation Discovery*.

"I'll make a note to ask him." I look around. I've made a dent in the clutter and cleaning, but it's nowhere near what the place normally looks like. "How did you know about Luke? At some point, we all take a leap of faith."

"But we had been together for over two years. It's different."

I could tell her we're going to have a contract, but I don't think it would help my case. "We've known each other for a long time. I think it's like eight years now."

"Yeah, but up until now, you've always hated him."

I need to stop this. I've never been able to lie to Mackenzie for long. She always figures me out. She'll undoubtedly figure this out too.

I shrug. "You know they say love is close to hate."

"*You love him?* Who are you and what have you done with my sister?"

"I don't love him yet." It's a relief to be able to say a true statement. "But I know this is the right thing."

"What if it doesn't last? What if you break up?"

"Couples split up all the time and still manage to co-parent. We're going to talk this all through before, so we know where we stand. We might even draw up a contract so there's no surprises."

That's honest too. I want to tell her that if we split up, it will be fine because there are no real feelings involved here.

"Erin, is this because of me? Are you obsessed with having a baby because I am?"

*Say what now?*

"I know about the Pinterest board. You accidentally shared it with me, even though it's still secret. I see all the things you put on there. The nursery layouts and the baby clothes and the ideas for baby showers. You're always adding new things. You're baby crazy."

I never told anyone about my passion for pinning baby things because I thought it would make me look pitiful and desperate. In all honesty, I started because I was planning Kenzie's shower for Trey. Then all these suggestions kept popping up and ... I couldn't stop.

It was the life I've dreamed of and thought I'd never really get. Until now.

"That's easy for you to say. You want a husband ... poof Luke walks in. Baby? Sure. How 'bout a boy then a girl? Great. Don't want to have defective genes? We wouldn't *dare* darken your doorstep with that."

I've had enough. I stand up to leave.

"Erin, don't be that way. I ... I want to be happy for you. I just think you're rushing it. Would it kill you to wait a little longer until you've been together a while?"

Oh God, she does not get it. Not one bit.

"Why yes, actually. It would."

# CHAPTER 21

"Ah, a meeting with a lawyer. How all good relationships start." I laugh nervously as we head in. Millie's friend Lisa recommended Paul Harris for family law.

Millie didn't ask why I needed a lawyer, and I certainly was not forthcoming with that information. I'm not ready yet. I'm not sure what to say after I let Mackenzie *accidentally* interpret the situation between Xander and I as a relationship rather than a business agreement. I'm still trying to figure out if there's a way out of that one.

At least she hasn't said anything to Mom or Dad.

Xander and I have met a few times after work to discuss *the thing*, which we now refer to as *the deal*. Surprisingly, we're pretty much on the same page with most of the details. It was a big sigh of relief when Xander brought up sperm donation and using a fertility clinic, so I didn't have to have that awkward conversation about why I don't want to sleep with him.

Sleeping together no longer seems as icky as it once did. But it would so complicate things. Especially because I may be looking at Xander with different eyes these days.

Can't have that.

I've also been able to omit from the discussion the fact that my sister thinks we're involved and that this isn't a simple transaction. That's a bridge I'm not yet ready to cross.

I sit down and knot my hands in my lap. I don't know why this is making me nervous. The weight of this man's opinion is not going to change my decision. It's my body and my reproductive rights. This is simply to make sure all of our rights are protected.

I give a lot of credit to lawyers because this stuff is so boring. Dry and tedious, and there's not even a cute animal to look at. I think I'm going to nod off right here right now. I should have taken the coffee the receptionist offered me.

I cannot pay attention for the life of me.

I have to say something. "I'm sorry, but this stuff sort of sounds like the teacher in Charlie Brown. Can I sum up and you can tell me if my understanding of these points is correct?"

Paul nods and Xander laughs. "I'm glad you said it. I was feeling the same way."

"Okay, let me take a crack." I square my shoulders and sit up a little taller. "Pending favorable outcomes of the health screenings, Xander will make the necessary donations to the clinic, which will then be used to ... " I falter a little, saying it out loud. "Impregnate me within the clinic setting. I am financially responsible for this procedure."

Xander interjects. "Erin, I told you I would split the cost of the insemination with you. I want it to be fifty-fifty, right from the beginning."

"Xander, I told you. Until there's a baby, it's all on me. Paul, don't change anything. I'm paying for that procedure."

It's the least I can do.

Paul nods so I continue.

"Following successful ... fertilization, I will move into Xander's house, into my own room. I will pay rent, and we will split utilities. Xander is the landlord and I am the rentee." After another nod, I continue.

"Xander is allowed to attend medical appointments and the birth of the child. He will be named on the birth certificate. Xander will put the child on his medical insurance, and I will pay half the difference of the insurance premium. We will keep a log of expenses for necessities and split these as evenly as possible."

"Hair bows do not count as necessities," Xander interjects.

"If she is bald and people keep calling her a him, then that does count." I've already bookmarked this great Esty site, Ella's Bows, for just such an emergency. I found them on Pinterest. Naturally.

Paul smiles at us.

After we finish going over the terms in plain English, I feel satisfied. That is until I stand up to walk out the door.

What happens if I don't get pregnant?

195

I say as much to Xander once we hit the parking lot. The days are long, now that we're into May and weak rays of sun slant toward my car.

"I think that's something you talk to your doctor about. You'll have my ... stuff ... so whatever works. But let's hope that we don't have to worry about that. Stay positive that this will work."

Suddenly I'm nervous that I won't be able to get pregnant at all. What if years of using birth control ruined my fertility? It's hard enough to know that using birth control could have increased my chance of developing breast cancer *even* further. While not prone to panic attacks, my breathing is coming in short little bursts, and I can't seem to get enough air.

Great.

"Hey, Erin, calm down. I think you take it as this. If you get pregnant, great. If not, it obviously wasn't meant to be, and you need to accept that the universe has another plan for you. Be grateful and accept either. We can always talk about other options, like adoption, but let's try this first."

Xander's right, not that I'll tell him that. While I've come to accept our new-found friendship and deeper bond, I can't go padding his ego.

He's still pretty cocky.

Though, the more time I spend with him, the more I'm starting to think it's an act. A front. He's sure of himself, in the things that he knows, but he's more than willing to admit when he doesn't know something. He's one of those people who is always looking to learn.

There's a genuine and earnest quality I didn't see beneath the swagger.

There is a lot I admire about Xander Barnes.

The least of which is the fact that he's not only helping me have a baby but to also be a parent to my—our—child.

~~~***~~~

I hate the human body. Specifically, the female body. Female hormones are stupid, and I hate them and I hate everything.

In a related story, I'm taking Clomid to increase my chances of getting pregnant. Dr. James doesn't think I'll have trouble, but he doesn't want to take chances either. I'm not like his typical fertility patients. As he put it, he wants me to get the most "bang for my buck."

If I could have just had a bang, I wouldn't have to go through all of this.

But also, if this works the first time, I'd be happy.

*Current mood: hormonal.*

I feel like I'm possessed. I'm on dose five of the Clomid. I don't know how women do this for months on end. My shorts are too tight because of the bloating. Also probably because I ate an entire bag of chips last night. I can't seem to stop eating, which certainly hasn't helped the shorts situation. As a result, they're riding up into my nether regions, and it's not going to be a good day if I have a perma-wedgie.

"Who pissed in your Cheerios?" Xander mumbles, as I slam the top down on the biscuit container. The edges aren't lining up and I can't—slam— get it—slam—to fit. Xander reaches around me and easily slides the top into place.

"I hate you and I hate everything."

He laughs. "This isn't you. It's the medication. Hang in there. Hopefully this is the only month you have to go through this."

I burst into tears. "What if I have to do this forever?"

He pats me on the head, like I'm one of his zoo charges. "It won't be forever. It could literally be this week. Buck up, little camper. This is what we want."

Why does he have to be so frickin' reasonable? As soon as his back is turned, I stick my tongue out at him.

*Current mood: irritable.*

It's been a long three months getting to this point. Some days it seems that I've been trying to get pregnant for years. Hard to believe that it was just the beginning of March when I decided to take a more active role in having a baby and tried online dating again. Now it's June and I've had more doctor appointments than I care to admit. I've had so much blood taken that I'm surprised I'm still alive.

And we won't discuss the invasive testing to make sure that all my bits and pieces are able to do their job and carry a baby.

FYI, I'm ship shape.

I also had another round of my cancer screenings. So far, nothing suspicious. Phew. I'd hate to get to this point to have to scrap it all.

Xander's been a good sport. More patient with me than I ever thought possible. Of course, I think all he had to do was to give some blood and some other samples. I do *not* want to think about those appointments. His job is done. Everything's been tested and washed, and all I need to do is produce an egg or follicle or whatever.

Today's the last day of Satan's pill and then I go in on Thursday for the procedure, if they detect a follicle.

I hope they light a candle or play some Sade at least.

Dr. James has mentioned several times the chances of a multiple pregnancy, but I'm choosing to ignore that. Having twins (or more!) is not in my plan, so it had better not happen. I haven't mentioned to Xander the possibility.

It's not going to happen, so why worry him?

Even with the prospect of combined residence and resources, two babies are so not in our financial plan. Zookeepers are notoriously overworked and underpaid. In fact, the only reason why this situation is able to work for the two of us is because Xander bought the house with money from his mom. It keeps the mortgage—and therefore rent—payments low.

I'm sweating like a stuck pig, which the sultry rainforest climate doesn't help. Good Lord, I need a mop.

199

"Erin, are you okay? You don't look good," Xander asks.

"I'm hot."

"Not really right now. You look a little crazy."

I grit my teeth. "I feel like I'm on fire from the inside."

He nods and smiles. "Ah. Hot flash. It's a side effect."

"How do you know that? Are you having a hot flash? Have you gained seven pounds? Do you feel like the Michelin Man? I don't think so. Back off."

Xander pats me on the head again, and I duck out from under his hand. "Easy there, killer. I am subject to your mood swings, so I deserve a little credit."

"Stop patting me on the head. You know I can't stand that."

Xander winks. "That's why I do it. Buck up. Things should get better, right?"

I shrug. They'll be better if I get pregnant. I can't even think about what would happen if I can't get pregnant. Each round is going to cost me about a thousand bucks. I really don't want to pay for more than one round. No matter how much I'll be saving on rent in the future.

Plus, the cancer thing. Every month, every week that goes by, I could be getting closer to it. Best case, I'm eighteen months out, give or take, from my mastectomy. I'm hoping to be able to nurse for about six months. I'd love a year, but that's time I don't have.

I'm lucky to be getting this time.

This chance.

And I owe it all to Xander.

Oh crap, here come the tears.

Did I mention mood swings are a side effect of this drug? Awesome.

I finish cleaning up Bonnie's bowel movement. She's in estrus again, which means she climbs down and goes every day. Can you imagine if poop was a lure for men?

She is also screaming a terrible sound, in hopes of luring a mate. With Barry in the enclosure with her at night, they have access to do whatever they please. Fun fact: while sloths are notorious for how slow they move, intercourse between sloths can last as little as six seconds.

Brings a whole new meaning to "wham, bam, thank you ma'am."

We're hoping that Bonnie and Barry do their thing. The gestation period for a Hoffman's two-toed sloth is about eleven months, we think. Much of the time, it's hard to tell when conception actually occurs. That means if all goes according to plan, Bonnie and I could be having our babies around the same time. While that's cool, it's a little nerve wracking as well. First time mother sloths are known to not always accept their babies, which would mean the zoo staff would have to hand raise the pup.

I know it's putting the cart before the horse, but these are the things I like to fret over in the wee hours of the night. They're so much more fun to think about than the other really big things in my life.

But I need to pull myself together. Today's an exciting day. I mean, everyday at Sloth Central is a happy day because someone's dreams come true. Today it will be more so.

When Millie approached me back in April about getting tickets for Piper, her boyfriend's daughter, I was happy to assist. I was able to not only get them on the schedule but was also able to close off their session so it's just the three of them in with Barry. Sure, I had to pull a few strings, but once Sterling told me his plan for the day, I knew I had to make it happen.

It's not everyday that your friend gets engaged at your job. On the other hand, it's not everyday that you take mood altering hormones either.

For the record, those two events are not the most compatible.

I manage to keep it together through their actual sloth encounter. I do my job, pretending to just take pictures when Sterling drops to one knee and pulls out a ring. I pretend that my tears are happy tears, which some of them are.

Millie's had a rough year. Her shirt reads "Previvor: By choice. My choice."

I'm making choices too.

It just so happens that my choices are making me a bit nutters at the moment. I don't know if I can do this again next month. I'm not sure I can handle it if I don't get pregnant.

# CHAPTER 22

"Are you sure?" Xander's voice is thick and hoarse.

"Would I be calling you if I wasn't sure?"

God, the man frustrates me. I know how to read a pregnancy test. I mean, it's not even as complicated as one line or two lines or a plus or a minus. The test *literally* says, "Pregnant."

It's been two weeks since the procedure. *The insemination.* While I certainly feel better off the Clomid, I still don't feel like myself. Xander wanted me to take a week off and go lay on a beach somewhere with my feet up in the air, but I didn't want to spend the money. Not to mention I'm not the best relaxer.

I've been afraid to go on Pinterest for fear of jinxing myself, so short of taking up knitting, I don't know how to relax.

I'm still in the bathroom. Yes, I washed my hands. The stick still sits on the edge of the sink.

*Pregnant.*

"Oh my God, Xander, I'm pregnant."

"Hang on. Crap. I'll call you back." He disconnects abruptly.

I'm not sure what he has to do that's more important than this but whatever. A feeling of dread creeps up that this is indicative of how he'll be with raising little ... what? What do I call it?

I walk out of the bathroom and look around my apartment. Guess I need to let my landlord know I won't be renewing my lease in September. Also, I need to start packing. I think I'm going to Marie Kondo this whole place so I don't have to move too many boxes.

On the other hand, what if I get rid of all my stuff and end up moving out of Xander's place in two years? Then I won't have anything, and it'd kill me to have to re-buy things I got rid of.

I need to convince Xander to KonMari his stuff so I can keep mine. Then when I have to move out, he's the one outta luck. Still, I've been in this place for nine years. There's probably a lot that can go.

When my buzzer rings, I'm sitting in a massive pile of crap that I've culled from all my miscellaneous drawers. You know, the drawers where you throw random things that don't really have a place? Turns out, I probably don't need the most of what's in these drawers. Not the graphing calculator from high school. Not the wooden puzzle that I could never figure out how to solve. Not the electrical cords from some mysterious gadget.

I will keep the thumbtacks and picture wire. While they don't spark joy, you never know when you might need them. Does Marie Kondo ever think about the practical side of purging?

It takes me a minute to get up off the ground and to the door.

I'm greeted by a large bouquet of the most gorgeous flowers I've ever seen. Delphinium, garden roses, lisianthus, and rice flowers, all in varying shades of blues, pinks, and whites. It looks like something off a Pinterest wedding board.

Okay, it looks like something off of my Pinterest wedding board, which is how I know what all the flowers are.

"Congratulations, Mama." Xander pushes the bouquet toward me, but I'm too stunned to react. "Okay, well, I'll just put these here." He walks around me and places the vase on my counter. He looks around. "What happened in here? Were you robbed?"

"I thought I'd start cleaning out because I guess I'm going to be moving."

Xander smiles. "I guess you are, Mama."

Mama.

I'm going to be a mama.

Without thinking I rush to Xander, throwing my arms around him. "Thank you. Thank you so much. For the baby and the flowers. No one's ever given me flowers before."

It occurs to me that I should call him Daddy or something, but that just seems creepy and weird.

What does not, however, seem creepy and weird, is that Xander hugs me back. Short of random body parts touching when we're handling an animal and his annoying head pats, I've never been in this close contact with Xander before. Doubly odd

205

considering I'm pregnant with his child. Yet somehow, it feels ... okay.

More than okay.

I pull back and look up at Xander. His eyes are shining. Immediately, mine fill in response. "I'm not crying," I announce.

"Neither am I." He wipes his eyes.

"I'm glad we are standing here, not crying with this momentous news."

Xander nods. He pulls me back into his arms, resting his chin on the top of my head. It's nice that he's tall enough to do that. "We're going to be parents," he whispers.

Parents. To a baby. That's going to grow in me and come out of me.

And then the thought hits me. I say, through my tears, "Yeah, but now I've got to get this thing out of me."

Perhaps I didn't think this all the way through. I've attended enough births—granted animal ones—to know it pretty much sucks for the mom. And what if I poop on the table? In front of Xander! OMG, he's totally going to see my lady bits!

I did *not* think this through.

"From what I hear, you're so uncomfortable by the end that you'll do anything to get it out."

"You're not helping."

"I'll make sure you get the good drugs. I'll bring a dart just in case, and throw a blind on you."

I laugh, picturing Xander shooting me with a tranquilizer gun like we use on the really big animals as

I'm in the painful throes of labor. Maybe he will be useful after all.

I step away and turn to look at the mess I created. Holy crap. I can't believe I've accumulated so much stuff. Suddenly, the trinkets and things don't seem so important. "I can't believe all I have to do. I'll never get it all done." I reach down and start grabbing handfuls of things, shoving them in the trash bag on the floor.

Xander leans on the counter, next to the flowers. "We've got time. When is your lease up?"

"September."

"Erin, it's only the first week in July. There's plenty of time. But not for me right now. I've got to get back to work."

"Oh God, that's right. Why are you here? Who's covering for you? Why did you leave?"

"I wanted to bring you those." He nods toward the flowers. I look at them again. The blues and the pinks are so pretty.

Blues and pinks.

"Did you get them because of the baby?"

Xander shakes his head as he turns toward the door. "Why else would I bring you flowers?"

Not romance. Obviously.

"But the colors—"

"Since we don't know yet, I decided to do both. We're going to find out, right? How soon can your doctor tell?"

"Um, I don't know. My sister found out at twenty weeks. I was there. Oh! I can bring her to *my* ultrasound!"

"Yeah, I gotta go. I'll talk to you soon." Xander looks at me and then shakes his head slightly before leaving. He can't keep the smile or expression of dazed wonder off his face. I know the feeling.

I look at the flowers and then around my apartment. It doesn't seem real. I stared down the beast and took a chance, and now it's about to pay off.

I'm having a baby!

# CHAPTER 23

I'm guessing this kid is going to be a rule follower, which is totally fine with me. Morning sickness didn't start until six weeks. It ended promptly at twelve weeks and contained itself to the morning. I am on morning six of no throwing up and loving life.

Mackenzie is not thrilled with my experience, as she's approaching thirty-eight weeks, is the size of a house, and is still puking at least five days a week. She takes little solace in the fact that she suffers from the same condition as Kate Middleton. She never looks on the positive side of things.

Killjoy.

Or maybe it's because she's the size of a house in the sweltering August heat.

It's been a surreal summer, for sure. I look around my new room and shake my head. This is my life. Doesn't seem real or possible. Yet here I am, living with Xander.

I've only been here one day.

This is going to take some getting used to. I vacated my apartment a week early so my landlord could paint. He let me out of my lease a month early as it was. I didn't mind. I was ready to go, and it saved me some money too.

I told my parents I was moving in with a "friend from work" because my building had mold. It has also helped me dodge them a fair amount because they wouldn't come near my death trap of a domicile, while it also accounted for me feeling under the weather.

Needless to say, I haven't officially announced my pregnancy. Only Mackenzie knows, and I made her swear on both her children's lives that she wouldn't say anything to *anyone*.

I think once I start telling people, it will all seem more real.

Once I'm talking about it, once I'm showing; then it will hit me that this is my life. That I don't have to keep my Pinterest board a secret anymore.

It won't feel surreal anymore.

Now that I'm over the first threshold, I'm telling the BRCA ladies. This might be the hardest news to share. My joy represents someone else's loss. I want to talk to Millie before the meeting so she's not blindsided. She's meeting me a few minutes before the meeting. I'm already at the Genevieve T. Wunderlich Women's Health Center because I had an appointment with Dr. Lee, who is also housed in this building.

Millie rushes in like a whirling dervish. I swear, she has the most energy of anyone I've ever met. I didn't realize it when she first joined UnBRCAble, as she was fresh off her mastectomy and still dealing. Now that she's one-hundred percent, I wish I could bottle her energy and take shots of it when I'm dragging.

"Hey, what's up? Are you okay?" She brushes the stray hairs back from her face, her bright diamond sparkling on her finger.

"I'm great. How's it going for you?"

"I'm getting there. My classroom is almost ready. I can't believe school starts next week. But it's so much better than last year. I'm a little nervous. According to my class list, some of the kids are tough, including two who don't always make it to the bathroom on time."

Sometimes, I think being a second-grade teacher is not that different from my job as a zookeeper but probably she doesn't get to hose everything down like I do.

It's now or never. Time to rip the Band-aid off. "That's good. Millie, I have some news that I'm going to share with the group, but I want you to know first."

Her face falls ashen. "Oh God, did something show up?"

The fear of every single one of us.

I give her a tight-lipped smile. "You could say that. I'm pregnant."

A brief look of shock flashes through her eyes before her face erupts in a wide grin, and she envelops me in her arms. "Oh Erin, I'm so happy for you! When? How? How far? How do you feel?"

"I did IUI. Just about thirteen weeks. I feel great. Due March fifth."

She hugs me again, but when she pulls back, I can see the tears in her eyes. "I'm sorry. It's why I wanted to tell you before."

Millie swipes at her tears. "Don't be sorry. This is great. It's like you found a way to beat this curse that we all have."

It makes me think about Xander who said he wanted to do this so that cancer didn't win again. For once, we outsmarted the curse.

We stand to go into the meeting. Other members have been trickling in.

"ERIN'S PREGNANT!" Millie screams before we even fully get through the door. Apparently, she's on board with this.

"Millie, you can't tell us that! It's not your news," Claudia jumps to her feet. I don't care. I'm not pregnant for the attention.

Through hugs and tears, I try to force myself to live in this moment and be grateful for this chance I've been given, especially when so many of my sisters have been denied.

After a moment or two, the excitement dies down and we all find seats on the comfy couches and chairs. In an effort to avoid the barrage of imminent questions, I start talking.

"I ended up telling a coworker about how I wanted to have a baby and was planning on using a sperm donor. After a fight with my mom who, unfortunately, pointed out the valid logistical reasons for why it wasn't a good idea, I gave up and was a generally miserable human being. My coworker offered to be the donor and that we could raise the baby together. Co-parent, if you will. Almost like divorced parents, but we live under the same roof."

There is a stunned silence.

"Erin ... are you sure?" Worry creases Claudia's forehead. She's always such a calming voice of reason that her concern immediately makes me second—and third—guess my decisions.

"Yes." Because it's a little too late for any other answer. I go on to explain the reasons why this is a *great* idea. When I finish with the fact that we have a legal agreement, I see shoulders drop and people exhale.

"At least you're protected," Frances says.

"Of course. Most of this was Xander's idea to begin with. He's been really on top of things, which I think bodes well for this project."

"Why?" asks Claudia. "What's in it for him?"

I've thought about this a lot too. "I think it's a shortcut to getting a family. He said he wanted kids and didn't want to be too old before he started. He's older than I am, so maybe his clock was ticking too." I never thought about men having biological clocks before. "His parents divorced, and then his dad took care of his mom when she was dying from breast cancer. I think he knows you can have a family without the traditional things."

"His mom died of breast cancer?" Frances asks.

I nod. "I think it's initially why he made the offer. He's already lost a lot to the disease and didn't want it to win again." I pat my non-existent bump. "And now it hasn't."

Tracey sits back and crosses one leg over the other. "Okay, the baby stuff sounds on the up and up.

But what about you two? Now that you've slept together, has it changed your friendship?"

I laugh. "We didn't sleep together. He didn't even ask. He, um, donated, and I had intrauterine insemination at the clinic."

A silence falls over the group. Finally Millie speaks up. "Damn. I was hoping for one of those love stories like in the movies. You know, where he can't stop thinking about you, and you realize all the tension between the two of you was sexual, and then you rip off each others clothes and ..." she trails off. "Was that inappropriate?"

I laugh. "Just a little, but rest assured, there's no chance of that happening. I don't see there being any way that we are compatible." I think for a minute. Nope. We're friends. Solidly friends.

That's what we need and that's how we'll stay.

Friends.

# CHAPTER 24

Damn you, Mille Dwyer.

Until she said something last Wednesday, I'd never even thought of being interested in Xander Barnes. I've never been one of those girls to fawn all over him. To titter and giggle and act like an idiot when he comes swaggering through.

I never want to be one of those girls, but here I am, a full week later, thinking about Xander in a whole new light.

Especially when I had to work today and he was off and I couldn't help but look for him, even though I knew he was at home.

Our home.

And now I'm at home with him, and OMG, I can't stop thinking about things I have no business thinking about.

Maybe it's the pregnancy hormones or something. Maybe it's his pheromones. Maybe it's because he's walking around without a shirt on and he's all sweaty, and I want to lick him.

Ugh, gross.

Yet somehow, it seems anything *but* gross.

I shake my head in an attempt to dislodge these crazy, errant thoughts. Xander and I are friends. Nothing more. I don't *want* anything more.

Well, I could go for some tacos but that's not the same type of want.

I don't know what to say to Xander while he's walking around, half-naked. We should have put a clause in the agreement about how much skin is allowed to be showing. His skin is fine and toned and well defined. I expected nothing less.

"Put your shirt on. I don't want to see *that*." I motion to him vaguely. "Gross," I add, hoping it isn't overkill.

"How was today? What's the news with Bonnie?" he asks as he pulls a shirt on.

Thank God.

I don't know how much more of that I could take. I was starting to think about some very inappropriate things, and it was only a matter of time before one of those lewd suggestions made its way out of my mouth. Cannot have that happen.

What I do appreciate about him, in addition to that six pack (and I don't mean of beer), Xander always wants to know how things are when he's been off. Can't say I'm not the same way.

"Dr. Val says her PdG concentrations are elevated, so they're thinking yes." Fingers crossed that this means Bonnie is pregnant too. Obviously Bonnie can't use EPT like I did, but apparently they can monitor her hormone levels through her waste products. Sort of the same yet so different. "We're going to take weight and girth measurements on a weekly basis now. They were talking about doing some blood draws too."

Xander's in and out of the kitchen while I'm relaying this news from the couch. We determined my couch was in better condition and more comfortable, so his couch went and mine stayed. I'm glad because I'm exhausted and my couch feels like home, even if nothing else does.

Finally, Xander walks out carrying a plate of food. "I made dinner. Help yourself."

He places his dinner on the coffee table. Holy snikeys, he made tacos! "How did you know I wanted tacos?"

"Because it's your favorite food. Also, it's Tuesday, and you usually get tacos on Tuesdays. Or days that end in y."

"I was lying here, wishing tacos would appear. You're the best!" I spring up and rush to the kitchen. Steak and chicken, all the fixins, hard and soft shells. Fresh guac and pico.

This is the best day ever.

I make my plate, piling it high with spicy goodness.

We munch comfortably in silence for a few minutes. That's the thing about being with Xander. We can talk for hours or sit in silence, and none of it is awkward. There's not many people I've had that kind of relationship with.

I'm mid-bite when Xander ambushes me. "When are we going to tell people?"

217

I try to swallow but an errant piece of lettuce slides down the wrong pipe, resulting in a ten minute coughing fit. When it's finally done, I think I pulled a muscle coughing, which probably is more an indication of my lack of physical fitness at this point. The only fitness I'm thinking about is fittin' dis taco into my mouth.

"I'm not sure when I'll be ready to tell people."

He gives a pointed glance to my midsection. "You won't be able to hide it forever. We are going to have to say something eventually."

We? What's with this we crap?

He's not the one who will have people eyeing his stomach suspiciously. He's not the one that people will tell they have to lay off the tacos.

My response is strong and visceral. "I will tell people when I'm ready. My parents don't even know." I conveniently leave out that I've told my UnBRCAble group last week. I also conveniently leave out the fact that I *may* have indicated to my sister that we were involved. He doesn't need to know those things. They don't affect him.

"*We* should figure out what we are going to say." The edge to his voice is unmistakable. "*We* should be telling people soon."

Perhaps he's getting a bit testy?

He's not the only one. "Why are you making a big deal about all of this? I'll tell people when I'm ready. I'm not ready." The admission startles me. I didn't know I felt that way. You'd think I'd be blaring it from the rooftops.

I should be ready. It's not like I was unprepared for this pregnancy. I literally made it happen.

Why don't I want people to know?

I have nothing to be ashamed of. I'm taking control of my own body and own health and own destiny. It's nobody's business but mine.

"My brother is coming to town tomorrow. I'd like to tell him."

"Your brother? Is he staying here?" I have no idea why these questions are popping into my head. They don't make sense.

"Does it matter?"

*No.*

I stand up. "Yes." It's like I'm not in control of my own facilities. Maybe this baby is a demon and is possessing me.

"He's not staying here. He has a work conference or something, but I'm meeting him for dinner. I want to tell him."

My throat gets tight as panic rises. You know it's bad when I can't swallow my taco. "Please don't. I don't want him to know. Not yet."

Again, this makes no sense, but I can't help the words spilling forward. Suddenly, I'm scared. What if the brother doesn't like me? What if he thinks I'm taking advantage of Xander? What if he convinces Xander to kick me out and sue for full custody?

I think I've lost my mind.

"Your sister knows."

"That's different," I scoff. How? I have no idea.

"This is bull. I'm telling him."

"You can't tell him. It's my body." I jump to my feel and put my hands on my hips in my best Wonder Woman, Helen Reddy pose.

It's official. I have totally lost it. But right here, right now, this seems like an important issue. It's my body. My pregnancy. I should be in control of it. If I'd gone with an anonymous sperm donor, I wouldn't be having this argument.

Xander stands up and shoots me a look that could kill. "Seriously, Erin? You're going to pull that shit on me?"

He storms out.

He can storm all he wants. It's not his choice. It's not his body.

I guess it's part of his body-ish.

But mostly mine. My decision. My timeline.

I storm upstairs to my room and call Mackenzie.

"You would not believe it. Xander is so unreasonable."

"Trouble in paradise already? Color me shocked." I am not finding her dry tone amusing.

"Would you stop? He wants to tell people I'm pregnant," I huff.

Silence.

"Kenz? Are you there? Are you okay? Hello?"

"Yeah, I'm here, but you've rendered me speechless."

"Right? Can you believe Xander?"

"No, I can't believe you. What's wrong with you? Are you touched or something?"

I don't say anything. She's not incorrect but I don't need her to get all reasonable on me and crap.

"Erin, it's his baby too," she continues.

Why does she have to be all reasonable and stuff?

"Yeah. But it's my body. I'm the one who wanted this." Okay, so I'm not the only one. If Xander didn't want to have a kid, I doubt he would have approached me with the idea in the first place.

She sighs. "Obviously he did too. He made it all possible for you. You wouldn't be pregnant if it weren't for him. You're a couple. Partners. If he wants to take out an ad in the New York Times, he should. Did it ever occur to you that he's excited about this?"

Traitor.

"Okay, fine. He can tell his brother."

"*You wouldn't let him tell his brother?*" Mackenzie shrieks.

I pull the phone away from my ear. "You don't have to yell. Jeez."

"You told me. You are being totally ridiculous in not letting him tell his family. And speaking of which, when are you telling Mom and Dad? They are going to flip."

I really hate when my sister makes sense.

At least we take turns being the voice of reason. We'd be screwed if we were ever both unreasonable at the same time.

And she's right about my parents, even without knowing the whole story. Dread fills me, even thinking about it.

221

"You still okay?" I ask, rather than continue the discussion I initiated.

"Still pregnant, if that's what you mean. I lost my mucus plug about an hour ago, so maybe things'll start happening."

Eeew. Gross.

"Do you need to tell me that?"

"I feel it is my duty as your sister to let you know all the fun things coming your way. Did I ever tell you about my hemorrhoids?"

"I don't care if it's baby related or not, I don't ever want to hear about your butt."

"I'll remember you said that," Mackenzie laughs. "Your day is coming."

"Does this mean you're in the start of labor?"

"I hope. I'm going to make Luke ravish me in a little while to get things going."

Double eeew.

Also, does that work?

Also also, would I be so desperate to go into labor that I'd ask Xander to do that for me? To me? Would he even?

Probably not.

Especially with him being mad at me currently. I'm still finding it hard to believe that this is a big deal to him. Either way, I can't believe that our relationship will change enough over the next six months enough to ask him to have sex with me to induce labor. I continue speaking my train of thought as if Mackenzie was in my head following along the whole time. "I don't understand why."

She sighs. "I don't know. I think it has something to do with the hormones in his ... stuff. Or maybe his penis breaks something open. I don't know. It worked last time."

There's not enough eeew in the world for the information my sister just shared. In a related story, I need to be more clear with what I say to her.

"So on that super disgusting note, I'm going to go."

Mulling over what my sister said, especially the disgusting things, I trudge downstairs to find Xander.

He's watching TV, something on the Nat Geo channel. In all honesty, it's probably something I would watch on a normal basis, but I'm not sure I want to hang out with Xander tonight. Oh, wait, it's about the coconut crab, otherwise known as the robber crab. It's the largest land-dwelling creature with an exoskeleton.

I sit down on the opposite end of the couch, watching these crabs which can have a leg span of over a meter and weigh over nine pounds. They have a penchant for carrying coconuts and stealing shiny human things, like pots and pans.

So cool.

I mean, they look like giant spiders, so I would probably freak out if I ever saw one close up.

I wait for a commercial. At the next break, I will tell him he can tell his brother. I know I was possibly not the most reasonable about it. Perhaps.

Maybe, with so much uncertainty about everything—from how my parents will handle this to if I'm going to be a good mother to how I might feel about Xander—I'm trying to control things. Stupid things. The wrong things.

You know, like my mom does.

And yes, it drives me crazy when she does that. I make a mental note not to be over controlling with the baby. As soon as Xander is speaking to me again, I'll ask him to remind me about that.

Xander doesn't even glance in my direction. Okay, I probably deserve it.

Not probably.

"I'm sorry. If you want to tell your brother, go ahead."

He shakes his head without looking over at me. He tosses the remote on the couch and walks out.

Well now what am I supposed to do?

# CHAPTER 25

Hallmark really needs to start carrying a line of cards for communication with your non-romantic baby daddy.

Ugh. I will not call him my baby daddy, though it's a pretty accurate term. Of course, to call him that would be to admit that I'm having his child. And whether I like it or not, that's exactly what's happening.

I wish I could pin down what's making me so squeamish about going public. It's almost like I didn't think it through or am having buyer's remorse.

Which I'm not.

I'm having a baby. I'm growing a life inside my body. A piece of me has been created and will enter this world, full of possibilities. But it's a piece of Xander too.

Okay maybe—*just maybe*—I didn't think this through all the way. In my desperation to become pregnant, I didn't think of all the ramifications. I wouldn't have these issues if I'd used a regular, anonymous donor. I wouldn't have to justify my freak aversion admitting I'm pregnant.

But I didn't, so now I need to serve myself up a piece of humble pie and swallow it down.

Tomorrow.

I don't feel like pie today.

Xander still hasn't talked to me since last night when I wanted to apologize in the first place. If he won't talk to me, fine. The apology can wait.

Plus, we're at work, which is neither the time nor the place to get into this. Xander continues to give me the cold shoulder. Unfortunately, we're doing tandem groups today, starting at ten a.m., which means we're going to have to at least pretend to be pleasant to each other.

Easy peasy.

And by easy peasy, I meant easier said than done. Apparently, a sloth encounter is the new in-thing for bachelorette parties. Which means we have a group of silly women, some of whom are single, and all of whom think Xander is the best thing since sliced bread.

He's been asked, in all seriousness, at least five times already, if he'd be willing to entertain the group tonight.

I definitely heard one of them whisper something about a stripper.

I narrow my eyes, like it was his suggestion in the first place. Look at him, being all smiles and jokes. He gets to flirt. He gets to show his white teeth and bulging biceps. He gets to get hit on left and right. He gets to have people oogle his tight backside.

I get to pray that my pants fit for one more day and hope no one notices my expanding backside.

Seriously, what's going on back there? I'm not carrying this kid in my ass.

"I take it you won't be home tonight?" I whisper as Xander and I head to the locker room at the end of our shift.

"Yup." The clipped tone of voice indicates he's still pissed. Most likely well-deserved, but I wish he'd get over it. One of us has to be easy-going and with my hormones out of control, I don't think that'll be me.

I can't even have rational thoughts. Jeez.

"Are you joining up with the bachelorette party from earlier?"

*Why the hell did I just say that?* I am a complete and total moron. This hormone surge and pregnancy brain is no joke. I don't even feel in possession of my own body.

Xander slams his locker shut. "Geez Erin, give it up. It's getting old. Don't you know me well enough by now to know—"

My phone blares, interrupting Xander's tirade. It's my emergency ring, the one that comes through even when my phone is on silent. I set it to get Luke's call when Mackenzie goes into labor.

"Oh, God. This is it. Kenz is having the baby!" I shriek before I even answer. "Hey Luke, is it time?"

"We need you now," is all he says.

My stomach drops, and my legs don't seem to support me anymore. I sag against the lockers. "What's wrong?"

"Just get here, as soon as you can. Like now."

227

I stare at my phone, blinking the duration of the call. Thirty-two seconds. What did Luke mean by 'we need you now?' Is something wrong? There must be something wrong.

Oh God, I think I'd die if something happened to my sister. Or her baby.

"Erin, what is it? Is she okay? Is the baby okay?" Xander's in my face, his hand under my elbow. I wonder why he's holding me until I realize if it weren't for his hand, I'd probably have fallen down.

I shake my head, unable to form words. I don't have any answers anyway.

"Let's go." He reaches down and grabs not only his knapsack but mine, never letting go of me. "Which hospital?"

I tell him and on the way out, he tells Carlos that we're leaving my car here overnight and not to have it towed. I still can't say anything, so Xander fills the space with useless chatter. "I figure the last thing either of us needs is a bill from the impound lot right about now."

I nod. What if something happens to Mackenzie? What about the baby? She's been super secretive about the name they have picked out, but knowing her, it'll be something traditional. Trey is really Lucas Andrew Mullin the Third, which is where they get Trey from. I bet they're looking at the grandmother names, which are Mary and Susan.

Xander glances at me. "I'm sure everyone will be fine. You have to relax. Don't stress too much. It's not good for you or the baby."

Right. It's not just me anymore. Now I start worrying that something will happen to my baby. Baby Bean. That's what I've been calling it. I'm thirteen weeks. I had to start calling it something.

As we draw closer and closer to the hospital, I feel my heart rate increasing. I don't know what I'd do if anything happened to my sister or her baby. I don't know what Luke and Trey would do. I don't know what my mom—

Oh crap.

My mom will be there. Obviously.

I've been avoiding her over the past two months. She thinks I've been ignoring her because I'm still mad. She's not necessarily wrong on that account either.

I don't like lying to her, but I've yet to figure out what I'm going to say so that she doesn't go ballistic. Who am I kidding? There's no way that she won't go ballistic.

Maybe I'll wait until she's holding her new granddaughter to tell her. That should make it harder for the ballisticness to occur.

Xander pulls up to the curb and puts the car in park to unlock the door for me. "You're not coming in?"

He shakes his head, looking forward. His grip is tight on the steering wheel, as if he's an Indy 500 driver, waiting for the green flag to wave. "I'm meeting my brother, remember?"

No, I didn't remember.

I'm beginning to hate this pregnancy brain.

"Right. Okay, well then see you later."

He practically burns rubber the moment my feet are on the ground. Sheesh. He's still really pissed off at me. But even still, it was nice of him to make sure I got here. I don't know how to make him un-pissed. I pull out my phone and text him quickly.

*Tell your brother.*

I want to wait for a response, but I need to get inside to my sister. Stupid siblings, always getting the in the way.

I rush in, only making four wrong turns before I finally reach my parents nervously pacing in the Labor and Delivery waiting room. Or should I say, my mom is nervously pacing. My dad is sitting still as a statue. When he's worried, he tends to withdraw inward. Seeing him sitting still makes my own worries skyrocket.

"What's going on? Is she okay? Is the baby okay?"

My mom, on the other hand, tends to freak out when she's stressed. And when I say freak out, I mean she becomes obsessive with controlling everything down to the little, nittiest, grittiest detail.

She should come with a warning label.

She stops mid-pace. "Dear God, what is wrong with you? You look terrible. Have you been eating everything in sight? I swear, your nose has gotten fat. Look at her, Bill. She looks like she's had a reverse nose job."

I should mention that when things are outside her control, my mom also loses all tact.

Good thing she has a good life and generally is not very stressed. I understand her control issues. I *may* possess one or two myself. But still, it's not fantastic to be on the receiving end.

I lean in and give my mom a quick hug before flopping down next to my dad. My mother certainly has a gift with words. "Nice to see you too, Ma. What's the update?"

My dad says, "They had to take her in for a C-section."

"Right." I knew that four months ago.

My mother stops. "She wanted to have this baby the old-fashioned way."

Huh? I *know* Kenz and I talked about this months ago. "She knew she couldn't VBAC. Was she stupid enough to try?"

"She and I talked about how C-sections aren't the best, and she should try to do what's best for her child."

Um, I haven't been through any child-birth classes yet, but I'm guessing a safe delivery is the best option. I start to say this to my mom when Luke comes out, dressed in scrubs. "Ada Suzanne is here!"

*Ada Suzanne?* Did the baby come out with a cardigan and eyeglass chain? Is she already an honorary member of the Golden Girls?

My mom rushes past, practically pushing Luke out of the way. It takes me a minute to stand up. My dad catches me under the elbow, not unlike how Xander did.

"Do you really think they're okay?" I ask my dad, like he has some psychic superpower or the ability to see through walls to get a preview.

231

"I think so. You mom didn't want Mackenzie to have another operation, so she was trying to convince Kenz to let nature take its course."

Something I could totally see Mom doing. When she gets on a bandwagon, there's no knocking her off. I make a mental note to not let Mom know I'm in labor until after Bean is here.

"She has an issue with thinking that just because she *wants* something to be true, it will be."

Like me and getting married.

Dad nods. "She only wants the best for you girls. She knows how it is when the deck is stacked against you. She doesn't want you to struggle that way."

This is not new news. It's why I give my mother as much leeway as I do. Her life, until she got married, was horrible. It's no wonder that she sees getting married and having kids as the only logical thing to do. It saved her.

We all give my mom a lot of leeway. Believe it or not, she's one of the most giving people I've ever met. She loves the three of us more than life itself and would do anything for any one of us. I'm half-surprised she didn't offer to be a surrogate for me.

Probably because I'm not married.

"Wait, if Kenz was fine all along, why was Luke in a panic when he called?"

My dad laughs. "He'd been trying to call you but your mother wouldn't get out of the way. An orderly finally had to pull her back. Luke was dialing you literally as they were wheeling Mackenzie into the operating room. She was in labor, so they had to get in there quickly. It wasn't an emergency, but there certainly wasn't a lot of time to spare. He was panicked that he wouldn't reach you before they went into surgery."

I want to sink back down. "I nearly had a heart attack thinking there was something wrong."

"Nothing's wrong. It's just Mom being Mom." My dad says this with a reverence to his voice. That would so *not* be my tone if I said the same exact words.

"Don't you think, Dad, that sometimes Mom being Mom isn't the best for us?"

"She means well. You need to give her a break."

I'm not sure I do, but my mom comes running back. "Come on you two slowpokes. There's a baby waiting."

Little does she know there's more than one baby waiting.

# CHAPTER 26

I am so hungry that I'm beginning to consider that baby might really be the *other-other* white meat. Every time I think about sneaking away to get something to eat, my mom hands me Ada again. So far, Ada's been handed off more times than a hot potato.

Mmmm ... potato.

"Here, Kenz. I think you need a minute or two." I stand up and hand the adorable little bundle back to my sister. For the first time in forever, I don't have that empty pit within. That feeling of longing and need.

Actually, that's a lie. There is a pit deep within me and it's my stomach and if I don't eat something soon, I may die.

But at least I'm not hungering for a baby. The feeling of peace, or maybe it's endorphins from smelling Ada's head, that courses through my veins is like none other I've felt before.

However, it's not enough to quell my actual hunger. "I'm heading down to the cafeteria to get some food. Anyone want anything?"

"How can you think of food at a time like this?" My mom sure is sensitive. "Your sister just gave birth.

They *cut her open* and pulled a baby out. And you want food? You could stand to miss a meal or two. Just sayin'." She puts her hands up like she doesn't mean to be offensive.

I get that she's still mad at me about the whole pregnancy-scare thing, but she doesn't have that right. It's like she takes my family planning differences as a personal rejection. But she can't see that me getting pregnant outside of marriage isn't me rejecting her. She can't be mad at me for living my life differently than she would choose. It's not her choice. Frankly, it's not really mine either. My options are limited. And I've made the choice that's right for me, given the situation.

I'm too hungry to have this fight right now. Plus, Ada shouldn't be exposed to family drama so early on. She's got her whole life ahead of her to deal with us.

"All righty then. On that supportive note, I'm going to bounce. Kenz and Luke, congratulations. She's beautiful. I'll see you around." I don't look at my mom as I walk out the door. This time, it only takes me two wrong turns before I find the parking lot.

Except there's no car to find in the parking lot because Xander dropped me off.

Shit.

And he's mad at me and out with his brother and I'm hungry and oh yeah, my bag—with my wallet—is in Xander's car, so I couldn't even buy dinner if I wanted.

There are not enough curse words.

Lucky for me, I have tears.

Unlucky for me, stupid Pittsfalls doesn't allow ride sharing, so what I don't have is access to a ride home with only my phone. I am so screwed.

As I see it, I have three options. One: I can hitchhike and hope Ted Bundy doesn't pick me up. Two: I can call Xander and grovel. Three: I can go back in and ask my dad to bring me home.

The serial killer thing might be the best option here.

I call Xander and it goes straight to voicemail. "Hey, it's me. Um, everyone's good here, but I'm sort of stranded. If you get this and can call me back, I'd appreciate it."

Then I wait. And wait.

I pace back and forth, staring at my phone as if it will provide some magic solution. Or turn into a taco, which I could really use about now. Looks like the only thing I'm swallowing now is my pride.

Knowing Mom, she and Dad will be in there all night, or until they kick them out, whichever comes first. A glance at my watch tells me it's after eleven. I haven't eaten in almost twelve hours. That's gotta be a new world record for me. Definitely one since I got pregnant.

Oh no, this won't hurt the baby will it?

I don't think it will, but I can't think straight enough to figure it out. I have no choice. I text Dad and ask him to meet me in the lobby, but after waiting for about twenty minutes, realize that he still doesn't check his text messages.

I'm so tired and my limbs feel like they're made of lead. Okay, I'm going to sit here for three more minutes before I get up and look for my dad.

"Miss, you can't sleep here."

"Erin, are you okay?"

"Oh my God, what are you doing out here like some sort of derelict?"

All the voices descend upon me at the same time, clashing and clanging but not quite clearing the fog in my head.

"I wasn't sleeping," I mumble, sitting up. My eyes feel like there is a wad of cotton under my lids. "I was waiting for Dad to text me back." I push myself up to standing.

The lobby of the hospital sways a little. No wait, that's me. I'm going to sit. Now.

"Erin!" Xander pushes through, his hands once again supporting my elbows. He lowers me down. "Are you okay?"

My mom pushes—*shoves*—Xander aside. "Erin, what's wrong with you? Is it the cancer? Is that why you look so terrible and bloated? It's cancer, isn't it. Oh, baby. Why didn't you tell me?"

I try to push her back. "I'm fine, Ma. I just haven't eaten all day. I left my wallet in Xander's car, so I couldn't even get chips from the vending machine."

And here are the tears. Again. Ugh, seriously?

"You haven't eaten all day? You can't do that. It's not good for—"

My mother whirls around, stopping Xander mid-sentence. "Who are you again? Why did you take her wallet?" For once, I'm glad she's going all tiger mom. The last thing I need right now is for Mom to find out I'm pregnant.

"Mom and Dad, Xander. Xander, my mom and dad. Mary and Bill." I wave my hands between them, like we're at some sort of garden party. Movement behind Xander catches my eye. Oh crap. Something's really wrong with me now because I'm seeing double. Maybe I do have a tumor, and it's already spread to my brain. There are two Xanders. Except this one is in a suit. And is about ten years older than my Xander. I squint, trying to make sense of what I'm seeing. My blood sugar is too low to process this.

"Yo, bro, what's the hold—hey, is this your baby mama? Are you okay? You look kind of peaked. Is your baby okay?"

Xander turns and punches—*actually punches*—other Xander in the arm. Who I'm now guessing is the brother. I don't even know his name. He's going to be my child's uncle, and I don't know what his name is.

*"What did you call her? Baby Mama? Baby?"*

Lord have mercy. Mary's been unleashed.

"Um, I mean, ahh ..." he stammers.

Shit. There's no getting around this now.

"Yes, Mom. I'm not fat. I'm not bloated. I'm pregnant." I stick my chin out, hoping she doesn't notice how it's wobbling.

And then my mother's face turns the most interesting shade of purple. Almost eggplant.

In other words, the color of doom.

"Erin Elizabeth McAvoy! I cannot believe you! After all we've discussed you go out and do ... do ... this!" Her hands are waiving and spit is flying from her mouth. The security guard is eyeing us suspiciously.

As well he should.

This might be worth it if my mom gets hauled in.

"Getting pregnant! How could you be so irresponsible? This is not how we raised you. Not what we taught you. I *asked* you if you were a loose woman!"

Of all the things for my mom to say, she comes out with *that*?

I look pleadingly at Xander. I don't know what I expect him to do because odds are he doesn't have a teleportation device in his pocket.

*Is that a teleportation device in your pocket, or are you just happy to see me?*

The inappropriate thought runs through my head and a bubble of laughter escapes.

"This is not a laughing matter, young lady. I can't believe you were so irresponsible. But that's how you've always been. Acting first and thinking later. Following your dreams instead of doing what's sensible."

Mental note: Never squash Bean's dreams.

"Mary, stop." My dad has his harsh tone out. It's about time. "I don't think Erin being pregnant is the end of the world."

"It's not like she can raise a baby. She can barely take care of herself!"

I cock my head and knit my brows together. My job is *literally* taking care of living creatures.

But Mom continues, "She can't even remember to eat! Who forgets to eat? People who have no business raising babies, that's who."

For the record, this is probably the first time ever that I've forgotten to eat.

Suddenly, Xander slides into the seat next to me, and his arm snakes around my shoulders. "With all due respect, Mrs. McAvoy, Erin is a wonderful caretaker. One of the best. And you don't have to worry. *We* will be taking care of this child. We've got it covered. All of it."

I look at him and know I'll never, ever be able to repay him for that. There isn't a cheesy Father's Day gift good enough for this man. He deserves so much more than a tie or a mug that says "World's Greatest Dad!" on it.

"Do you plan to make an honest woman of her before the baby is born at least?"

I swallow hard and look at Xander. That's not what he meant. I know it. He knows it. His brother knows it. But when I look at my mother, I see the disappointment is gone and there's hope in her eyes. It shouldn't matter, especially not after all the things she's said, but it does.

I don't want to let her down. I never have.

I put my hand on Xander's knee. "We're still discussing all that. Obviously, we're going to keep things quiet and small." No big white wedding for me. Ironic considering how this baby came to be. Technically, I could be a pregnant virgin.

I'm not of course, but *technically* ...

I feel Xander's quads go tense under my hand. "We're going to keep things quiet and small?" he says through gritted teeth.

Turning to him I say, "Yes, honey. It's not like we can have a big church thing, with me in this condition. That's frowned upon."

His eyes are blazing. I see him glance at his brother and then back at me. "Erin, what are you talking about?"

I plead with my gaze, imploring him to see that I need him to play along. We can always "break up" in a few months. "Obviously we didn't want to steal the spotlight from Mackenzie and Luke with our news, right?" My grip on his thigh tightens. He places his hand over mine, attempting to pry my fingers out of his taut flesh.

"Erin—"

"Don't worry, Xander. I'm sure my sister will understand. After all, it was your brother who really spilled the beans." I glance up to see scarlet rising in Xander's brother's cheeks. "We can finally tell the world. We're getting married and having a baby!"

# CHAPTER 27

"You have to talk to me at some point."

"I don't."

"You just did."

I'm met with a stony silence. He's been this way since we dropped Allen off. Allen is Xander's brother. I now know all the names in the family. Thanks to Allen, of course. Xander won't speak to me.

For the record, they're all 'Al' names. Alyssa, Albert, Allen, and ... wait for it ... *Alexander*. He was Alex growing up but thought Xander sounded sexier.

Like he needs any help being sexier.

Also, when he's this pissed, Xander does *not* appreciate being poked fun of. At least Allen was doing most of the mocking. I think he's trying to get on my good side after screwing up so royally back there.

"I didn't know what else to do. You saw her. She was totally flipping out. It's no big deal. In a few months, we'll tell her we decided not to get married for one reason or another. You just have to play along until then. We'll barely see her anyway."

We pull into the garage and Xander turns the car off but makes no move to get out. "I'm sorry, Xander. I really am. I panicked. Plus, I was seriously disoriented. I plead temporary insanity due to extreme hunger."

Xander's head is against the headrest. Even with his eyes closed, I can see the fatigue on his features. It's after one. Tomorrow—er, today—is going to suck when the alarm goes off in a little over five hours.

"I can see why you did it," he says finally. "She's a little intense and a lot nuts. There are definitely some bats loose in her belfry."

I try not to smile. "She has her beliefs, and there's no swaying her from those."

"Do you feel the same?"

"I'd say obviously not, but that's not entirely true. I never wanted to have a baby on my own. I was only looking into it because I'm out of time. I'd been putting it off, thinking that it'd eventually happen the way I wanted. But every few months, I'm going through all these tests and it's horrible. Absolutely, completely awful waiting to hear if I'm clear or not. Wondering if this is the time that I pushed it too far. That I waited too long."

I look over at Xander. He hasn't moved. I'd almost wonder if he fell asleep, but the tension in his jaw indicates he's still listening, so I continue.

"I had a cyst right before I t—told you." I stumble, thinking about that trip to the E.R. "It scared me. A lot. It was the day I found out I got Sloth Central, and then I thought I was dying. It's interesting what shakes out when you're dealt a hand like mine. Six months ago, I wouldn't have considered having a baby without being married. But having a baby is more important to me. My chances have run out."

He still doesn't say anything, so I keep going. "I'll make this right with my parents, but if you can go along with it for a little while, I'd appreciate it. It's not like we're actually going to get married. I'm so sorry for this. And for freaking out about you telling your brother."

He sighs. "I'm tired and need to sleep."

I nod. I agree.

I also need to eat. I made short work of the protein bars in my sack once I got into the car, but I need something a little more substantial. I head straight for the kitchen and polish off a bag of chips and an entire jar of salsa before falling into a fitful sleep.

Tomorrow is going to suck.

~~~***~~~

"Allen says he owes it to us."

I sigh. I don't want to go out to dinner with Xander and his brother. I want to go to back to bed the minute I fall through the door, but that's at least ten hours away. I've developed some significant heartburn and apparently Bean doesn't like salsa and let me know all night.

I'm going to have to have some words with this kid.

"You owe me."

I finally meet Xander's gaze. He's right. I'm going to owe him big time, if the flurry of text messages from my mother this morning are any indication. I also have a series of voicemails from my sister, yelling at me for not telling her that things had become so serious with Xander.

My phone vibrates again, and I'm thankful the sound it turned off. The constant dinging would drive me crazy.

"Who is texting you?" Xander glances over, his eyes darting away from the road for a minute.

"Eyes on the road, buster." I'm tired and cranky and my mother won't stop blowing up my phone!

"Let me guess. Your mother. I hope she's apologizing for acting like a lunatic last night."

Right. Apologizing. That would make sense. Instead, my mom is texting me possible wedding venues.

As if.

"Yeah, she's super sorry," I say dryly.

"So what's she really saying?" Xander raises an eyebrow.

"You don't want to know."

He reaches over to grab the phone. "Oh, but I do."

I pull the phone over to my side. "Both hands on the wheel, bucko. You've got precious cargo here." I open up the latest message and sigh. "She's not sure what she can do on such short notice, but she went to a wedding once at the K of C, and it wasn't that tacky."

Shit.

"Okay, I will do dinner with Allen tonight. I will do whatever you need me to do. I'm going to owe you more than one. More like a million." In reality, I won't ever be able to make up for what my family is going to put him through. I quickly re-assure him. "I'll handle her. Don't worry. Nobody will have a shotgun, I promise."

He gives me the side-eye, but at least he's still looking at the road.

"Fill me in on all things Allen. I feel like I probably didn't make the best impression last night."

"He probably feels the same way. Allen is the football player turned CPA."

"Isn't your sister a CPA too?" I thought he said something about that when we were talking about careers and family.

"Al is too. As is my dad. I'm the black-sheep."

"Did you know that the most rare type of sheep is the Jacob's sheep, which produces fleece that is black and white spotted?"

Xander smiles. "I did know that. Also, I recently read about a white ram and thirty-seven ewes that produced an *entire flock* of black sheep. I think there were like sixty of them."

"So much for recessive genes. That certainly beats the odds."

"Speaking of which, what do you think Bean will have? You know from us. Hair? Eyes? Skin?"

It takes me a minute to realize that Xander referred to the baby as Bean. How did he know? I'm saved answering the question though, because we're pulling in through the staff gate. My car, lonely and sad, is sitting where I parked it yesterday morning. It's sort of stupid that we're not carpooling. It would make sense to. "This was nice driving in together. We should take turns. Save on gas."

Xander doesn't say anything as he pulls the key out of the ignition and opens his door.

Yet because I'm a moron, I keep talking. "Unless you don't want to. Like if you want to give rides to other people. Like Dr. Sophie. *Sophia*."

I seriously don't know what's wrong with me. Apparently I am much more like my mother than I care to admit.

Xander turns and looks at me. "Really Erin?"

Heat fills my face, and I can only look down at my feet. "No, I'm sorry. It didn't come out right."

At least I can apologize. It'd be better if I didn't say the stupid things in the first place, but Rome wasn't built in a day you know.

"No, it didn't." He starts walking and I struggle to keep up.

"What I meant was you shouldn't feel beholden to me. You don't have to carpool with me. I just thought …"

Xander stops, right before we enter the employee gate. Other people are arriving. "Beholden? Are you touched? We live together. We're having a baby together. Your mother is planning our wedding. It wouldn't surprise me if she ambushes me for my tuxedo measurements during the middle of our shift today. Yet you still doubt me! What is wrong with you?"

He whirls around and storms through the employee entrance. He's mad, as he should be. I don't know what's wrong with me. I don't know how I keep

247

messing this up so colossally, but here I am, queen of the mess yet again.

While I'm hungry, as always, I'd like to start the day without my foot in my mouth. For once.

It doesn't taste good.

I hurry in after Xander, totally ignoring the dozen or so co-workers gawking at our tiff.

"Xander, wait! You know I'm super good at saying the wrong thing, especially around you." I grab his arm and he spins around. Sucking in a deep breath, I continue, "You've done so much for me, and we both know I'll never be able to repay that. I don't want you to think you have to spend time with me or whatever. Or that you can't spend time with your other friends or whatever. Or that we're even friends or whatever."

So freakin' eloquent.

Or whatever.

Xander looks at my hand on his arm and shakes his head. I pull it back.

"I'm teaching this kid how to talk to other people. Maybe you could learn sometime too," he hisses through gritted teeth.

He heads off to the locker room, while I still stand there, stunned.

"I *knew* it! I told you two weeks! But this—*this*—is totally unexpected. You're getting married! And having a baby! It's so romantic. And I didn't even think you were the type for romance," Terry gushes and envelops me in a crushing hug. I never would have believed her a hugger, if I wasn't a frequent recipient.

"Um, it's not—" I attempt to protest. To tell her the truth.

"Let me see your ring! When are you due? This is so romantic. You should have your wedding here at the zoo!"

I look down at my empty left hand. Crap. This has gone too far, if Terry's asking me about my ring. It's one thing to be in this mess with my family—that's complicated and will take a while to sort out.

And it's bad enough I'm lying to them. I'm a big fraud. Erin "the Fraud" McAvoy. That's me.

Work is a different story though. I don't owe these people anything. They don't have expectations of me, other than I show up and do my job. I can't let this go on.

"Um, I'm due—"

"But where's the ring?"

"It's a long story. I'll tell you the whole thing in a bit."

Shit. This is so bad. If Terry jumped to this conclusion, I bet everyone else has. Damage control is going to take a while.

Xander is going to kill me.

*Current mood: screwed.*

Of course, he was the one going off on me in front of everyone. It's really all his fault. He's the one who mentioned wedding and tuxedo. There, I'll put the blame squarely on his shoulders. Yes, that's it. This is all his fault.

Even though I know it's not. It never has been and never will be. I'm the only idiot here.

Bean only has a fifty-percent chance of being an idiot.

I quickly rush through my morning prep and head out to Sloth Central. I've got to catch up with Xander to tell him that the news of "us" is spreading through the Pittsfalls Zoo like lice in a kindergarten class.

The word lice makes me want to stop and scratch my head.

"Hey," I pant. I think that's the fastest I've moved in a while. Probably since my last Lola the rabbit chase. "We need to talk. People heard us and—"

He nods and then tilts his head to where Ed is keenly observing us, as if we were animals in an exhibit. I rise up on my toes and whisper in his ear. "Everyone knows I'm pregnant and thinks we're getting married. I'm so sorry. So, so sorry. I—"

Xander quickly reaches up and clasps my hands in his, pressing them to his chest. I can barely move. I'm not sure that I want to. And *then*, he starts yelling. "What do you mean you forgot your ring? *Forgot?* How do you forget your engagement ring? It's a priceless ring from my grandmother and you forgot it? My mother gave it to me on her deathbed and made me promise I'd only give it to someone who truly deserved it and now you're not even wearing it!"

Xander steps back, releasing me from his grasp. I stumble forward a step. He may have lost his mind.

Job hazard from hanging out with me.

Xander reaches down and grabs my left hand again, holding it in front of him as if this is something we always do. "Do you even know where it is? How could you be so irresponsible? Again."

His hand is warm on mine. I'm starting to sweat. He pulls me in close for a moment, his breath hot on my neck as he whispers, "You created this circus. Now take care of the monkeys."

I think I know what he's doing. Here I go, taking a chance. If I'm wrong, I'm going to seem like an idiot.

More of an idiot.

"Xander, we went through this. I cannot wear your grandmother's ring to work. You know what our hands go through. It would be too hard on the ring. I don't want anything to happen to it. I know how important it is to you. It's in a very safe space."

So safe I don't even know where it is.

"But how are people supposed to know you're my woman?" A smile flashes briefly but is quickly replaced by a stern frown.

*His woman?*

That almost makes me choke, but I stick with the charade. "I told you before; get me one of those silicone rings. I won't wear anything but that here at work. *But*, if that's not enough for you, why don't you ask Don if I can change my uniform to a shirt that has *Property of Xander Barnes* in big, bold letters on it? You know how I love my T-shirts with slogans." The shirt I'm wearing under my uniform polo today is my favorite and says, "If you don't like tacos, I'm nacho type."

A slow, devilish grin spreads on his face. "You do have to get a new maternity uniform. Two birds, one stone." His eyebrow cocks up and my blood rushes south. Yowza.

I return his grin, energy coursing through my veins. This is fun. "Only if you wear a shirt that says *My Heart Belongs to Erin McAvoy.*"

"Oh, look at you two. You're adorable. Xander, why didn't you tell me?" Dr. Sophie strolls by. "I talked to Matt last night, and he didn't say anything about it. And you know he can't keep a secret to save his life."

"He doesn't know yet. We're only now telling people. Apparently. Erin's been unpredictable about wanting to go public." He looks at me, a hint of seriousness behind the devilish look. "Plus we wanted to wait until she was through the first trimester, obviously."

Dr. Sophie embraces me tightly. I don't know that I've ever even shaken her hand before and now we're hugging. Swell.

"Oh, this is so exciting. I can't wait to tell Matt! He's going to be super jealous that I know first." She pulls back and looks over her shoulder at Xander, who has the most amused grin on his face. It's almost as if he knows how much I *don't* like to be hugged. "Xander, you are so lucky to have found Erin. She so much better than the hag in Dallas. She was so prickly and hated all of us and never wanted kids. She didn't get how important family is to you and how much you wanted kids. This is fantastic!" She hugs me again.

Interesting. Very interesting.

While I'm sure we're bound to play twenty questions all day, we're given a momentary reprieve by the fact that there are hundreds of hungry animals who could not care less that Xander and I are having a baby and pretending to be engaged. Speaking of which ...

"What was all that with the ring?" I whisper as we're measuring out Bonnie and Barry's breakfast.

He smiles without turning to look at me. "I just thought it would be funny to make you squirm. Plus, it gives you a reason why you're not wearing your ring, other than I haven't given you one."

I elbow him slightly and go on about my work. "But seriously, what are we going to do about the engagement thing? People are going to notice if we never get married."

Xander shrugs. "Lots of people have long engagements, especially when they accidentally get pregnant."

"There was no accident. I scheduled an appointment."

He cocks his brow as if to say, "This was no accident. I could impregnate you just by giving you a sultry look." Instead he says, "I know that, but they don't. It'll be fine."

Xander moves to the other side of the pen, and I watch him walk away. My heart does a weird little flutter thing.

Wait—my heart isn't supposed to flutter. This is only a fake engagement.

Oh no.

# CHAPTER 28

"Absolutely not. It's dumb and don't ask again."

Sheesh. He doesn't have to be so sensitive.

"But Xander—"

"Oh my God, Erin. No. I am not having a gender reveal party. You are not having a gender reveal party. We are not having a gender reveal party. We're finding out the gender during the ultrasound and when people ask, we will tell them. That's it. End of story."

I cross my arms over my chest and pull them in tightly, but I keep forgetting that I now have boobs and tiny little belly in the way. It takes me a minute or two to get them into a comfortable position. I can't believe Xander won't let me do a gender reveal party. Doesn't he know all of the great things I have planned? I mean, on Pinterest I found a whole bunch of ideas for a gender reveal fiesta, complete with "Taco Bout a Baby" spelled out in large balloons over a taco bar.

It's like the creator of that knows my soul.

And yes, the reveal would be done via piñata. What else?

I could save the taco bar for the shower, but the fiesta decorations would clash with the zoo theme I have planned. Or that I'm trying to plan. I can't settle on what direction I want to go in, and the more I look, the more indecisive I become.

The only thing I had decided on was the gender reveal party. It's annoying that Xander is being so stubborn about this. I don't even understand why he cares. I mean, we get to find out what we're having.

I stand up and hurry (okay, not hurry *exactly*) to the kitchen where Xander's unpacking his lunch bag. "Can you at least tell me why not?"

"You don't want to know," he mutters without looking up. He puts his dishes in the dishwasher and sets about prepping his lunch for tomorrow. As he leans forward into the fridge to assess the leftover status, he asks, "What are you planning on tomorrow?"

"Dinner leftovers. I put them all in individual containers, in case you want some too."

I step back and admire the view of his backside. I'm only human, and these second trimester hormones are killing me. Plus, he's packing lunches. Not just his, but mine. He's on lunch duty this week while I'm on dinner. Sure, our chore chart is sort of geeky but considering we've both been on our own for a long time, it seemed efficient.

Also, it was totally Xander's idea because he's a closet neat-freak and organizer. He doesn't need to KonMari his house because he's a minimalist to begin with. The chore chart is his way of keeping me in line.

Or at least his attempt to.

And not that I'd admit it to him, but things have been flowing smoother with plans in place. On the other hand, I'm much better at meal planning and prep than he is, so he's happy that there's a constant stream of food in the house.

It's almost like we're compatible.

*Except* for the topic of the gender reveal party. At fifteen weeks now, my ultrasound is in three short weeks, which doesn't give us long to schedule a party. Especially considering how hard it is to coordinate time off at work.

Even though Xander's house is cleaner than my place ever was, there'd still be a fair amount of prep work to get it party ready. It would be nice not to have to do that. Maybe Xander's right.

Of course, I won't tell him that.

"Fine, I'll drop it, but I want to know why you are so adamantly against it."

Xander puts our lunch bags back in the fridge, all ready to go for morning. "You want coffee in the morning?"

I shake my head. Though Dr. Lee said one cup a day is fine, the smell of it turns me off. "Thanks though."

Xander sets up the coffee maker for the morning, complete with his travel mug underneath. I'd always thought this sort of organization would be annoying. I was wrong. It's sort of a turn on. Damn those hormones again. I really can't wait until I give birth and my hormones settle down, and I can stop thinking about Xander this way.

Dirty ways. Sexy ways.

Only twenty-five weeks until that happens, give or take.

Also, I can't wait to pack a sandwich for my lunch then too. Who knew pregnant women couldn't eat lunch meat?

I miss ham.

We finish up in the kitchen and meander into the family room to watch TV. I'm about ready to go to sleep, but I want to know what the deal with the gender reveal party is all about.

As soon as we're settled, I raise my eyebrows, willing Xander to continue. He takes a deep breath before starting. "Fine. It's your mom. I don't want to have to deal with her any more than necessary."

That was *not* what I was expecting to hear.

"My mom? Why?"

Now it's his turn to raise his eyebrows. "You're not serious, are you?"

"I mean, I know she can be a *little* trying at times." Like ebola is a *little* infection.

"At times? You—we're—in this whole mess because of her. Because she couldn't let her own shit go long enough to want what's best for you. Because she wouldn't stand by and support you no matter what. I said before that my mom wouldn't have been thrilled with my sister if she got pregnant, but it would have been a momentary blip of disappointment, followed by unwavering support."

I look down at my hands, folded loosely over my barely there bump. Xander's not wrong about any of this. My mom has been really crappy to me throughout. I hate all the lying about the wedding planning. To be clear, I'm not planning anything. She's taking over,

257

sending me suggestion after suggestion. The good thing is that it's all through text and email, so I don't have to talk to her. I hate lying to her, but I don't know what else to do at this point. She barely even acknowledges that I'm pregnant. It's like it can't be true unless I'm married.

It's sort of ironic. She has all these issues and chips on her shoulder because her parents thought the sun rose and set on her brother, while she could do nothing right. She attributed that to the fact that she was adopted. Yet she does that to me, and I am her own flesh and blood.

"You can't let me do that to Bean," I say quietly.

"I won't let you do that to her," he says clearly. Strongly. Determined.

"*Her?*"

Xander's staring straight ahead at the TV, though it's not even on. "Yeah, it's a girl. Can't you tell?"

Honestly, I have no idea. Shaking my head I say, "Not really. Plus, I was sort of mentally prepared for a boy. Everything I've read indicates that the environment created by the insemination process favors boys." I don't say this out loud, but if it's a boy, then he will have a lesser chance of developing cancer, even if he has my defective BRCA gene.

"Yeah, but she's different. A strong swimmer."

Yuck. Gross. I don't want to think about that.

"We'll see in three weeks." I think a little more about what Xander had to say regarding my mom. "So you really hate my mom then, huh?"

He clicks on the TV and starts tooling around, looking for something to watch. "I wouldn't say hate, but I don't have a tremendous amount of respect for her either. I don't like that we feel the need to lie to her to make *her* more comfortable. This isn't about her. It's about us. You really."

*Us.*

I reach over and take Xander's hand. "No, it's about us. All three of us." I place his hand on my belly. "No matter what happens in the future, and no matter how it all came to be, we're a family."

Xander's breath hitches as he puts his other hand on my bump. I slide down a little to give him better access. His hands, big and warm, are gentle as they explore the contours of the growing life inside me. His hands still and I see him close his eyes. Suddenly, they fly open and his hands pull back as if on a hot stove.

"Was that ... did she just ... I felt something!"

Yeah, most likely my dinner digesting. "I don't think so. They say for first time mothers, it can be anywhere from sixteen to twenty-five weeks before you can feel the movement."

Xander's face falls, making me want to do anything to put that look of happiness back on it. It wasn't even happiness. It was pure joy.

Oh my God, he loves this baby.

I don't know why I expected anything less from him, but I guess a part of me still thought this was about what he could do to help me. It's not about me at all.

It never has been.

I've been a selfish, stubborn ass.

Xander wants to be a father. It's why he made this offer and invited me into his home and puts up with the cockamamie antics of my family and goes along with the engagement.

"Why aren't you married with kids?" Suddenly, I have to know. It's such the polar opposite of what I've thought about him for so many years. That he was the perpetual bachelor. A player. A dog.

He's none of those things. So why did he act as if he was?

Xander shrugs, still staring straight ahead at the TV, though he's yet to settle on a program. "Never the right time I guess. Never the right person."

Dr. Sophie's comment about the "hag" in Dallas dances through my mind. Did she keep him from having the family that he's always wanted? Would he have had a baby with her if she asked?

I glance down at my midsection. "And now is? Why didn't you do this the old-fashioned way?"

"Why didn't you?"

Rolling my eyes, I straighten up a little, though I'd love nothing more than to stretch out along the entire length of the couch. "You know. You saw who was on my dating profile. The pickins were slim, to say the least." I sigh, not sure why I'm admitting something so personal. "And I've never been so great at the dating thing."

"Same."

Yeah, no. "Sorry, I don't believe that. Literally every female and probably some males who work at Pittsfalls have thrown themselves at you."

"You never did." Xander finally looks at me.

"You never did to me. Why should I have with you?" I'm not even sure that sentence makes sense. "Or whatever. You know what I mean."

"You're different, Erin."

Oh, here we go again.

"Yup. I know. I'm not *like other girls*." I make air quotes around that phrase. Which I hate, by the way. "I don't care how different she may be, we will never say that to our daughter, if Bean is a girl."

"Bean is a girl, and I'm fine with not saying that to her, but why not?"

"Because what it really means is: you're not pretty, you're not cool, you're not like one of us, and we don't want you. It was hard enough growing up looking like I do. I didn't need—and still don't—need to hear that at every turn."

I stand up, years of rejection and harassment fresh in my mind. I start to pace, not sure what else to do with these feelings, ripping open wounds I didn't know I had.

"Erin, calm down."

Never, in the history of calm down, has telling someone to calm down every actually calmed them down.

Xander stands and puts his hands up, in the universal "calm down" gesture. Also historically ineffective.

"I'm sorry that's how you interpreted it." He's staring at me, those brown eyes intense and soulful.

I raise my eyebrow and put my hands on my hips. When did my waist get so thick? Damn, it's pretty solid there. I've only gained ten pounds. Okay, twelve.

Thirteen.

"I didn't *interpret* anything. That's what people mean."

"It's not what I meant, and that's what I'm apologizing for. When I say you're not like other girls, it's with a sigh of relief. You see more than my face. You see me. It's because you understand my love for animals and my need to be there for them, even more than people. You're smart and sassy. You understand how to take a joke and how to give it right back."

His words start to soothe raw wounds deep within until I realize the one thing he didn't say. About my looks.

It stings, but if he doesn't find me attractive, he doesn't. There's nothing he can do about that. It's not like I can change my features or the texture in my hair or my height.

And let's not forget, my nose has apparently become fat.

I wonder if when I have my mastectomy, I can convince the breast surgeon to do a little nip and tuck on my nose as well. It can't hurt to ask.

I still haven't said anything back to Xander. I'm afraid if I do, I'll start crying. He takes my silence as a need for more reassurance.

"Erin, I've only had limited interactions with your mom, but I can kind of see why you're not secure in who you are or in who you want to be. I get it. My dad was—is—hard on me. He's a good guy, obviously, but it didn't stop him from wanting something for me I didn't want for myself. I had no interest in football like my brothers. You know I'm not a number guy. He can't let that go. I hope he gets over it eventually. We didn't have the best relationship to begin with, and none of that helped it." Xander shrugs and looks over to the corner.

Well crap.

"Look at us, a bunch of disappointments having the next generation of disappointments," I say glumly.

Xander's head whips back in my direction. "Are you disappointed in her already?"

I laugh. "No, not at all. I got pregnant right away. It's not multiples." I cross myself quickly. Thank goodness *that* prayer was answered. "I don't care if it's a boy or gir—"

"It's a girl," Xander interjects quickly.

I smile at his confidence. I don't doubt him one iota, though statistics aren't necessarily in his favor. "I want Bean to be healthy and happy. If I can only request one thing, it would be that she—*or he*—doesn't get my stupid mutated genes."

"I think your mutation would be a cool thing."

*What?*

"How can you say that? That undoubtedly has to be one of the stupidest things I've ever heard you say!"

Xander takes a step toward me and pushes a strand of hair behind my ear. His touch is light and, well, exhilarating. "Don't you know that blue eyes are the result of a specific genetic mutation that occurred somewhere between six and ten thousand years ago? Before that, everyone had brown eyes."

I try to say something but instead resort to my fallback of repeatedly opening and closing my mouth like a big-mouth trout out of water.

But then, I do something even worse.

I look into Xander Barnes's big, brown eyes and something inside me melts. Before I know what I'm doing, I throw my arms around his neck and pull him tightly toward me. My mouth crashes on his with such force that I probably bruised him.

Oh my God, what am I doing?

I'm kissing Xander Barnes. That's what I'm doing.

# CHAPTER 29

This is bad. Like so bad. Like worse than lying about being engaged bad. I shouldn't be doing this. *We* shouldn't be doing this. There shouldn't be kissing and groping and touching and exchanging of bodily fluids.

But there is and it's soooooooo good.

My nether region is screaming and dancing. I swear, I just heard my lady bits say, "hallelujah!" as Xander's hands wandered over my chest. Okay, I may have started this by attacking him, but Xander definitely appears to be a willing participant. I pull him closer to me and our bodies press together. Oh yes, he's definitely willing.

Holy crap.

*Current mood: turned on.*

He's now kissing my neck, and I swear my legs are about to buckle. Xander's hands wander down and are playing with the bottom of my T-shirt. Just as he starts to pull up and a breeze hits my back, his phone rings to the tune of the Imperial March from *Star Wars*. He freezes immediately. "Shit, that's my dad's ring. He never calls."

I step back, panting and breathless. Holy hell, what was that?

"Hey, Dad. What's up?" Xander's also trying to catch his breath. I keep backing up, moving toward the stairs. Xander puts a hand on his forehead, effectively covering his eyes. I take the opportunity to bolt up the stairs and secure myself in my room.

For lack of knowing what else to do in a time like this, I text Mackenzie.

*I just made out with Xander.*

*Eww. Gross. I don't want to hear that. Cant text. Trying to nurse Ada but it hurts like a mo-fo, and I don't have a lot of milk.*

I call her, whispering so Xander can't hear me, even though I know he's still downstairs. "I *made out* with Xander. Definitely first base. Sort of second too."

"Okay, yuck. I don't need to hear these details. I don't tell you every time something happens between Luke and me."

"Yeah but you did the first time. I had to hear *all* about that. It took me months to even be able to look at Luke again. Do you even know how long it's been since I've had sex?"

"I'd say about three and a half months."

Oh shit.

"Right. Of course right. Yeah, back then. In June. Obviously," I scoff.

My sister is not fooled by my sly answer. "Erin, what's going on? Is Xander not the father?"

I swallow. "No, he is."

"Are you sure?"

266

There's literally no other possibility.

When I don't answer, Mackenzie asks again, "Erin, what's going on here?"

I guess she kept all my secrets the first time around. She won't tell Mom. "Xander was my sperm donor."

There's silence on the line. Maybe she's attending to the baby or to Trey or was suddenly abducted.

"Kenz? You still there?"

"What do you mean by sperm donor? Do you mean like a friends with benefits sort of thing?"

"No, I mean literal sperm donor. This baby was conceived in Dr. James's office."

"I don't understand." Mackenzie sounds lost. Maybe sleep deprivation has fried her brain cells? What's so hard to understand?

"Remember I had decided to use a sperm donor and insemination? Then you tried to talk me out of it. Mom succeeded in talking me out of it. But Xander came up with the solution that he could father the baby and then help me raise it. It seemed like a good idea. I tried to tell you that, but you jumped to the wrong conclusion that we were together. I *possibly* didn't correct you."

"But you told Mom you were getting married!"

I cringe, thinking about that awful scene in the hospital. "I didn't say we were getting married. I said we were thinking about our future, and that we'd keep things small. That's all true."

"Oh come on, Erin, that's splitting hairs. You know it. We all thought you were in love and marrying this guy. Sure, things are a little out of order, but if he's good to you and the baby, that's all that matters, right?"

Exactly.

"Xander is good to me. He's going to be fantastic with the baby. So then whether we're in love or not, it doesn't matter. We decided to have a baby and raise her together."

"*Her*? Did you already find out? What about your gender reveal party?"

Damn it.

"Xander is convinced it's a girl. I guess I started drinking his Kool-Aid. And we're not doing the party. He doesn't want to, and I respect that." His point about avoiding my mom struck a nerve. I'm in this whole mess because of her and the less I have to deal with her, probably the better.

"But Mom has all these ideas. She was talking about these mini-sandwiches and some sort of veggie platter."

*Veggie platter? What about my taco bar?*

I sigh. A big blow up with Mom is coming. There's no way to avoid it. She's totally out of control. "How did we never see that Mom has serious control and boundary issues before this?"

Kenz is silent for a minute. "Luke's pointed things out, but he doesn't get it. Mom has had a difficult life."

"Lots of people have, and they don't all act like this. Look at Dad."

"Gramma and Grandpa were awesome to him. They loved him so much."

"I know they did, but *look* at Dad, especially in relation to his siblings. One of these things is not like the other. You know he had a hard time, getting harassed for being black."

"He's biracial." Kenz adds quickly.

"Yes, but in a family of pasty Irish kids ..."

We're both quiet for a moment. Dad never complained. He told us about the teasing and bullying growing up, but he made it seem like it was the same that thing that everyone goes through. Like when I got teased for being tall. Only now as an adult, do I realize it was something entirely different.

"You know I heard Mom and Dad talking about us once. They thought we were asleep, but I needed a drink." I can still remember that night, my Power Ranger pajamas. "And Dad had just been passed over for a promotion at work. He was crushed, and Mom was trying to bolster him up."

"See? She's not all bad," Mackenzie interjects.

"I know she's not. But anyway, I heard Dad say, Kenz is so fair she won't have to deal with this, and at least Erin can pass. I didn't know what they meant. I thought they were talking about that you are fair, like a maiden in a story, and that I'd be able to skirt by even though I wasn't pretty like you."

It's one of those moments that's etched in my nine-year-old brain but floated around like a dandelion puff, never really attached to anything. Now I see the stem and roots of the comment. Mom's reply also finally makes sense. "As long as she does something with her hair."

"I never really thought about that." Mackenzie says quietly. "Poor Dad."

"Poor Dad. Poor Mom. Poor me. Poor all of us. But that's not the problem here. The problem is that I almost just had sex with Xander!"

The memory of his hands—and mouth—on my body instantly makes me flush. Holy cow.

"I don't think sleeping with the father of your child is generally considered a problem."

She has a point there. We end the phone call because Ada's screaming and Trey is screaming and there's a good chance Luke is about to start screaming.

Babies.

I should probably talk to Xander. We need to figure out what we're going to do about my mom. And when I say we, of course I mean me. This isn't Xander's problem, though he's a good sounding board.

And is obviously good at coming up with solutions.

I would also not be opposed to picking up where we left off. The memory of his kiss still has power over my body. No, I would not mind that at all. I wander down stairs, but he's nowhere to be found. Back upstairs, I see his bedroom door is closed.

Huh. There's no mistaking or confusing what he means by that. His light's on, but I can't hear him talking. So he's awake and not talking to his dad, but does not want to see me.

Message received.

He's probably sitting in there, flooded with relief that he had an escape. Even better than the friend emergency call on a blind date. I bet his dad talked some sense into him, and he's trying to figure out how to get out of all of this. I would be if I were him. I mean, look at me. I'm a hot mess with an overbearing, sometimes irrational family. Why would he want this?

And we're not even going to mention the cellulite that has suddenly sprouted on my backside. I was ready to combat stretch marks but cellulite? Really? Now? Someone up there has a sick and twisted sense of humor.

Whatever the reason, it's probably good that he's in his room. I need time to cool off. To think things through. Sleeping together will only complicate things. Although this is the one time I wouldn't have to worry about getting pregnant.

As I wash my face and get ready for bed, regret fills me. Why did I have to kiss him? Just because he complimented my eyes? Personally, I've never thought they matched with my complexion. Just another part of me that wasn't right.

I can't believe I messed this up so much. I took a good thing, the best solution in a trying time, and totally ruined it.

But man, I'm sort of glad I did. Xander Barnes knows how to kiss.

# CHAPTER 30

"So, how 'bout those—" Crap is it still baseball season? Football? What do they play in September? "That sports team you like?"

Xander glances over at me and a small smile momentarily dances across his lips. He's barely said two words to me this morning.

I hate it.

I've become accustomed to Xander's company. His comments, jokes in the morning. How he asks me everyday what the weather forecast is, even though he's in the room when channel ten reports the weather. Also, because we're working with animals from Central and South America, except for in the dead of winter, we're better off wearing shorts. The enclosures and habitats are pretty steamy.

Not unlike that kiss.

No, no, no. I will not think about it. I cannot think about it. It's obvious Xander doesn't want to talk about it. It's fine.

It's not fine.

"So, what's up with your dad? Everything okay?"

Xander closes his eyes for a minute, which is only okay because we're stopped at a light. The car behind us honks indicating that we're not moving fast enough. Xander opens his eyes and begins to slowly accelerate.

He can be evilly passive aggressive.

"No," Xander says finally. We're about two minutes out from the parking lot. Not enough time to have a meaningful conversation. "He's pissed."

"Okay. Does he have reason to be?" I can't imagine why. He and Xander don't talk a whole lot.

Xander nods. "He ran into Matt."

Matt. Why does that name sound familiar? The way Xander says it, I know I should know who he's talking about. But for the life of me, I don't.

I should probably work on my listening skills. Or maybe it's the pregnancy brain that I've heard about. Matt ... Matt ... Matt.

And then it hits me. Where I've heard that name. "Matt who can't keep a secret, Matt?"

Dr. Sophie, who also apparently can't keep a secret's brother.

He nods as he puts the car into park. He doesn't look back at me before getting out, grabbing his backpack out of the backseat, and walking toward the employee gate. Just a guess here, but I guess Xander's dad is no more thrilled about this than my mom was.

Now that she's planning a fake wedding, she's happier than a pig in you-know-what. She's still not really acknowledging the baby thing though. It's like it won't exist until after we're legally married. Like saying "I do" is what creates a baby.

Xander's covering the cats today, as it's Henry's day off. I'm split between sloths and popping over to primates in between encounters. Barry and Bonnie are pretty low key and clean, so in between interactions, we let them sleep. Bonnie especially can get pretty grumpy if she doesn't get her beauty sleep, often lashing out at us if we bother her too much.

I think Bonnie may be my spirit animal.

It's a good day not to be near Xander. I still cannot make heads or tails of what happened last night, but the fact that he's been so closed off ever since is not a good sign.

He certainly has made no indication of wanting to pick up where we left off.

But he's *such* a good kisser though. Wait— what if I'm not? What if he was grossed out and is trying to figure out a way to throw me out or something? He can't do that. We have a legal contract!

We should have put something in the contract prohibiting a romantic or sexual relationship. If it didn't cost a lot of money for Paul to amend the contract, I'd call him right up.

Though I do have to admit, my living expenses have gone way down since moving in with Xander. Not only is the rent less and we split utilities, but I'm better about grocery shopping and I don't waste nearly as much food. Now that we're carpooling, my tank of gas lasts at least twice as long. Suddenly I can see why the DINKs (Dual income, no kids), as my dad calls them, can save money for things like nice houses and cars and vacations.

Not that we have that much longer being DINKs, but I'll save while I can. Though my wardrobe is no longer fitting, and I'll have to spend some of my savings on that. I should go shopping on my next day off. I found a shirt that I need to order that says, "Don't eat the watermelon seeds". Mackenzie has sent a few things over, but it's not enough. I thought she'd send more but apparently is still wearing a lot of her maternity clothes.

This is a judgment free zone over here. Those in stretchy-pants houses cannot throw stones.

And those who need to buy larger pants, including grandma panties to accommodate a rapidly expanding backside, should not be thinking about getting frisky with anyone. Let alone someone with a tight, firm butt that I bet I could bounce a quarter off of.

Yum.

Dammit, I'm thinking about Xander again.

But it's clear, as we finish up our ZIMS accounting and paperwork, that the last thing on his mind is picking up where we left off. He's sullen and silent.

"Hey, I know I wrote down that I was planning tacos for tonight—"

"Shocking," he mutters, barely audible.

But audible enough.

I suck in a deep breath before continuing, "but I was thinking about making chicken parm instead. I'll do a quick run to the store and get dinner going."

"Fine."

The night we went out to dinner with Allen, he and Xander talked all about chicken parm and how much they loved it and how it was the best dinner their mom cooked. It's the least I can do for all he's done for me.

The very least.

You know what doesn't help a grumpy man's mood? Having to wait almost three hours to eat his dinner. I couldn't help it. It was after six by the time we got home. My "quick run to the store" turned into a forty-five minute ordeal because of a car accident. It took me forever to trim and slice and pound the chicken out. Then I realized we didn't have any breadcrumbs, so I had to go back to the store.

Not to mention the kitchen looks like a bomb went off. Flour and I do not get along. Apparently also neither breadcrumbs or marinara sauce like me.

"What did you do in here?" Xander looks from me to the mess and back again. "You have flour in your hair."

"But was the dinner worth it? Was it just like your mom used to make?"

He closes his eyes and shakes his head. "Not even remotely. But seriously, look at this kitchen!"

I blink, trying to prevent the tears from falling. Twenty-four hours ago, we were about to rip each other's clothes off. Now I'm nothing but a failure and inconvenience and ...

"I'll clean it up," I mumble glumly.

I set about trying to make order out of the chaos I've created. My phone pings once, then twice. I'm sure it's my sister complaining about some postpartum issue or mother with even more wedding ideas. I have to tell her that there will not be a wedding.

That there never was.

That can wait until after the dishes are washed and the food is put away and the floor is mopped. Yes, I am that messy when I cook.

Perhaps it's why I like tacos so much. There's not a way to be neat while eating them, so no one realizes that I wasn't neat to begin with.

Add that to my ever growing list of faults: not thin enough, talks about animals too much, too nerdy, looks funny, odd sense of humor, bad T-shirt collection, lies to family, terrible kisser, and messy in the kitchen.

I can't believe I would even entertain the idea of Xander being interested in me. I should have seen it when he never, ever made the suggestion of sleeping together to conceive a child in the first place. What guy wouldn't jump at that chance?

A guy who finds the girl repulsive, that's who.

I pack our lunches for the morning and click off the light in the kitchen. It's after eleven and I'm exhausted. My feet hurt and my back is beginning to ache. I plop down on the couch. I need to rest before I walk all the way up the stairs to my room. Let me just sit for a few minutes here ...

I bolt upright, suddenly awake. What time is it? What day is it? Where am I?

It takes me a minute to realize that I'm on my couch in Xander's living room. A watery light coming in through the window tells me it's got to be early morning. I glance at my watch. Shit! It's almost seven. I have to shower.

I fly off the couch, the blanket sliding to the floor. Wait— blanket? There wasn't a blanket here last night. I look a little closer. I think this is the blanket off of Xander's bed. He has one of a similar color and texture that I've seen when I casually stroll by, obviously not snooping.

How did Xander's blanket get down here? And there's a pillow too. Where'd that come from? He may not like me or want me, but at least he was still nice to me.

And there I go, setting my bar super high again.

It's no wonder I'm single.

But now, it's even worse. I think I'm falling for my roommate.

# CHAPTER 31

"Erin, there you are. You didn't answer my texts last night." Dr. Sophie comes jogging up to me the moment I walk through the employee gates. It's Xander's day off, so I drove in myself. I didn't see him this morning, which is a good thing. I'm too tired to handle that much rejection so early in the morning.

"Your texts? Oh gosh, I assumed it was my mom or my sister harassing me. We— I had a bad night, and I didn't want to deal with them. Sorry." Then it occurs to me that Dr. Sophie has never texted me before. I didn't know she had my number.

Oh no, what if something happened to Barry or Bonnie? "Is something wrong? Is it one of the animals?"

She quickly shakes her head. "Something's wrong, but it's not the animals. It's Xander. I'm so sorry. You have to tell him sorry for me. He won't take my calls."

"What are you sorry for?" I want to ask if she kissed him too, but that's not an answer I want to hear.

"He didn't tell you?" We've walked as far as we can together. I have to head to South America while she's attending to the hospital today.

"No, he's not speaking to me right now. I—" I break off before spilling it all. "I did something I shouldn't have, and it crossed a line. I'm trying to make it up to him, but he won't let me. I even made him a special dinner last night, but all he did was get mad that I'm a slob in the kitchen. I didn't mean to be but ..." I trail off, unsure of why I'm telling her all this.

"He's mad at me too. I ... I opened my big, fat mouth when I shouldn't have, and it's stirred up a hornets' nest. Look, I have to run, but next time you see him, tell him to call me, will you?"

She jogs off. What on earth could she have done that's worse than my physical attack?

I don't get much time to think about Xander during the workday. Terry's out, so I'm filling in for her, along with running two encounters. We've realized that we only need one person per sloth encounter now that we are more comfortable with everything. They still use both Xander and I for travel exhibits. We haven't *exactly* approached them with not wanting to travel together after the baby is born, but I'm sure Ed has to see that coming.

We've got another event this weekend. If he's not speaking to me, it should be nice and interesting. I don't blame Xander. Not at all. He went and did this great thing for me, and I ruined it.

I changed the terms. I threw myself at him for no reason. Just because he was being nice and supportive and likes my eyes. But deep down I know that it's more than physical.

I'm in love with Xander.

280

Not friend love either. The romantic kind that wants the engagement to be real and this baby to be a product of our love.

He's right to hide from me.

I'm such an idiot. It couldn't be any more clichéd.

Today sucks. And because of the upcoming travel schedule, I'm working today, a Wednesday, which means I get to go right from work to UnBRCAble. It's not ideal, and I'll have to go back into work after the meeting to finish my paperwork.

Actually, tonight I'm happy for a reason not to be home.

"Don, I'll be back to finish my ZIMS. I have my appointment," I call as I pass by his office at the end of the day. We negotiated this arrangement when my schedule started changing, but I don't know that he remembers.

"Oh, right. Make sure to get your charting done."

As if I don't usually.

Heading into the UnBRCAble meeting, I'm relieved that someone else is more crisis than me. Well, not crisis per se but struggling. And don't get me wrong, I'm not happy that a fellow sister is having a rough go. It's nice not to be the only one with a complicated life.

"I think he's cheating on me," Tracey says. "He comes home late at night with ridiculous excuses. He's evasive. He's always on his phone. And ..." her voice breaks as the tears finally come through, "he won't touch me."

There are several nods. Marg-with-a-hard-g, a newer member, speaks up. And that's how she introduced herself during her first meeting. "My name is Marg, with a hard g. Like Margot, but don't call me that. Don't call me Marge either. Just Marg with a hard g."

Marg-with-a-hard-g is looking at Tracey sympathetically. "I'm sorry to say, but it sounds like you're right. If a man gives you reason not to trust him, you should probably listen. Men say what they mean. If he won't tell you, then he can't."

I don't appreciate the way Marg-with-a-hard-g lays it all out, but she's not wrong. It totally sounds like he's cheating. Tracey hasn't ever been the best judge of character. This latest guy is no exception.

Maybe she needs the hard truth like Marg needs her hard g.

"Most of the guys I've dated love that I have implants. He doesn't seem to care," Tracey laments.

I see Millie make a face and Claudia looks at me knowingly. I wish Tracey could find a man—not a guy— who is good and decent.

Hell, I wish I could too.

Marg-with-a-hard-g is talking again. "My husband loves the implants. He's happy I won't get sick and everything, and he never would have said I was too small before, but he likes the girls now. I'm so lucky to have him."

I don't think Marg-with-a-hard-g means for the comment to be condescending, and maybe my emotions are a little raw, but that's totally how I take it.

Claudia tilts her head slightly, her inner counselor coming out. "How do *you* feel about your implants, Marg? How do they make *you* feel?"

Her confidence crumples slightly as her shoulders draw in and her head drops, the façade disappearing. "I wish I had my old chest back. They don't feel right. But Mike's happy so ..." she trails off.

"Listen, it's hard for all of us to come to terms with the body we used to have with the one we have now. None of us are here because they *want* to be," Millie says quietly. "And I miss real boobs too. Even if they were tiny."

This is a familiar statement, repeated over and over, in this group. We're all trying to make a silk purse out of a sow's ear. It's hard for me to complain about anything at this point because I still have my body intact. I have breasts, getting large by the day. I have a new life growing in me. This group is for the people who have lost.

I've lost nothing.

Except for Xander.

I need to leave. Now.

"Um, ladies, I have to run back to work. My schedule's changing, so I don't think I'll be at meetings for a while. Good luck to everyone." I stand up, rushing toward the door.

I don't belong here anymore.

I don't belong anywhere.

I make it outside the door before the gaping wound inside my soul opens, the longing to belong somewhere—anywhere—greater than any physical need I've ever had.

At least I'm comfortable at work. It seems like the only place that fits me anymore. I can't go to my parents' house. Mackenzie has too much on her plate to deal with me. Xander doesn't want me. I don't even have a place of my own at this point.

This all sort of sucks.

It should be a happy time in my life. Instead, I'm miserable.

Living in a web of lies is no fun.

Once I talk to Xander and apologize for crossing the line, I'm telling my parents. It's going to make things infinitely worse. This may be the deal breaker for my mom. I hope that someday my dad will come around and that neither will make Kenz choose between being a daughter or a sister. I still don't think I've done anything wrong, other than mislead them, but they—she—won't see it that way.

By the time I finish up at work, and trudge home, I'm almost too tired to eat. Almost. I swing through the drive-thru and make quick work of a cheeseburger and milkshake before I pull into the driveway. While I know I need to square things up with Xander, as well as try to smooth things over for Dr. Sophie, all I want to do is sleep.

Growing a person is tiring work.

Especially when you are spending a tremendous amount of energy ruining your own personal life.

Relief floods me when there are no lights on downstairs and Xander's door is closed. I won't have to talk to him tonight. He obviously doesn't want to see me.

There's no way to digest that without a massive ego blow.

And, accompanying the ego blow, copious amounts of tears.

*Current mood: defeated.*

As long as I feel this down, I might as well tell my mom. It's not like I can feel much worse.

Yet I remain a coward, so I shoot out a quick text.

*Xander and I are not getting married. I don't want to talk. Good night.*

So there, that's done. I didn't even apologize. I don't owe her one and I will not give her one. I will be strong and ...

*Ping.*

I jump, dropping my phone on the bed next to me. I reach over and turn it off. I may be a coward, but I'm not stupid.

Yet I did not consider the tenacity of my mother, who, a brief twenty minutes later, is pounding on the door. Impressive, considering my parents' house is at least twenty-seven minutes away.

As I head downstairs, I see Xander stumbling out of his room. He hasn't shaved and his hair is standing straight up. He's also pulling a T-shirt over his head. Gah, the sight of his abs distracts me. As I turn my head to get a better look, my foot misses a step and I slide on down the last four steps.

"Oh my God, Erin!" Xander rushes toward me, picking me up and righting me back to my feet. "Are you okay? Is the baby okay? Do you need to go to the hospital?"

The only thing wounded is my back where I whacked it on the edge of the stairs and my ankle which rolled under the force of my slide. "I'm fine. I have to get the door."

"Who could possibly be knocking on our door at this ho—"

"ERIN ELIZABETH MCAVOY, I KNOW YOU ARE IN THERE."

Xander rolls his eyes. "How did I not guess that one?"

"I texted her that we're not getting married, so no more planning."

"*You texted her?* Are you crazy? Didn't you know she'd flip out like this? Why did you do that, especially now?"

"Because it's not fair. It's not fair to you and it's not fair to me to pretend we're something that we aren't. To make you lie and act like you're in love with me, when we know it's a big fat lie. I'm surprised people even bought it as long as they did. There is no way you and I could ever be together."

I pull open the door and face the wrath of Mary. At this point, Typhoid Mary might be more pleasant to deal with. "You drove over here for nothing. I don't want to talk. I had a long day, and I want to go to bed."

I start to close the door on my mother, but she will not be silenced so easily. "Xander Barnes, how could you do this to her? To break her heart like that? Don't know you what this will do to her? She might lose the baby, and it'll be all your fault. I demand you make an honest woman out of her."

I close the door practically on her face and am tempted to call the police. If I do that, our relationship will never rebound. I open the door a crack. "Mom, it's not Xander, it's me. I don't want to marry him. I want to have this baby on my own. It's not him, it's me who is putting an end to this. Be disappointed in me. I'll talk to you tomorrow. Good night."

And *now* I close the door.

I hear her get in the car and drive away. While I wouldn't *actually* call the police on her, I might not necessarily be that upset if she got a speeding ticket on the way home. It would serve her right.

I turn to Xander. I would normally expect my heart to be pounding a mile a minute, but I don't feel it. I don't feel anything. There's a whole lot of nothing where my body and feelings should be.

"I'm sorry. She had no right to say those things. She's really gone off the deep end. It's never been this bad. I didn't think she'd take any of this well, but I didn't see her reacting this poorly either. I'm so sorry. If you want me to move out, I will."

Xander looks at me and blinks once, then twice. "You don't want to get married?"

"No. Not like this. Not now. I don't want to get married because our—my—parents force us to. I don't want to be married because I'm pregnant. I don't want to settle, and that's what this is, don't you see? It's a great solution to a problem, but it's not the end of the road for me. I hope ... I hope someday I meet someone who loves me for me."

Angrily, I swipe at the hot tears that refuse to stay confined to my eyes. "Who can accept that I have a child with someone else. Who can accept that my body will never produce more children. Who can accept that I'm surgically reconstructed to look like a woman, but that I'm not really anymore. And that's on top of my crazy family, my bad T-shirts, my penchant for tacos at every meal, and the fact that I might care more about a rodent than I do my spouse. Who won't mind that I spend more time with animals than with him."

Xander looks at me, blinking slowly. "And you don't think that's what we have going on here?"

"You don't love me, Xander. In fact, you have laughed—*laughed*—at me when I've mentioned dating you. I get that you don't see me like that, and it's fine. Really. I will never, ever be able to repay you for what you've done to help me out here. And we'll be friends forever as we raise this great little person into a great big person."

He's quiet for a minute, staring at the ground. He looks down so long that I have to look too, just to make sure there's not something interesting, like a million dollars, on the floor.

"Is that really what you think we should do?" he says quietly.

"I think it's for the best. We don't have to make any big announcements at work. If people ask, we can simply say that we've—how did Gwenyth put it—mutually uncoupled."

"I don't know what that means." Xander finally looks up at me. I try to read what's going on behind his deep brown eyes. Relief?

But right now, relief looks like pain.

Maybe I'm projecting. Every ounce of my body is filled with pain right now.

I laugh, the taste bitter in my mouth. "I don't either, but since we never coupled in the first place, it would be hard to define uncoupling for us."

I look down and rotate my foot around, trying to work out my ankle. "I can move out, if you don't want me around. I'd understand that totally. I can find a place to live nearby. We'll still share custody and everything, obviously. Nothing's changed with that."

"Erin, wait. You've got it all wrong. Nothing's changed."

I shrug. "But that's where you're wrong, Xander. Everything's changed."

"Because of your mom?"

I can't tell him. He won't understand. It'll make things worse. "No, because of me."

I start toward the stairs, limping a bit. My ankle and back hurt for certain, but my pride and my heart bear the brunt of his injury.

All because I had to go and fall in love with Xander Barnes.

Not even a taco could make me feel better right now.

# CHAPTER 32

"We might as well drive together since we're both going in." Xander hands me my water bottle, all filled up. "Did you take your vitamins? Dr. Lee's office called to confirm you for your appointment. Fourth month check up."

I look from my water bottle to him and back again. Has he lost his mind? Does he not remember what happened last night? Or is he so relieved that I won't be forcing him to pretend to love me anymore that he's in a great mood?

"Yup. Sixteen weeks today. Sure, fine. Good." I don't even know what question I'm answering. "I'm almost ready."

I'm moving slowly this morning because my back hurts, my ankle hurts, and I barely slept at all. When I did, I dreamt the brakes didn't work in my car and I had no control over it. It slid into multiple cars before stopping in a giant pothole. When I got out, the pothole turned into a water-filled sinkhole and my car sank to endless depths, complete with my cell phone and knapsack and all. I had nothing left.

Doesn't take a genius to figure out what that's all about.

Also, I need to get a handle on my control issues before I act with Bean like my mom acts with me.

Once I slide into the driver's seat of my car—my day to drive—I finally remember to give him his message. "Dr. Sophie wanted me to tell you to call her. She's really sorry." I hope it's not too late to relay that information. I had my own stuff to deal with last night.

Xander immediately bristles. "She needs to stay out of it."

"Stay out of what?"

"My business."

Okay. Whatever that means.

Once I pull into my parking space, I look at my phone for the hundredth time. Nothing from my mom. I shouldn't be surprised. But nonetheless I am. I thought for sure she'd have a lot to say.

This is it. I've officially reached the *disappointment* status that she always threatened. Don't pierce your navel otherwise we'll be *disappointed* in you. Don't drink underage otherwise we'll be *disappointed* in you. Don't get pregnant without being married otherwise we'll be *disappointed* in you.

Achievement unlocked.

And it feels about as crappy as one would expect.

My mom's not speaking to me, I sprained my ankle, I'm quitting UnBRCAble, and I have to cancel my fake wedding. All in all, this week sort of sucks.

Oh, and I fell in love, and he doesn't love me back.

And Xander's mad. I can't tell if it's about the kiss, my off-her-rocker mother, the thing with Dr. Sophie, or because Mercury is in retrograde.

To be honest, I don't even know what that really means, other than it's bad.

Regardless, despite his politeness this morning, Xander is making it crystal clear that he wants nothing to do with me outside of a professional capacity. It's a good thing he came to his senses before I took my clothes off. At least I was spared *that* embarrassment.

As I'm grabbing my morning paperwork to sift through, Ed pokes his head out. "Great! Erin, I was about to email you. There's been a change in plans for this weekend. Instead of a Saturday only event, we need you and Xander to drive out tomorrow. Similar to Albany."

"Where to this time?" It never matters to me. Xander drives and all I need to know is if I need a toothbrush or not. This'll only be the second overnight since we started. Last time, I came home with plans to have a baby.

I doubt the souvenir for this trip will be quite as nice.

"Lexington, Kentucky. There was an issue with the sloth from Columbus. She's in estrus, so can't travel. The guy from Cincinnati is booked elsewhere, so they want us for two days instead of one."

Great. The whole weekend with Xander. That shouldn't be strained or anything.

"Okay, so the front office is reserving us rooms then right?"

"Oh, right. They wanted me to ask. One room, right? You don't need two anymore?"

Uh ...

"Just double checking. I think you guys are great together. You're perfect for each other and are going to make great parents. I can't believe it took you guys that long to get together, but I'm just glad you did."

Uh ...

"And I don't know if you've made plans or not, but, um, well, my wife is getting into the wedding planning business, if you need help. She asked me to give you her card." He hands me a business card that he happened to have right next to his computer. Handy no?

Uh ...

"Okay, I think that's it. Check your email for the hotel confirmation. You'd better get out there. It's disinfectant day, and you know how Terry is with Tyler if you're not there to get him started."

I walk out, a bit in a daze. What am I going to do? We need to stage our breakup and quickly. There is no way I can share a hotel room with Xander.

But I didn't think I could stand up to my mom either. Let's face it, I didn't really. I'm a big coward, scared and running. Running from my family, from the women in the group, from Xander. What I truly want from Xander and how I really feel about him.

That I've fallen for him.

But because of that, I need to make sure he finds someone who deserves him, and we all know that's not me. He needs someone smart and gorgeous and who appreciates his intelligence and wit and giving nature.

Hell, even this morning, he was taking care of me.

He doesn't have to. He doesn't want to. But he does.

He deserves someone who can give him so much more than I can.

I start over to the South American primates, but decide Tyler can fend for himself with Terry for a minute. There's something I've got to do.

"Hey Doctor—I mean Sophie—do you have a minute?"

Sophie exits her office. "Did you talk to him? Did you tell him? Is he still upset?"

"Yes, I tried, and yes, but some of it might be with me. It's hard to tell."

"Why's he upset with you?"

I sigh. It's time to reveal this charade for what it is. "I changed our arrangement. I kissed him. I threw myself at him." I sink down in the chair across from her desk. "I know, totally pitiful and clichéd."

"I don't understand. How is it clichéd?"

"It's like one of those romance novels my sister reads. The fake marriage trope where they pretend to be in love. Except I was stupid enough to fall in love with him." My hand flies over my mouth, but not in time to capture those words.

I just told Sophie I loved him.

Sophie puts her hands up. "Wait, hold up. You're not engaged?"

I shake my head, my hand still clamped tightly over my mouth in fear of what else will come out.

"But you love Xander."

I nod my head.

"Are you really pregnant?"

I nod again.

"Is it Xander's?" Her eyes light up. "Please tell me it's not," she asks hopefully.

I'm sure the pain I feel in my gut isn't actually physical, but it wouldn't hurt any less if Sophie stepped back and landed a roundhouse kick to my abdomen.

All I can do is nod in the affirmative. I don't understand as she wilts, obviously disappointed that I am carrying Xander's child. Though this is more of the reaction I expected. I'm so far out of my league, it's not even funny.

"Yes, it is. I need to go." I jump to my feet and hurry out. I can't believe I tried to talk to her. I can't believe I told her I love Xander.

And the more I say it, the more in love with him I seem to fall.

What's not to love though? He is caring and genuine and intuitive and thoughtful and he gave me the one thing that no one else cared to. All out of the goodness of his heart.

I unlock the primate enclosure, sliding inside and checking the lock behind me. I need to be extra cautious today, because with my mind on my earth-shattering self-realizations, I'm likely to let an animal—or twelve—out.

They frown upon that.

I see Terry glancing my way. Ugh. I can't. I simply cannot today. I can't talk to anyone about anything, but especially not about my lies and deceit. And especially not about Xander.

And definitely not *to* Xander.

I head into the office and tell them I need to go home sick. I've never done this before, but I can't be here now. Frantically texting my sister, she sends Luke, who is still on paternity leave, to fetch me.

I've got to leave the car for Xander, after all. He wouldn't leave me stranded. I slide the house key off the ring and hang the rest up in his locker and head outside to wait.

This is bad. So very bad.

"Um, you okay?" my brother-in-law asks nervously. Apparently hysterical crying makes him nervous.

"Sure. Fine." *Sniff, sniff, sniff.*

"Is it a baby thing?"

Luke hardly talks, let alone to me. Certainly not about emotions or relationships or girly things. "Really?" My boat is about to go over the precipice of the waterfall and everything's on the tip of my tongue.

"Well, Kenz will grill me. Is it the baby?"

Despite myself, a chuckle slips out. There's no doubt Kenz will give him the third degree the minute he pulls into the garage. If she wasn't in the middle of nursing when I texted, she would have come.

"The baby's fine. I'm a mess, but the baby's fine. Tell her I'm fine too. I don't want her worrying. I'm fine. We're fine." I keep repeating the word fine, as if I say it enough and it will be true.

It will never be true. I will never be fine again.

"Good. As long as everything's fine."

"I kissed him and then he hid from me. He hates Mom, as he has good reason to. Something happened with his Dad or best friend, and he won't tell me anything because I mean nothing to him, and I realized I'm in love with him and he will never see me that way." The words spill forth, the dam breaking loose.

Poor Luke.

He pulls up to my house. "I don't know what to tell you, Erin. You mom is out there sometimes, and she certainly complicates things, but she loves you and only wants what's best for you. I don't know what's going on with this Xander dude, but you need to talk to him. You're having a kid together. You can't run away from this."

That's the most Luke has ever said to me. Probably cumulatively.

"Thanks for the ride and thanks for being a great brother-in-law." I hop out of the car, digesting what he says.

I have a lot of difficult conversations coming up.

But first, a nap.

# CHAPTER 33

It's late afternoon before Xander starts blowing up my phone. He didn't realize I wasn't at work until then. In his defense, I was supposed to be in primates.

Though it makes me a little sad that he didn't look for me before four p.m.

I shouldn't be surprised. I mean, not really. He's very thoughtful, but it's not like he's waiting by my locker to catch me passing in the halls like we're in high school. Not that I ever stalked someone like that.

Sorry, Nate Clemmens.

I sigh and text him back. Let's play two truths and a lie.

*I'm fine. Had a headache. Needed a nap.*

His answer pops up immediately. I'm impressed with how fast he can text.

*Do you think it's your blood pressure? I'm coming home now.*

I look at the clock. It's only ten till five. He still has over an hour left.

*You don't need to come. I don't need to be checked up on, especially not by you.*

Crap. That's way harsh. It's not his fault he's irresistible any more than it's my fault I'm totally resistible.

*What I meant was, you don't have to take time off. I'm fine.*

There's no response. What if he's on his way home? I can't talk to him now. Gah. Why am I so bad at this? It's no wonder Xander runs and hides. I have *got* to get myself in check. We have to go away together this weekend. We have to work together. We have to raise a kid together!

I'm beginning to think this was not a very good idea. Either that, or I've totally lost it and gone off the deep end.

Probably less of the former and more of the latter.

I so cannot see him right now. I need space.

Or to run and hide.

I throw my things in a bag and high tail it for my car. Crap. He has my car.

Well, now I have his. He'll understand. It's not forever.

As I'm speeding down the block, I'm almost positive I see him pulling in. Crappity crap. I hastily pull the car over and send out a quick text.

*I need a little space. Will meet you at work tomorrow.*

But here's the thing: I have nowhere to go until tomorrow. My parents most likely won't let me in. Mackenzie has her hands full, not to mention that's the first place Xander will look.

I could really use a friend right about now.

The odd thing is that if the problem weren't *about* Xander, I could totally see myself spilling this to him. Seeking his advice. Turns out, he's a good problem solver.

The thought of losing him as a friend is worse than losing him as a potential lover. Gah, I feel so cheesy saying that. *Lover.* Good for me, I won't have to worry about what to call Xander. Friend will be fine. Better than nothing.

I turn the car around and head home. *Home.* It is. This place, these four walls may shelter me from the elements, but Xander makes it feel like my home.

Xander feels like home.

I rush through the front door, dropping my bag in the foyer. "Xander? Are you here? Where are you?"

The kitchen and living room are empty, as is the dining room. His bedroom door is wide open and dark. I whirl around, wondering where he could be. My car is in the driveway. The door was unlocked. He has to be here.

And then I see it. The sliver of light sneaking out from under the door. He's in the nursery.

Tentatively, I turn the handle, inching the door open. I don't know what I expect to find, but it's not Xander, sitting in an old rocking chair, eyes closed. His face is tight and drawn.

"Hey," I say quietly.

He doesn't say anything.

Okay then. I guess it's still my turn. "You know I'm really stupid, right? Like smart about book things but stupid about people things. So, here's the thing. The main thing. The only thing. I don't want to pretend to marry you. I don't want to pretend to be engaged. I don't want to have to lie about us. I know I started it because—well, see previous note about being stupid—but I can't keep going. And it's not because of my parents either. They'll be disappointed in me or they won't. They'll accept this baby or they won't. I can't change that, and I can't change them, and I was stupid for thinking lying makes it better. It doesn't."

Still nothing.

"I know I can't have what I want," I continue, "because that's not how things work for me. I know I can't have you as ..." my voice falters. "You're too good for me to really have. I understand that you don't want me like I want you, but I need you, Xander. I need you to be my friend and be in my life."

"You don't want me," he finally says quietly. I have to strain to hear his voice.

I sit down on the floor in front of him, hands on his knees. "Yes, Xander, I do. Look at you—who in their right mind wouldn't want you?"

"Who in their right mind would?"

I have never heard him so dejected. Suddenly, it's quite apparent that this is less about me and more about him. I kneel down in front of him. "Xander, talk to me. Tell me what's wrong."

"I can't."

"You can. You can tell me anything. I can be your friend. Let me be your friend."

His face is down in his hands again, his head inches from mine. "You're going to hate me."

301

I run through my mind and try to think about what could make me hate him. "Did you get me fired from Sloth Central?"

He shakes his head, face still buried.

"Did you get me fired from the zoo?"

Another shake.

"Did you switch your semen with someone else's so I'm carrying some rando's child?"

That gets me a look. At least his face is out his hands. Granted, he's looking at me like I'm certifiable, but I still see it as an improvement.

"Did you tell my mother that the marriage thing was a sham?"

"You did that on your very own."

I shrug. "So I did. Then as I see it, I can't fathom a single reason why I might hate you. Or why I ever could."

"I ... I want to tell you, Erin, but look at you right now. Sitting before me, so hopeful. So beautiful. You're positively fucking glowing and radiant, and I'm going to dampen that light forever."

"Xander, I understand that you don't feel about me the way I feel about you. I ... I didn't mean to fall in love with you but somewhere along the way, I did."

"You don't mean that."

"That I didn't mean to fall in love? You're damn certain I didn't mean for this to happen. It was only a few short months ago that I hated you. You picked on me. You were so flirty, but never to me."

"I respected you too much to blow smoke up your ass, Erin."

"But not too much to insult me?"

"That was for fun. You weren't any less insulting to me."

This is not untrue.

"I didn't want to like you, Xander, but damn you, you made it impossible. You're a truly good and genuine person. How could I not fall for you?"

He looks at me, pain ripping through his eyes. "Dammit, Erin, why now?"

I can't tear my gaze away from his. "Maybe it's my hormones. Maybe it's because you sacrificed your whole life to make sure I could have the one thing that eluded me. That kind of noble deed usually leaves the women swooning."

"I'm sorry," he whispers, leaning forward to rest his forehead on mine. Our hands are clasped in his lap.

"Sorry for what, Xander?"

"Sorry that I didn't know sooner. That I didn't understand. Sorry that I gave you a baby."

I scramble back, standing up so quickly the room spins for a minute. "What?"

Xander's on his feet. "Hear me out, please. I talked to my dad the other night. You know, he called."

The memory of Xander's lips on mine flashes through my brain and I touch my lips with the tip of my finger. "I remember."

"He'd heard from Matt, who'd heard from Sophia, of course, that we were having a baby. Dad went ballistic."

Kind of glad I'm not the only one with parents who aren't totally on board. "I know the feeling."

KATHRYN R. BIEL

"No, that's not why. Al, my brother, apparently had to have a lump removed. It was in his chest. Initially, he thought he tore his pec while lifting."

I'm failing to see what this has to do with why I'd hate Xander. "That's too bad."

"It was cancerous. Stage two."

I say nothing. It's terrible news of course but has nothing to do with the baby or me.

"It was breast cancer."

I frown. You don't hear a lot about males with breast cancer.

"He got tested. He has an abnormal PALB2 gene. Mutations in this gene make it so the BRCA-2 gene cannot repair cells and inhibit cancer growth."

"So he's got the BRCA-2 mutation?"

"No, he's got the PALB2 mutation which means that the BRCA gene can't work, and therefore places him at high risk for cancer. They're thinking this is what Mom had."

"Okay ..."

"Essentially, by not leaving you well enough alone, by having to swoop in and save the day, I just ensured that one way or another, our child is almost guaranteed to have cancer."

# CHAPTER 34

I don't know what to do. Not about Xander. Not about his family. Not about the baby. The only thing I can think of is to send him back to Columbus. He's got to be with his family right now. Talk things out. Figure out what's going on.

Get tested for a hereditary cancer risk.

While Xander's packing, I call Ed. I've never called him at home before. I hope he takes this well.

"Um, Ed, it's Erin."

Historically, in times of emergency, the vets are the ones who get to call the directors. Don, usually. Ed, as Director of Education, is most likely not used to getting late night calls.

"This can't be good."

It's like he already knows. Probably from the fact that I'm calling him in the first place. "It's not super awesome. It's about the trip."

"Columbus pulled out. We can't leave them hanging."

I feel like there's a sloth joke in there somewhere, but I'm too tired to find it. "Um, Xander can't go. He—he has a family emergency in Columbus, actually—" I look over at Xander and give him a tight smile.

"What is going on in that state?" Ed sighs.

"I'm not sure, but I'm relatively confident that the two are not related. He has to leave tonight to go home. He can't do the trip."

"Are you going with him?"

"No. I mean, I can't." *Because he feels too guilty to be around me.* "I figure I will still do the event, but I need someone to go with me."

I hear Ed shuffling papers for a minute. "It would probably be easiest if I just go with you."

"You're getting your own hotel room, right?" Lord only knows why *this* is what flies out of my mouth. Xander looks up, startled.

Ed laughs. "Yes, Erin, I will get my own hotel room. We can talk about how we will run things on the drive. Tell Xander I hope everything's okay."

I nod, though Ed can't see it through the phone. "I'll make sure to pass it on to him. Thanks for understanding."

"I'm glad you found each other. Finally."

Something occurs to me, since Ed is under the impression that we are a real couple. "Ed, did you ship us?"

"I have no idea what that means."

"Did you try to get us together?"

"What does that have to do with a ship?"

Honestly, I'm too old to know too, but there are a lot of interns and kids right out of college who work at

306

the zoo, and I try to keep up with them. Makes me feel younger.

"You know, like a relation-ship?"

Ed sighs. "Good night, Erin. I'll see you tomorrow."

I disconnect and turn back to Xander. He looks no better, and I think is feeling no better. "Ed totally shipped us. Well, tried to. Sometimes I forget that we're not together."

He stands up and walks by me, stopping only to pick up his bag by the door. It's for the best, him going to be with his family for a few days. They need each other. They're all getting tested for this mutation. They should probably meet with a genetic counselor. Julie really helped me out when I got my BRCA news.

Man, what are the odds?

Fifty-percent, just like mine.

*Of all the mutations in all the genes, you had to mate with mine.*

I tell myself over and over not to worry. That there's literally nothing that can be done either way. This kid had a fifty-percent chance of inheriting this kind of crappy luck from me anyway.

I wish it were Wednesday so I can talk to the UnBRCAble girls about it. I guess I'm going back to the group. I need them right now.

Xander opens and closes the door without saying a word. I want to run after him, to tell him that it'll be fine, to tell him that I love him, to say *anything* that will make his heart stop breaking.

Breaking for this child, this great gift, that he gave me. What if he can't look at her without feeling this grief?

He already can't look at me.

I run out the door, waving my arms wildly. Xander's backing out of the driveway. He looks up, to see me flailing about like an uncoordinated pelican. But then I'm at a loss for what to do. I give him a little wave.

I see his hand go up, and perhaps even, a little smile on his face. Then his car changes direction, and he's driving off into the night.

Okay then. Now that my life's totally in the crapper, I guess I'd better pack to go on a business trip with my supervisor. No pressure there.

If I had any more pressure on me, I'd turn into a freakin' diamond. Maybe that's why diamonds are a girl's best friend. They remind us of all we survive, hopefully with dignity and grace.

Although with me, there's no hope for either of those.

As I sit in the now-empty house, I think about all I've lost while on this quest to have a baby. My parents, the man I love ...

And while I don't—can't blame him in the least—now there's a larger chance that our child will develop cancer.

So glad I decided to seize the day. Carpe diem is bullshit.

~~~***~~~

I have been late to work everyday this week. Without Xander here, I'm having trouble keeping on schedule. Trouble staying organized. Trouble not crying.

It also doesn't help that I was away Friday through Sunday with Ed and Barry and have then had to work everyday to make up for Xander being away. No rest for the weary and yes, I'm weary. It's contributing, heavily, to my inability to get up in the morning and get moving in a timely fashion.

Xander's due back on Friday, from what I hear, but that won't help me as I'm scheduled to work through next Monday. The thought of it makes me want to cry.

I can do this though. I can do this for Xander.

I take a picture of the front of my T-shirt and text it to him. Every day I've sent him a pic of what my shirt says. Today, it says, "Thou shall not try me. Mood 24:7."

Today, like every other day, there's no response.

I mean, he didn't even respond to the picture of the sloth wearing a sombrero, eating a taco. It's the best shirt ever. I bought three, in case something happens to one. Or two.

But now the tears I'm finding building up in my eyes are the angry kind. Anger with my mom for cutting me out like I was a bad crust of bread. Anger with Xander for walking away without looking back. Anger that Xander has to go through everything I've gone through with finding out he has a hereditary cancer risk. Anger that I couldn't accept my losses in the first place like a mature person would have.

If only I could have lived life without a baby, I wouldn't be here. I'd still be in my crappy little apartment, eating tacos and pinning pictures on Pinterest for a life I'd never have.

If only I didn't need it in my life.

But I need this baby ... and Xander ... like I need air to breathe.

At least tonight is my UnBRCAble meeting. Ed said I can leave early so I can make my "appointment." I'd say a little white lie never hurt anyone, but that'd be a lie, now wouldn't it?

"Um, Ed." I shift nervously from one foot to another. "About me leaving early today—I don't have a doctor's appointment."

"If you don't tell me that you're getting a follicular resection, I'll pretend I don't know, and we'll call it even."

My brows knit together. "Follicular resection?"

Ed laughs. "It's what my wife says when she's going for a haircut. A color, in her terms, is a pigmental acquisition."

I laugh. "No, no cut and color for me. I had my one for the year." Though now that he mentions it, my hair is growing superfast and could use a bit of a trim. "I, um, I have a support group. For women with BRCA. The BRCA mutation, actually. I have it."

"Oh, okay. Sorry, I guess? I don't know what the correct response is. But anyway, it sounds medical so I hope your appointment goes well." Ed gives me a nod and then he's back to his work.

Maybe being truthful isn't the worst thing in the world.

When I pull into the parking lot, I take a deep breath. I'm still not sure I belong here, but I have nowhere else to turn. No one who might possibly understand.

Claudia calls the group to order, not because it's an official meeting but because we'd never stop chit-chatting otherwise. I'm sitting next to Millie who's been rambling on about her school year and Sterling and their wedding plans. She leans over after Claudia starts leading introductions. "Um, do you think you might want to be in my wedding?"

"As what?"

"A bridesmaid, dummy. I have Lisa as my maid-of-honor, and I want you and Claudia and my co-worker Amy to round us out."

I look down at my small bump. "Depending on when your wedding is, I might really round things out." Dear God, please let her date be in about a year so I can have the baby and get back into some semblance of my old size.

"December seventh."

That's less than three months from now. "Of this year?" My voice rises, and the rest of the group turns to look at me. "Sorry," I mumble.

Marg-with-a-hard-g is talking. Again. Something about her rubs me the wrong way. Or maybe it's because my underwear is riding up again. Whether I want to admit it or not, it may be time to break out the larger size granny panties.

"And so he bought me this great red dress. Look at it!" she waves her phone around. Yes, Marg-with-a-hard-g, we get it. Your reconstruction was great. Your rack is great. Your figure is great. Your husband is great.

"Anyone with any other news they'd like to share?"

I raise my hand, slowly at first. The ladies here know the true deal with Xander. I'm sure there'll be some knowing glances. I can practically see the "I told you so's" written on their faces.

"Things aren't working out with Xander so well. First, I told my mom, who as predicted, went ape shit." I recount the ordeal with Mom, the call from his dad, the realization that I love him, and his terrible news.

The raised eyebrows go from condescending to sympathy with lightning speed. "He's finding out what he can, and it's a wait and see. I was rolling the dice, but now they seem stacked against us. Or at least against the baby."

I rub my belly.

*Dear God, please let Bean be okay.*

Millie wipes a tear away and reaches out for my hand. "It doesn't matter what it lands on. It's still the luckiest roll. Let's face it, we're all here because of our risk of hereditary cancer. Even with the risk, it doesn't mean all of us will get it. Statistically some of us will be fine, and I can't believe I used statistically in a sentence."

"Correctly no less." Claudia smiles. "Erin, we're here for you. We're here for your baby, but that's mainly because we all want to hold her. Him. Them. Whatever. We're here for Xander, should he want to join."

"You can't have a man join this group!" Marg-with-a-hard-g wails. "We talk about personal things here." She leans forward. "Breast things," she says in an exaggerated whisper. "Nipple things. Sex life things."

Claudia remains casually slouched in her chair. If it were me, I'd be on my feet, yelling and shouting. "We're here for whoever is living with hereditary cancer risk. End of story."

Millie jumps in. "I'm getting married. In December. We set a date and have a place, and it's going to be so great. I know it's quick, but it's not. Not when you know you're right for each other."

Naturally, my mind flashes to Xander. I don't know how I can know we're right for each other but he doesn't. One of us is wrong here, and I have a terrible feeling it's me. I shoot him a quick text.

*Finishing up my meeting. You should come next week.*

As soon as I send it, I wish I could unsend.

*Current mood: really, really sad.*

And wanting tacos.

# CHAPTER 35

Xander's still gone.

He hasn't responded to my texts. I get the message. Not to mention, today was my ninth straight workday. I'm grumpy and sad and wishing I could do something—anything—to make this better for him.

Before I pull out of the parking lot to head home, I text him again.

> It's Thursday, so I'm seventeen weeks. Not sure if I feel Bean moving or if it's gas. Maybe I should lay off the beans and see if I still feel it?

No response.

Not to mention, the elastic snapped on my socks this morning, which means I've spent the entire day trying to wiggle my toes and tie my boot tight enough to keep my socks up.

Needless to say, it wasn't a good day.

So of course, now would be the time that my mom shows up. She's waiting for me in the driveway when I get home.

This day keeps getting better and better.

"Can I come in?" she asks as I breeze by her, pretending she's not there.

I roll my eyes. Short of slamming the door in her face, I can't keep her from coming in. She trails behind and stands in the foyer until I motion for her to go into the living room to sit down. I take my time putting my lunch bag away and getting a drink.

Let her sweat for a minute.

Finally I go out to her, choosing to sit across the room on one of the dining table chairs. It keeps me sitting ramrod straight, and my hands naturally gravitate toward my belly. Her eyes lock in on that. I try to guess what her expression means, but I honestly have no idea. She could be here to tell me I'm allowed back in the family, or she could be here to formally shun me.

It could go either way at this point.

"Erin, I need to beg your forgiveness," Mom says.

That I was not expecting.

"Did Dad put you up to this?" I could see him advocating for it. He wouldn't go against her, but it didn't seem like he'd be okay with permanently cutting me out. It's not like I killed anyone or anything. All I did was get pregnant.

"No." She clears her throat. "I came on my own."

"Mom, if we're going to hash this out, the least you can do is be honest with me."

"Dad *may* have encouraged me to reach out. He only suggested I call. I decided to come over, so he didn't *technically* put me up to this." Finally, she's able to raise her gaze from her feet to my eyes.

Un huh.

315

"Mom, quit wasting my time. I've got things to do." Like find a new place to live. There's no way I can be here when Xander gets back. It's too hard on him to have me here. To see me. To think about the baby.

She looks around. "Where's … um … Xavier?"

Okay, that's it. I've had enough. Standing up, I put my hands on my hips. "Enough, Mom. You have one minute."

"How am I supposed to know his name? I didn't even know you were dating anyone. You never mentioned him. You never said things were getting serious. I thought we were close, and then you spring it on me in front of all those people that not only are you getting married, but you're pregnant too. How did you think I was going to react?" Her hands are flailing. Now I know where I get my uncoordinated pelican moves from.

"I knew damn well how you were going to react, Mom. You made that very clear. And ask yourself how close we really are that I have to lie to you about something like this. That whenever I approached you about wanting to have a baby, you freaked out. Do you remember the incident where you called and screamed at me on the phone? How about when you threw my beer? So how, *exactly*, was I supposed to break this news to you?"

"You should have told me you were dating someone." She crosses her arms over her chest.

"I'm not, Mom. There was nothing to tell."

She opens her mouth, but I do not want to hear what I know is coming next. "And no, for your information, I'm not loose. I got pregnant on purpose. I went to a fertility doctor and did all the testing and made and appointment and got pregnant. Xander is my sperm donor."

This has rendered her speechless. For once.

"I'm running out of time to do this. Aside from my career, having a baby is all I've ever wanted. I can almost live with the mammograms and breast MRIs and ductal lavage every few months, waiting for cancer to rear its ugly head. But there's not great screening for ovarian cancer and by the time that shows up, game's over. Ironically, not having kids in the first place increases your overall risk for ovarian cancer."

Isn't that a kick in the ovaries?

"You yourself pointed out all the ways in which I'm unable to provide for a child. Xander, who lost his mother to breast cancer by the way, thought if we raised this child together, we'd both win. We'd both get to be parents. And we'd both be happy. But that isn't good enough for you. Nope, it has to be first comes love, then comes marriage, *then* comes baby in a baby carriage. Not everyone gets the fairy tale, Mom."

I leave out that most fairy tales, in their original forms, are actually horror stories. There are very few that end with "and they all lived happily ever after."

"Don't you think I know that not everyone gets their fairy tales?" The bitterness permeates her words.

I roll my eyes. "Mom, you have to get over it. You can't keep holding onto it. It's weighing you down. Dragging you under, and us with you. Look at us! Is this what you want? All the secrets, all the lies—all because you can't let go of the past and embrace the present and the future. Do you want to be a part of my life? Of your grandchild's life? Because I'm telling you right now, if something doesn't change, you won't be."

Tears burst forth from her eyes. "You can't reject me too. You can't throw me away too. I'm your mother. You're supposed to love me."

And though she's sixty-years-old, I hear the small, scared child within her.

"Then don't throw me away, Mom. Don't reject me. Love me *and* my child."

She stands there, tears streaming down her cheeks, shoulders rounded, and head down. "I do love you. I don't want you to struggle. I want you to have what I have with your father and you girls. I want you to have it all and have the perfect life."

I step toward my mother and pull her into a tight hug. "Can't you see that I do? This way, I have my baby and my career and my health. As long as I have my mom, I'm all set."

Her hands cling to my arms and after a moment, I wonder who's supporting who. And then I realize it doesn't matter. This is what family does. This is what love does. We hold each other up.

After a few minutes, she steps back and wipes the tears from her eyes. "I'm sorry."

"I thought 'love means never having to say you're sorry.'" I say, quoting Mom's favorite line from the old movie, *Love Story*. Which, by the way, if you ask me, is totally stupid. Love means you respect the other person enough to admit you were wrong.

"Well, that doesn't fit here, I guess." She pulls me back in for a quick hug. "I am sorry, honey. I love you and I love this baby and I'll love your baby daddy too as soon as he lets me apologize."

Baby daddy. Ugh.

"Um, Xander's not here. He's having some family issues. I actually was thinking he might need some space when he gets back. Because of his family ... stuff ... it's hard for him to look at me and think about the baby. I'm thinking I might try to stay out of his hair. Can I come stay with you?"

Why did I say that? I must have lost my mind.

"So you're pregnant, estranged from your baby daddy, homeless, and moving back in?"

I sigh. "Yup. We should probably see if we can get on *Maury Povich* or something. I fit the criteria."

"No, it's a bump in the road. I'll get your room ready." She squeezes my hand and smiles.

"Who are you and what have you done with my mother?"

She leans over and pulls my head down so she can kiss the top of it. "I love your father and you girls more than anything. I just want what's best."

"I know, and I know how hard it is for you to admit that something different than your pre-set expectations might be what's best."

"Stable is best."

I want to reassure her that Xander is stable, but considering I just asked to move back in with her and Dad, I'm not sure my argument holds water.

"I'll make sure Bean has a stable life."

"Bean?"

"We don't know what it is yet, so that's a nice middle of the road name."

My mom exhales and sags slightly. "Oh good. I was afraid I'd have to get excited about that name, and it was going to be hard. Please don't name your baby Bean. Or Apple. Or Kindle. Or any other inanimate object, really."

"I promise, we won't. We haven't discussed names yet, but that won't be on the table."

"Don't name it Table, either." My mom starts walking slowly toward the door. "I'm sorry, again. Sorry I doubted you. I know you'll be a great mother and do everything you can to give this baby a stable life. And you know what they say—it takes a village. Remember I'm in your village."

Oh, Mom. How I needed to hear those words right now. She must see how much I need her support. Thank goodness she came through. Suddenly, I don't feel quite as tired and alone anymore.

Well, I'm still pretty tired. "You're the busybody mayor of my village." I laugh.

"If you need help moving things over ... let your father know. I'm the mayor so I know how to delegate."

When she leaves, I'm alone. Truly alone. But I don't feel that way. Things are better with my mom, and I'll have a roof over my head. Not that Xander said anything about me leaving, but I don't know that he'll want to see me anytime soon.

I'll get over it someday.

It's not like I have to see him all the time anyway. Oh wait ...

I pack my clothes and toiletries in a few bags and boxes. He can keep my stuff here until I find a more permanent place. Before I go, I walk in the room that's going to be the nursery.

He's painted it a soft, pale, dove gray.

I didn't even notice the last time I was in here. All I saw was him in distress.

I never even told him that's what I wanted, but of course it's what I wanted. He knows me better than I know myself.

I'm never going to find someone like him.

Ever.

I look at my duffle bag and my knapsack, stuffed to the brim. I don't want to retreat to my parents. I want to stay *here*. In this house. With Xander. With our baby.

It's time to stop being passive and get off my duff and go for what I want.

Carpe diem, baby.

*Current mood: determined to win him back.*

# CHAPTER 36

I don't exactly have a woo-ing plan. Not yet. I'm binging on romantic movies, looking for ideas, as well as combing Pinterest and reading Buzzfeed articles about clever ways to win him back.

Nothing jumps out, but what I do do is get an emergency appointment with my genetic counselor, Julie. She's always been such a great help and reference source for me on my BRCA journey. It's hard finding out through the internet that you could have this terrible, possibly fatal flaw in your very cellular makeup. Having a real-life person, not just the scary Google, to give answers, has been a huge relief.

Even when the news isn't great.

Which is sort of where I am right now.

"As you know, Erin, there is a fifty-percent chance you will pass the BRCA-1 pathogenic variant onto your baby, just as there was a fifty-percent chance that Xander's mother passed the PALB2 pathogenic variant onto him."

"Patho—what?"

"Pathogenic variant. It's the most up-to-date terminology, but mutation is still widely accepted."

"I prefer mutation. It makes me feel like I have the potential to be one of the X-men someday. My superpower will be eating tacos."

Julie smiles. "So Xander has a fifty-percent chance of having the mutation from his mother. If that's the case, then in terms of your baby, here's the breakdown: Twenty-five percent chance that he or she inherits neither variant; a twenty-five percent chance of inheriting just your BRCA-1 variant; a twenty-five percent chance of inheriting just his PALB2 variant."

When she pauses, I add up the numbers in my head. "That's only seventy-five percent."

A nod. "And then there's a twenty-five percent chance that the child will inherit both variants. This would indicate a very high probability of cancer at some point." Julie looks up at me and closes her computer screen. "This isn't what anyone wants to here, but there's time. Lots of time. And scientific advances being made everyday. In fact, they are working on ways to edit the DNA in human sperm. The first variant they are looking to edit out is BRCA-2, so change is on the horizon. You know. You're aware. Your child will be aware, and you can monitor properly."

I nod.

She hands me some papers from off her printer. "Take these and read through them. Let me know if you have more questions. If Xander wants to come in, I'd be happy to meet with him."

"I'm not sure when he'll have his results, but I'll send him your way."

When I see him. He's due back today. He'll be coming into work this afternoon, which I conveniently have off to make my appointment with Julie. The Zoo has been great about my appointments.

And now that appointment is done and I'm free. In the past, I would've gone back into work. Today seems like a pedicure day. If I have pretty toenails, maybe it'll give me the strength to stand up to Xander and say what I have to say.

Second thoughts fill my mind as soon as I walk into the nail salon. I can see right to the back and Marg-with-a-hard-g is there, just sitting down. Maybe if I quickly back out ...

"Hello. How can we help?" The technician stands up from her table and walks forward.

"Um, pedicure?" I hate that I always sound so uncertain. Probably because I don't get these regularly enough to ever feel comfortable.

"Pick your color."

Seven gazillion colors sit before me. Um ... I quickly grab a nice sage green. It's not like anyone's going to see my toes anyway.

As I'm led back, I pray that Marg-with-a-hard-g doesn't see me. Unfortunately, the only open chair is next to hers. Great.

"Oh Erin! How nice to see you! This is great. I was supposed to come with my friend, but she had to cancel on me at the last minute. I hate being here alone. Now I'm not."

Well, poop. Marg-with-a-hard-g has always irritated me in her perfection. Her perfect marriage with her perfect kids and her perfect house. I'm surprised the BRCA *variant*—I inwardly smile at using my new word— dared mess with her perfection.

"I had an appointment this afternoon and decided to do this rather than go back to work."

"Playing hookey? Good for you. Self-care is important. Remember that after the little is born."

"What'd you do for self-care?"

"I'd read for ten minutes every night."

That's it?

"Ten minutes a day doesn't seem like a lot." In fact, it seems like nothing.

"With reading, it would take me someplace else. An escape. If I could read for longer or more times each day, I will. But ten minutes of me time is my minimum."

"And your husband doesn't mind?"

She giggles. "You know what they say: happy wife, happy life."

Her perfection is a little too much for me sometimes.

Or maybe it's my own inner jealousy.

"That's good advice. I'm not married, so I guess I'm on my own to give myself a happy life."

"Make sure you do. You deserve it, Erin. We all do."

Maybe Marg isn't so bad after all.

I'm sitting comfortably under the foot dryer when my phone pings. And pings. And then pings again.

Three pings mean it's got to be a crisis from someone.

Xander.

My heart drops all the way to my newly painted toes.

Quickly I flick open my screen, pretending my hands aren't shaking.

*Anything been off with Bonnie lately? She's not eating well.*

*She's not right. Dr. Val wants to do testing at the hospital.*

*Can you come in?*

Shit.

I look around the salon, unsure of what to do. I hate to slide my feet back into my socks and sneakers, so I waddle out, still in the disposable flip-flops with the spacers between my toes. I put my car heater on high and blast my toes. On the other hand, if I smudge the polish, it's not a big loss.

Bonnie is worth worrying about. Toe nail polish is not. What if there's something wrong with her? What if it's her baby?

I'm so panicked about Bonnie that I don't have time to think about what I'm going to say to Xander. I know in this moment, we'll pull together and work as a team for Bonnie's sake. The animals come before our personal problems.

Just how it will be with our child.

I pull into the employee lot in record time, taking only the briefest of moments to shove my feet back into my socks and shoes, before I race to the gate. And by race, I mean walk as absolutely fast as I can while sucking in air and trying not to die.

I really need to start working out.

And lay off the tacos.

I don't know if I should head all the way back to Sloth Central or to the on-site hospital. Carlos meets me at the gate.

"They're waiting on you."

"I got here as fast as I could."

He nods, his mouth set tightly. Oh God, this is not good. What if I'm too late and something happened to her?

I'm not prepared to lose her.

Carlos walks with me, using his keys to unlock gates and doors. I'm relieved, as I'm not sure my hands would work properly at this time. He gets one of the golf carts out, which means she's still in Sloth Central. It can't be that bad if they haven't taken her out of the habitat.

Unless she's already gone.

Tears well in my eyes as I grip the roof post to keep from falling out as Carlos takes a corner particularly sharply.

"I get that this is an emergency, but I'm carrying precious cargo here. Can you slow down a bit?"

Carlos continues with his iron grip on the wheel but lessens the pressure on the accelerator. "I thought you'd want to get there."

"I do ... in one piece." Worrying that I sound ungrateful, I quickly add, "Thanks for driving me out there."

The only time I take a cart is if I'm transporting an animal, and even then, I let someone else drive. It'd take me at least ten minutes to walk all the way to Sloth Central from the employee gate.

Carlos screeches to a halt at the opening to South America. "I've got to get back to my post. Good luck in there."

Taking a deep breath before I head in, I tell myself to be strong. I can handle whatever happens. Bonnie will not be the first animal I've lost, nor will she be the last. It's part of the job. I'm allowed to be sad, but I have to be professional.

I can do this.

The door to the building is unlocked, which is not the standard operating procedure. Maybe because so many people have been in and out? Maybe because they knew I was coming? There's an eerie quiet though. I don't hear voices. Certainly not the loud ones that usually happen when there's a medical crisis going on. Because the sloths are such low key creatures, we usually leave them in their indoor enclosure at night, rather than putting them in their cages, so it's no surprise that the cage room is dark.

A small, faint light sneaks out from under the door to the enclosure. This door isn't locked either.

Something's terribly wrong.

"Xander?" I call out.

"In here," he says, as I push open the door to Barry and Bonnie's inner sanctum.

My eyes immediately go to the trees where I see two balls of fur hanging in the dim light. Wait—two? That means Bonnie's on her perch. I strain to see if there is movement of her breathing, but it's too dark. Only then do I see Xander.

Sitting at a small table in the middle of the space. The light is provided by a few candles on the table, as well as the space heaters in the ceiling.

A table? Candles?

What?

# CHAPTER 37

"Where's Dr. Val?"

I have no idea what's going on.

"Bonnie's fine." Xander stands, wiping his hand on the front of his pants. The heaters keep this room at least eighty-five, which makes everyone who walks in here sweat.

"Is she doing better? Is she on antibiotics? What does Dr. Val think it is?"

"Bonnie's fine," he says again.

"But she wasn't a little while ago?"

"No, she was."

Huh? None of this is making sense, and why is there a table in here? Is it a new enrichment Xander wants to try out? Why didn't he just tell me?

"Erin, sit down." He motions to a chair.

Tentatively I slide into the seat. "Xander, what's going on here? What's wrong with Bonnie?"

He sits down, shaking his head. "Nothing. She's fine. She's been fine all along. Feisty as ever, but fine."

What the hell is going on? I'm so confused. If I didn't know better, I'd say this looks like the set up for the grand gesture in one of those romance movies on the *Hallmark Channel*.

Obviously, that's not what's going on.

So what else can it be?

Suspiciously, I sink down into the seat.

Xander looks down at his side and then back at me. He leans over and picks something up. "Here. I got this for you."

He passes a pink gift bag across the table, lifting it high enough so it doesn't catch on fire. I can see trying to explain that one. "Xander, what—"

"Open it." He shakes the bag in front of me. "I'm sorry I didn't answer your texts while I was away."

I wave my hand, not taking the bag. "Don't worry about it. I just wanted to make you smile and let you know I was thinking about you."

He wiggles the bag again. "They did. They were the highlight of my day."

As I'm grabbing the bag, I see the tattoo on his wrist. I have to know. "What does your wrist say?"

The sad smile on his face tells me everything. It's about his mom. "It says 'Never forget to love.' My mom told me that right before she died. She was afraid that I'd end up alone without her to encourage me on."

My eyes fill. "Don't tell my mom, otherwise she'd have us tattooing things all over our bodies, like 'don't forget to brush' and 'fooling leads to crying.' We'd look like the tattooed man at the circus by the time she was done."

Xander laughs, still holding the bag. "I can totally see that. The secret's safe. Now will you *please* open this?"

I put the bag on my lap and peek inside. Nestled in the tissue paper are … T-shirts?

I hope he isn't trying to get me to wear more respectable—i.e. dull—T-shirts. "Um, thanks?"

He smiles. "Look at them."

I pull the first one out. From the back it appears to be a plain—albeit large—heather gray shirt. I turn it around. "Filled with tacos … and a baby." The next shirt is white and says, "Tacos for two, please."

Tears fill my eyes. The thought of tacos truly does bring me that much pleasure. "Oh, Xander, these are great. Perfect."

"Keep going." He smiles, expectantly.

There's a charcoal gray shirt that's rolled up. When I unroll it, a smaller piece of fabric the same color drops out. The larger shirt—but it's not a maternity shirt—says "Taco" while the smaller one—a onesie actually—says "Taquito."

Tears fill my eyes. He got Bean and me matching shirts. Goofy shirts. Taco shirts.

"There's one more."

In the bottom of the bag is a tiny pink onesie that says, "I'm cute. Mom's hot. Dad's lucky."

That pushes me over the edge. Tears well and swell out of my eyes. "Oh Xander. I'm so sorry about everything. About my mom and the kiss and my bad genes that make your bad genes even worse."

He reaches across the table and grabs my hand. First one and then the other. "No, Erin, don't be sorry. I freaked out."

"You had reason to. But I messed up first. I'm sorry I broke the deal and ruined our friendship by falling for you."

"Erin, that's not what freaked me out. Not at all."

"You're not freaked out that I fell in love with you?"

He smiles. "Never. I've sort of been waiting for it to happen. I figured I could live with just being your friend and raising the world's most awesome kid together. But if I had to choose, I'd rather it be more. It would be a distant second option, but better than just trading jabs all the time."

Say what? He wanted me to fall in love with him? Why? That doesn't make sense. If he wanted me to love him, why did he freak out?

"But you freaked."

"Yes, because I love you and the baby so much, and I probably gave her a death sentence. If I had just minded my own damn business—"

*Hold. The. Phone.*

Did Xander just say he loved me?

"Um—" I try to get a word in edgewise.

"If only I'd stayed out of it, Erin, then she wouldn't be born with cancer looming over her head."

I can't respond to this love thing, but I know my statistics about pathogenic variants.

"There'd still be a fifty-percent chance that this baby would have the BRCA-1 mutation from me."

333

"But fifty-percent is a much better gamble than one-hundred."

"Xander, you didn't know about your genetics. Did you get tested? You might not even carry the variant."

He nods. "I did it through the clinic where my brother goes. I won't know for about six weeks."

"Then we'll deal in six weeks, one way or another."

"But what if—"

Now it's my turn to cut him off. "We'll figure it out. It's too late for any other answer. There are never any guarantees in life to begin with, you know. This is more of an advantage, because we have the superpower of knowledge."

Xander raises an eyebrow. "A superpower? Are you sure about that?"

And then it hits me. I jump up out of my chair, pumping my arms in the air. "I'm a mutant with a superpower. Do you know what that makes me?"

Xander stares in disbelief.

"I'm finally one of the X-men!"

He laughs. "You're nuts."

"That too." I join in his laughter, sinking down into my chair.

"But you know this means that she's most likely going to get cancer."

"She has the same chance of having that high risk of cancer as she does not having any genetic risk." I explain what Julie told me earlier today. Gosh, was that only a few hours ago? It seems like a lifetime ago.

"You know I'm not good with numbers." Xander looks down. "My dad kept telling me I was blowing this out of proportion. But then he followed it up with a whole bunch of *statistics*." Xander says the word like it leaves a bitter taste in his mouth. "Your explanation is much easier to understand."

He looks like a little boy who worked so hard in class only to fail the test again. I get up and walk over to him. Without waiting to be invited, I sit down on his lap.

"Xander, look at me. We're in this together."

I pause, letting that sink in. I smile at him and then continue. "You did a tremendously honorable thing, giving me this gift. It takes a special kind of person to do something so selfless."

"It wasn't selfless. I wanted kids. I always have. And I knew, even if you didn't want to be in a relationship with me, you'd be a fantastic mother. I mean, it's not like I was plotting this out for years. Like I said, it was a shower idea."

"Xander, what do you want?"

"Right now?"

I nod.

He pushes the hair back behind my ear. "The day you told me you had to get a mastectomy, it felt like the floor dropped out on my world. I'd been trying to think of a way to ask you out for months—years actually—but you were always so quick with the retort that I knew you weren't interested in me like that. I thought you wanted someone to spar with, so that's what I gave you. I kept thinking that I had time to woo you and win you over. But if you didn't have a lot of time left because of cancer, I had to do something. I couldn't waste one more day not being in your life."

"Woo me?" I'm having difficulty processing this information.

"And then you started talking about having a baby, and I was so filled with jealousy until I heard your plan. Your reasons for wanting a baby, as well as not being able to have one, were all so justified. I thought that maybe you didn't want me, but at least I could do this for you."

"Why?"

Xander may have a hard time with math, but I apparently am unable to understand the English language at this point.

"Erin, I love you."

That—that, I can understand.

I wrap my arms around his neck and pull his face to mine, closing the distance between our lips. This kiss is different than our last. It's a different type of urgency. Because though we are desperate for each other—to touch and explore and express our love—it's clear we have all the time in the world.

We also have an audience or at least the potential of one via the monitors.

"Hey," I say breathlessly. "Do you want to go home?"

Xander laughs. "But I have dinner ready."

"I'm not hungry."

"Liar. I brought tacos." He tips his head toward a box on the floor filled with foil-wrapped packages.

Mmm ... tacos. "As good as that might sound, there's only one thing I'm hungry for right now."

Xander stands up, lifting me right off him and placing me on my feet. "Let's go."

Despite our rush to get home and pick up where we left off, we take a moment to clean up the table and bring the food with us.

I have a feeling I'm going to be very hungry later.

# EPILOGUE

As I help Lisa yank up Millie's Spanx, I am filled with relief that I don't have to be stuffed like a sausage into a similar scuba suit. It's one of the advantages to being a pregnant bridesmaid.

To be clear, a Pinterest search informed me they do make the restrictive, supportive undergarments in maternity wear, but ain't no way that was happening here. I've got a bump, boobs, and a butt, and I'm proud of them all.

But mostly I won't need one because the bridesmaids' dresses Millie picked are extremely flattering on all of us with their silver beaded and sequined V-neck top and flowy, blush skirts. Perfect for a winter wonderland wedding.

Even Claudia, who admits to last wearing a dress at her high school prom in the previous century, has the glow of someone who knows how stunning she looks. We all feel that way.

But we all pale in comparison to the blushing bride. Millie has a radiance I didn't know existed. This is what true happiness looks like. Piper, Millie's soon-to-be stepdaughter, is taking her responsibilities as junior bridesmaid very seriously, including advising her not-so-wicked step-mother on makeup tips.

"I think you need a little more highlighter. You really want those cheekbones to pop."

Claudia leans over and whispers, "Any more highlighter and she'll look like she stepped out of a 1980s music video."

I tend to agree, but what do I know about makeup? Mackenzie had to come over and do mine. That's twice this year I've worn foundation. It's a new record for me!

As we zip and button Millie into her form-fitting, figure hugging gown, I admire her courage. The neckline is low and gives more than a hint at her cleavage. Millie arranges the girls—her foobs, as she calls them—and a look of panic crosses her face. "I should have gone with a higher neckline. What was I thinking?"

Millie's aunt Polly swoops in. "You were thinking that you have a nice rack, and this dress is perfect for you to own it."

I don't know if this is the right thing to say to Millie or not. I still have my breasts. Hers are reconstructed.

Millie smiles and I let out a breath of relief. "You're right, Aunt Pol. If it weren't for my journey with these—" she waves to her chest, "Sterling and I might never have found each other. And now we're getting married! Eep!"

Eep indeed.

As I march down the aisle, bump leading the way, my eyes land on Xander immediately. If I thought he looked hot as a zookeeper, I was not at all ready for how sexy he'd look in a suit. Yowza. If I wasn't holding a bouquet of flowers, I'd fan myself.

The ceremony is short and sweet, to my relief. Though I'm only six-and-a-half months pregnant, my feet have started swelling with prolonged standing. Especially while in heels. Seriously, why didn't I get flats? I hope I'm not limping on the procession out, not that anyone is looking at me.

Pictures take forever and all I can think about is taking my shoes off. Though I'm quite certain once I do, it'd take heavenly measures to get the shoes back on my feet.

We've lined up in endless permutations on the steps of the venue, in front of the building, down by the park, leaning against cars. We're back inside now, thankfully, because that December air is cold.

There's a room just for pictures, and we're in there. On the other side of the heavy oak doors, cocktails and hors d'oeuvres are being passed. I wish they'd bring some in here. I'm starving.

"One last series, folks!" the photographer announces. Thank goodness. I want to eat and sit and probably eat a little more.

Xander comes strolling in, shepherded by the photographer's assistant.

"Hey, what are you doing back here? Did you come to rescue me? Do you have slippers and food for me?"

"Millie sent for me. Told me, by 'royal decree of the bride,' I was to come back here." He makes air quotes. Millie is so not a bridezilla that this statement of hers makes me laugh.

Xander laughs and my heart melts even more. The past two months have been bliss, being together and preparing for the arrival of our baby girl.

Because Xander was completely right. Against the odds, I'm carrying a girl.

Also against the odds, Xander was found to be negative for the PALB2 mutation, which was an enormous burden off his shoulders. It wouldn't have mattered to me one way or another, but he's relieved.

Millie looks at Xander and smiles. Xander goes over to Millie and gives her a hug. He shakes Sterling's hand, giving him the traditional guy chuck on the shoulder. I love that he's back here with the bridal party. All this love in the air made me miss him. Plus, did I mention the suit? Yowza again. Not to mention he's always so kind and thoughtful, checking up on me.

I sit in a chair while the photographer arranges Sterling's siblings and Piper, with Sterling and Millie in the middle. Xander walks over to me, squatting down in front of me. "You look ravishing."

"Ravishing? That sounds like something Sterling would say. Did I detect a hint of a British accent there?"

"I've heard the ladies think it's sexy."

"These two ladies right here don't think you need any more help."

He leans in and kisses me softly right in front of my ear. "But you do look ravishing."

"Awww, you guys are so cute. Dennis, can you get a picture of them?" Millie squeals.

Xander helps me to my feet and steps behind me. "Where are you going?"

"I want to make sure they can see your bump. It's our first family portrait."

"It doesn't matter where I stand. You can see this bump from outer space."

Xander chuckles as he reaches his arms around my middle and places them over my belly.

"That's great guys. Erin, tilt your chin up slightly. Xander open up your hands a little."

Millie is right behind the photographer, watching us. "Hang on. May I?"

She walks up to us and takes Xander's hands in her own and rearranges them slightly. "There. That's better. Erin, what do you think?"

I glance down to see Xander's fingers making the outline of a heart over my stomach. I smile and look again. "Can you get a close up of that?" I ask the photographer again.

He steps in to take a picture and then turns the camera around to me for a preview. "Is that okay?"

On the tiny screen, I see the heart over the soft blush fabric of my dress. But wait— what's that? Is there something on my dress? Did some of my sequins fall off and down the front of my dress? I hope it didn't ruin the rest of Millie's pictures. "Can you zoom in?"

Except it's not a sequin beneath Xander's hand. It's a ring, slid half-way up his index finger. I whirl around to find Xander on his knee, holding the ring out to me.

"Erin, love of my life, mother to our daughter, will you do me the honor of making it official and becoming my wife?"

My hands fly to my mouth. "But ... I ... how ... why ..." I sputter. Movement to my side catches my eye. Millie is holding Sterling's hand, leaning into him. "Xander! You can't do this here and now! It's Millie's day. I mean it's Millie and Sterling's day!"

Millie laughs. "You got me. Turn about is only fair! I approached Xander about this weeks ago. We've been planning it all along! Now answer the damn question!"

"Yes!" I scream and Xander jumps up, sliding the ring onto my finger before pulling me into his arms and kissing me senseless.

Millie whispers *loudly*, "See Sterling? This is how you do a proposal. He never once mentioned anyone's vagina."

I break our kiss, laughing. "Except now you did, Mil."

The room erupts in laughter and Millie and Sterling step forward for a big group hug. The photographer keeps snapping away.

I wipe a tear from my eye and pause to look at the ring Xander gave me. The design indicates it's an antique. "Your grandmother's?"

He nods. "I have a silicone one for you to wear to work, but at least you have this for nice occasions."

The photographer steps in and gets a close-up of my hand. This has worked out well. Engagement photos as well as a maternity shoot. "Thanks. And I'll be in touch about these pictures, as well as to book you for our wedding."

He winks. "You'd better."

Millie asks, "Are we ready to go into the reception now?"

I look around frantically. "Don't anyone say *anything* about this! I will not be one of those girls who steals the scene at someone else's wedding!"

Millie flicks me away with her hand, and I bet she's going to make an announcement. She never did get over that Sterling and I planned out her engagement. She had to one-up me.

Oh well, it's her day. I'm not going to say anything, but I doubt anyone can stop Dynamo Dwyer here.

In all the excitement, I almost forgot how hungry I was. Almost. The pangs hit full force and all I want to do is stuff my face. "Let's go. I'm not getting any younger, you know."

Xander takes my hand as we prepare to be announced. "Now entering the reception, bridesmaid Erin McAvoy and her fiancé, Xander Barnes." *Fiancé*. I like the sound of that.

And just when I think this day cannot possibly get any better, a waiter walks up with a silver tray of hors d'oeuvres.

"Mini tacos?"

*Current mood: Blissfully happy.*

And eating tacos.

# THE END

# ACKNOWLEDGMENTS

To Erin Huss: I had to name this character after you. I'll bet that sometimes you feel like you live in a zoo. Thank you again for your inspiration and guidance. This is an important series, and if it reaches or helps one person, it's because of you.

To Julie Lundberg: Thank you for sending me articles and helping me understand the role of genetic counseling. Your information will hopefully reach other people.

To Joy-Anna Wulff: Thank you for sharing some of your online dating experience. It makes for great comedic material.

To Bria Quinlan: I'm glad you pushed me and were hard on me. You are what I need to put forth the best story I can. Thank you for being my editor.

To Tami Lund: Thank you always for your editing assistance. I'm relieved this wasn't a "fork in the eye" book. And also, in regards to the hair description, that was purely coincidental.

To Michele Vagianelis: I don't know what I'd do without you. That is all.

To my accountability team: Becky, Melissa, and Wendy, thank you for encouraging me and not letting me give up.

To Kristan Higgins: Thank you again for your assistance with my cover and blurb. I appreciate you taking the time to help a small, little author like me. May you be rewarded with a visit from Tom. Or Idris.

To my writing sounding board: Ginny Frost. Thank you for sitting in my booth.

To Sophia: Thank you for liking sloths. They are pretty cool. But even better than meeting a sloth was seeing your excitement when you found out we were doing the sloth encounter. That will forever be one of my favorite days.

To Patrick and Jake: Hey men, what can I say? I appreciate the patience, always.

To Mom and Dad: You definitely come in first place as my own personal cheerleaders.

# ABOUT THE AUTHOR

Telling stories of resilient women, Kathryn R. Biel hails from Upstate New York where her most important role is being mom and wife to an incredibly understanding family who don't mind fetching coffee and living in a dusty house. In addition to being Chief Home Officer and Director of Child Development of the Biel household, she works as a school-based physical therapist. She attended Boston University and received her Doctorate in Physical Therapy from The Sage Colleges. After years of writing countless letters of medical necessity for wheelchairs, finding increasingly creative ways to encourage insurance companies to fund her client's needs, and writing entertaining annual Christmas letters, she decided to take a shot at writing the kind of novel that she likes to read. Kathryn is the author of numerous women's fiction, romantic comedy, contemporary romance, and chick lit works, including the award-winning books, *Live for This*, *Made for Me*, and *Paradise by the Dashboard Light*. Please follow Kathryn on her website, www.kathrynrbiel.com and sign up for her newsletter at bit.ly/KRBNews.

Stand Alone Books:
*Good Intentions*
*Hold Her Down*
*I'm Still Here*
*Jump, Jive, and Wail*
*Killing Me Softly*
*Live for This*
*Once in a Lifetime*
*Paradise by the Dashboard Light*

A New Beginnings Series:
*Completions and Connections: A New Beginnings*
*Novella*
*Made for Me*
*New Attitude*
*Queen of Hearts*

The UnBRCAble Women Series:
*Ready for Whatever*
*Seize the Day*

If you've enjoyed this book, please help the author out by leaving a review on your favorite retailer and Goodreads. A few minutes of your time makes a huge difference to an indie author!

Made in the USA
Monee, IL
29 July 2021

74491537R00203